STRANGE WORLDS, NEAR AND FAR

ALSO BY JAMES C. GLASS

Synths
Eagle Squad
Sedona Conspiracy
Touches of Wonder and Terror/ Voyages in Mind and Space
Imaginings of a Dark Mind (collection)
Toth
Visions

STRANGE WORLDS, NEAR AND FAR

JAMES C. GLASS

WILDSIDE PRESS

"Beneath the Ice of Enceladus" originally appeared in *Analog*, September, 2014. "Evolution" originally appeared in *Analog*, December, 2016. "Time Heals" originally appeared in *Analog*, March-April, 2017. "Skirmish at Heklara" originally appeared in *Digital SF* #3, September, 2011. "Beneath a Red Sun" originally appeared in *Analog*, March-April, 2019. "Daddy's Little Girls" originally appeared in *Pulphouse*, July, 2018. "Oscar Peterson's Meadow" originally appeared in *Best of Northlight*, Concordia Press, 1988. "Georgi" originally appeared in *Writers of the Future. Vol. 7*, Galaxy Press Press, 1991.

Published by Wildside Press LLC.
wildsidepress.com

CONTENTS

HISTORICAL INTRODUCTION

This is my fourth story collection, and it contains stories that have been turning points in my publishing history. My writing career has always been a part time activity. I made my living as a physics professor, department head, and in later years as an academic dean. My day jobs kept me busy with teaching, getting research grants, and publishing papers in molecular biophysics and superconductivity. Until I retired in 1999 I only found the time to write short stories, and my current ten novels have been published since academic retirement.

I've been classified as a science fiction writer, but I've also written and published mystery, fantasy and horror, and even mainstream fiction. Some stories outside of science friction are included in this volume, and all have historical significance in my development as an author.

For me, writing was a natural result of voracious reading at an early age. My first science fiction read was Robert Heinlein's *Red Planet*, and my early interest in science led me quickly to the genre. By junior high school I was writing stories and sending them in. At age fourteen I got a hand-written rejection note from the *The Magazine of Fantasy & Science Fiction*. In high school my best friend was an artist. And for two years we published a fanzine, running off copies from ye olde ditto masters. One of our authors, Joel Nydahl, published a story in *Galaxy Magazine* when he was thirteen.

After high school, life pushed my writing aside. There was college, working in industry to build ion and arc jet engines, marriage and kids, then graduate school and a demanding academic career. I was a dropout of The Famous Writers School after finishing half of the course, but learned a lot about craft. I wrote a story or two a year, and sent a few things in. Over the years, I've kept all of my rejections slips and notes. They are the dues I paid to become a published writer.

Around 1986 the writing bug gave me a terminal bite and I began writing more, but still only a few stories each year, and still no sales. Friendly, hand written rejection letters kept me going, and my first published story was "Oscar Peterson's Meadow, which appeared in a Concordia College literary journal in 1988. For this work, I received a free copy and a warm handshake. The same year I sold "Bodyguard" to *New Black Mask Quarterly*, but that magazine ended up in legal problems over their title and folded before my story came out. Nonetheless, I was paid a kill fee of $188, and so "Bodyguard" became the first story I was actually paid for.

I entered the Writers of the Future contest twice. The first time I didn't even survive the first cut. I heard later that the writing was fine, but the idea had been used to death. The second time I won first place in a quarter contest, then the 1991 Golden Pen Award for my story "Georgi," which is included in this volume. This was indeed the jump-start for my writing career.

I've been writing regularly since that time. There have been ups and downs, good years and dry spells, all of it working part time, enjoying conventions and my associations with writers, editors and publishers. I wouldn't trade the experiences for anything.

Four stories in this collection are appearing for the first time. Several others have undergone minor revisions, and "Sally and the Zero-Point Field" has been given an entirely new ending that makes it a new story indeed. My hope, dear reader, is that you will enjoy the variety of stories in this volume and want more of them, because I'm still having a good time doing work that allows me to conjure up new worlds for me to live in, if even for a short time.

—James C. Glass
Spokane, Washington
June, 2019

TIME HEALS

"You haven't called your father yet, John. Don't you care about how serious his condition is? He could have died last night."

Her voice was raspy, and penetrated to his bones. *How convenient that would have been*, he thought. "I'm on my way out of town, mom. I haven't had the time yet."

"So make the time. He's the only father you've ever known, and he did his best with you. You were not an easy child to raise, you know."

"I've heard that before, mom. Sorry to say his best wasn't so hot. I'll call when I back on Thursday. It's only five days."

Hopefully he won't be around to receive the call, thought John.

"Promise?"

"Promise."

"A hospital visit would really lift his spirits, John."

"I'll try. I have to go, mom. The shuttle is here," he lied, and broke the connection before she could answer.

Ten years of physical and emotional abuse, and she had never acknowledged it. His step-father had been a man's man and clearly wanted him gone. John's hatred of the man had become a living thing, darkening his soul and stealing the joy from his life. He wanted it to end. He wanted the man named Carl Anderson to cease existence, and for the past year, with growing frustration, he had been trying to achieve that.

Now he had another chance at it.

He finished packing, and a shuttle took him across town to the dome of Time Adventures, where he checked in and was assigned a cabin in the transfer module, a tiny space at the center of the great dome overhead. Laser ports there were like pixels, flickering. The mechanism behind time-travel was the most closely guarded secret in the industrial world, and had something to do with laser compression of space-time. John had made several trips, and the effect was always the same: a moment of disorientation, an instant of unawareness, and it was over, during jumps up to seventy years.

The man who checked him in was a condescending shit. "Don't kill anyone over there," he joked. "We don't want to stretch the limits of quantum corrections, and have a paradox to deal with."

"Do I really seem that stupid?" snarled John, and the man's grin faded.

"Don't be such a fool, and buckle me up."

A lifetime of put-downs was enough for John. And as for killing someone, that was exactly what he had in mind.

Officially this was a business trip, and another attempt to locate and reproduce the many precious books and manuscripts lost or destroyed in a terrible fire when John had been museum archivist for barely two years. His efforts had met with some success, and a fat federal grant fed Time Adventures' coffers for expensive time jumps back to acquisition times for his targets.

The door to the transfer module closed, and he was alone, on his back, staring at a featureless ceiling. This was his longest trip so far, and potentially most useful for two reasons: a large acquisition of medieval books and two Greek manuscripts from the first century had been made fifty-three years ago, and all were now missing, and his step-father had grown up in the inner city, was a boy of thirteen at that time. With some luck on John's part, dear Carl Anderson would not reach the age of fourteen.

There was the usual moment of fear. Outside the transfer module something monumental was happening, but there was only a thumping sound and a high-pitched whine before cool air blew on his face and he felt himself slipping into a kind of reverie preceding sleep. He was aware of a passage of time, a few seconds, and the cool air flow ceased and there was a creaking sound in the ceiling above him.

Occasional amnesia had been observed as a side effect of time travel, but John had yet to experience it. Little in the way of weirdness had been seen in the limited number of time jumps through the continuum, but John had experienced a few of those and had learned from them. Some called it quantum weirdness, but for John that was a misnomer, for the weirdness extended to macroscopic objects. If the butterfly effect existed, it had not been observed, but somehow space-time had found ways to avoid paradoxes. Such events were simply not allowed to happen.

It was this fact that John had to get around in order to solve the problem of Carl Anderson. And so far, he had not been able to do it.

There had been two trips, and two fumbling attempts to eliminate the man. The first time John had planned an accident. Carl was then twenty, already a street tough, and there were stories about him beating his own father into a senseless state from which the man had not yet recovered. Carl lived in a brownstone, and sat on the stoop after dinner every evening. One such evening, John climbed to the roof, loosened a large tile and dropped it with what he felt was perfect accuracy. He jerked back from the edge of the roof and waited for the sound of a melon bursting.

Nothing happened. He looked down. Carl Anderson was still sitting there. There had been no shattering of a tile, no exploding skull due to impact, no screams, nothing. The void was still there on the edge of the roof where John had removed the tile. So where had it gone to when he dropped it? He'd been fully awake and aware the whole time, yet there had been an intervention. And when he went to a neighboring building and dropped another tile into an empty street there was the sound of porcelain shattering and a yell from an apartment below him.

His second attempt had not been so subtle, a handgun and cartridges smuggled past Time Adventures people who didn't even bother to check his luggage. Carl was now twenty four and doing muscle work for a local bookie to earn money for trade school, where he would eventually become a machinist. John's opportunity arose when Carl was busy beating up a slender man in the middle of the street. People in the surrounding buildings had shut their windows to block out the noise. John stood in a dark alley, braced his wrist on a dumpster and took careful aim. The distance was fifteen yards. John pulled the trigger smoothly, and the hammer fell. There was a click, but no shot rang out. He tried twice more, jacking in new cartridges, but the result was the same, and then the fight was over, Carl gone, another opportunity ending in failure.

There was a faint mark on each cartridge where the firing pin had struck too weakly for ignition to occur. John carefully disassembled the gun and assembled it again. Still, the weapon would not fire, and by then he had run out of time and had to do the job the museum had sent him to do. But when he returned to his own time he took the gun to a local range and, surprised at first, went through an entire box of ammunition without a single misfire.

Guns, it appeared, did not travel well through time, but that problem was solvable. There were other ways to kill a man. This time would be different, and he'd be dealing with a young boy who was hopefully more vulnerable than a street-toughened adult.

Upon arrival, he dozed for a moment. The module door was opened by a Time Adventures Link Officer, a young, attractive woman who greeted him warmly and helped him from his couch. His luggage, a single suitcase, awaited him by the door. He exited the dome and found himself inside a vast warehouse with broken windows and smelling of oil and other chemicals. A car awaited him outside the abandoned-looking structure, surrounded by a high fence and a locked gate. The tall buildings of the central city could be seen in the far distance. A folder on the front passenger seat contained the current currency and identity cards he required. There was a hotel address and a key to his room. No check in was required.

In two hours John was settled in his room. The museum was visible from his tenth story window, and it was less than a mile from where Carl Anderson had grown up in the inner city. John's syringe and chemicals went into the little refrigerator provided for him, and he loaded his wallet with cash and new identity cards before leaving the room.

He had lunch at a deli three blocks down the street. The food was excellent, but in thirty years the business was destined to fail. Another two block walk and he found the pawn shop he had researched from police records. The owner, a pleasant Italian gentleman, would later get into considerable trouble over his record keeping and the clientele he serviced. John paid him an outrageous sum, in cash, for a forty-five caliber automatic and a box of cartridges. He used a false identity card and filled out a form, knowing full well that no record of the transaction would be kept by the store. And he left with gun and cartridges neatly wrapped in a package under his arm.

He had dinner in the hotel and enjoyed television shows from another age until bedtime. In the twilight of approaching sleep he was again nagged by a questioning mind. He was plotting the death of a human being, based on a hatred he had allowed to consume him. Wasn't this an evil thing? In the time of the act, perhaps, but with success there would be no object of hatred in another time, the historical time of his own existence. There was the paradox, of course. How would his existence change in the absence of Carl Anderson? He had no answer for that. He only wanted the anger and hatred to be gone, and then sleep came.

* * * *

For three mornings and early afternoons, John did his work for the museum. Using his false identity as a professor of medieval studies he was granted access to the vault where a new collection of books and letters was being held for study and analysis. Everything on his list was there, and he was given a private cubicle for his work. The staff was polite and didn't bother him for hours at a time. On two previous occasions he had failed to physically bring back books with him through time. They simply disappeared from his luggage during transition, either stolen by a Time Adventure employee or lost by space-time weirdness. Those books had been lost forever, but then he had begun photographing every page of every document, experiencing a delightful surprise when every picture he took survived transition, and the contents of all documents or books were preserved. It seemed to him that paradoxes related to physical objects, but not information, for whatever reason. So for three mornings and early afternoons, he took over two thousand pictures of text that had been lost to the future.

In late afternoons, he pursued his other mission.

In this time, Carl Anderson was a few weeks from his thirteenth birthday. John was shocked when he first saw the boy. Even at age twenty, Carl had looked like a neighborhood thug, with buzz-cut hair, thick chest and heavy arms, and here he was at twelve, a slender, frail-looking lad with a full head of blond, curly hair. John watched from a store entry across the street as the boy returned to his brownstone, leaning under the weight of a grocery bag he carried.

John began following him. Every day at three, Carl walked to a neighborhood grocery up the street. He remained there for an hour or two before emerging with the heavy grocery bag and returning to his brownstone. On the third day of his observations, John entered the store minutes after his quarry had done so. It was a small, family-owned store. A tall man behind the counter smiled in greeting. There was a magazine stand near the front of the store, and Carl was sitting on the floor in front of it, head down, a magazine in his lap. He did not look up while John was there.

There was potential here, for what John had in mind. There were several rows of shelves with narrow aisles not visible from the counter. Sooner or later the kid would do his shopping. John could work quickly and silently.

He found some crackers near the back of the store, a small brick of cheese in a cooler, and he paid with cash.

"You have a kid over there getting a free read," he said softly to the man who took his money and returned change.

"No problem," said the man. "The kid needs the escape, and he's a good customer. He comes in every day to pick up his old man's beer. Old Joe isn't doing so well since his wife run off a few years ago."

"A boy needs a mother," said John, and the man handed him a little bag containing his purchases.

"You actually let a young kid like that pick up his daddy's beer?"

The owner's eyes narrowed. "You a new cop or something? We have an understanding."

"Nah, just curious."

"Joe is a mean cuss, but he pays his tab on time. He doesn't go out much, and the cops are happy to keep it that way."

"Makes sense," said John, and smiled. "You have a good day."

Outside, John felt a twinge of sympathy for Carl Anderson, but quickly pushed it away. This was a kid who would later beat his father into a senseless condition, become a feared thug and then spend years brutalizing a young stepson after somehow charming a clueless single mom into marrying him.

He waited one day and then returned to the store to make his move. The syringe was in his coat pocket, the needle capped with a thick plug of rubber to protect the user. Inside the syringe was a carefully formulated cocktail for instant unconsciousness and quick death that had had been used in prisons for a time in the future.

Carl had been in the store for over an hour when John arrived, and was in his usual position on the floor, reading. There was a large bruise on his forearm, and Carl rubbed at it as he read. John picket up a small basket and went to the back of the store quickly when he saw the owner was not at the counter. He put a couple of items in the basket and rested it on the floor when he heard the owner come out of a back room and return to the counter. The beer cooler was in a back corner of the store, and John positioned himself adjacent to it. The boy would be turned away from him when he came down the aisle. One jab and it would be over. John heard Carl get up from the floor, the faint slap of a magazine being replaced on a shelf.

The cap came off the needle and John was poised at the entrance to the aisle. He heard footsteps, saw a moving shadow on a wall, and pulled back half a step, readying to strike.

His elbow struck something. It felt like a can, and then there was a terrible crash behind him. A small display of soup cans tumbled to the floor from a flimsy display stand he had bumped into.

"I didn't do anything! I didn't do anything!" screamed Carl. "I was just going back for the beer!"

John quickly capped the needle and got the syringe into his pocket just as the owner came around the corner.

"Sorry," said John. "I didn't see the display there, and backed into it. I'll pay for any damage."

"Please don't say anything to Joe," sobbed Carl. "I've got to get his beer to him."

"Easy, boy, and get your beer. It's all on the tab. This gentleman had a little accident here, that's all. Damn flimsy display stands don't hold anything anymore."

John was on his hands and knees, picking up cans. Carl came up behind him. A cooler door opened and closed. "I'm late again," said Carl, and left them.

"Poor kid," said the store owner, stacking cans again. "I don't know what would happen to him if his old man didn't get his beer on time."

John checked out and started to leave, but noticed an open magazine lying on the floor by the magazine stand. He picked it up and put it back on the shelf. It was the latest issue of *Dark Tales of the Orient*, and patterned after the old pulps of years past.

"He forgot one," he said.

"Likes adventure stuff," said the owner, and smiled.

* * * *

That night, John struggled to understand how Carl could change so much between the ages of twelve and twenty. His reaction in the store today was that of a dog abused often by its owner. John again fought back sympathy for his intended victim. Whatever his history, Carl Anderson had become a brutal person, and John had taken the brunt of it for a decade.

He called up the memories of being slammed against a wall, choked and slapped, all the while being told how spoiled and worthless he was while his mother just stood there and watched with a submissive pose. Over the years John had managed to partially forgive his mother; his real father had run away, his mother without marketable skills, and there were bills to pay. There was a room she could rent, and Carl Anderson had rented it. The rest was a study of a woman's effort to survive.

John could forgive his mother.

But for Carl Anderson there must be a reckoning or, better still, his removal from the history of John's world, even if it meant killing a seemingly innocent boy.

On this trip, he had one day left to accomplish it.

In the morning he had breakfast in the hotel, and packed his bag. His transition in space-time was scheduled for eight that evening. His work for the museum was finished, so he read and hovered around the restaurant much of the day and had a leisurely lunch there.

Near four in the afternoon he put his locked and loaded gun into his coat pocket with the safety on. He carried his light bag seven blocks down the street and through an alley to take up a position at the next street where the boy sat on his brownstone steps each evening. A small dumpster was there, and he lounged behind it to read a newspaper.

The street was empty and quiet while he waited, but at one point he heard yelling from across the street, and then a window slammed shut. Moments later, a door opened and Carl came out of the building. A burst of noise came with him, with sounds of a fight beyond the doorway. Carl leaped down the stairs and hurried away before John could get a hand on his gun. Someone slammed the door shut, but there were still the muted sounds of a fight going on, and then it was suddenly quiet again.

John could only hope that Carl was on his daily beer run for his father, and would be returning soon.

He had just thought this when the door opened again and a man came outside on unsteady legs and sat down on the stoop. He had a can of beer in one hand and a red bandana in the other, with which he swabbed his face often. His pants were rumpled and he wore a tee shirt stained brown. After a few minutes, John could smell the man's stench across the street.

This must be Daddy Joe, thought John, and immediately despised the man. *Waiting for his beer.*

John took the gun from his pocket, and clicked the safety off. *Maybe I can do two for the price of one*, he thought nastily, and then wondered why he'd thought that.

Old Man Joe rocked on the stoop, humming a tune and sipping beer until the can was empty and thrown casually into the street. Time began to drag by, and Joe grumbled to himself, wiping his face over and over.

The kid was late. There must have been a fight. Would he even return from the store? When John checked his watch again it was well after five. Old Joe wasn't happy about it either, his grumblings getting louder and louder.

Suddenly he stood up on the stoop, grabbing a banister when his legs wobbled, and he looked up the street.

"You're late, boy. Get your ass over here," he shouted.

Carl slowly approached his father, the grocery bag held tightly to him. "They were busy. There was a big line," he said.

"Bullshit," growled Joe. "You were reading that crap again. I know what you do there. C'mere, worthless. Can't even do an errand on time."

Carl pulled the bag tighter to him as John rested his arm on the top of the dumpster and raised the gun to a firing position. Local gun, local time, nothing could go wrong this time.

"I have your beer," said Carl faintly, and stepped forward to deliver the bag.

John had just put his finger on the trigger when the old man exploded in rage and grabbed his son by the throat, slapping him hard and repeatedly.

"You piece of shit! I don't know why I ever sired you!"

Carl dropped the bag, which clattered to the street, and one can ruptured, spraying beer onto the stoop.

John's finger tightened on the trigger, but his arm wavered as a terrible sound came from the boy he intended to kill. It was both a moan and a cry, a sound of sadness, helplessness and despair, and at that instant John felt something break inside him, something that had been there a long time and did not want to go away.

Carl screamed in agony, and Joe released him, stooping down to grab the bag and stagger up the steps, unaware that across the street the sights of a heavy caliber pistol were now lined up perfectly with the middle of his back.

He went inside and slammed the door behind him while his son slumped down on the steps in a puddle of beer and cried his misery away.

John still focused on the sights, but could not pull the trigger. A kind of paralysis gripped him. He stepped away from the dumpster and started to lower the gun.

And at that instant, Carl looked up and saw him standing there.

Their eyes locked. The boy's sobs abruptly ceased, and they looked at each other silently for a long time, and then John put the gun back into his coat pocket, picked up his bag and followed the alley back to the neighboring street, walking away from everything.

* * * *

John made the call the morning after returning to his own time. A familiar, gruff voice answered.

"It's John, dad. I wanted to see if things were going better for you now."

There was a long pause, then, "This is a surprise. I didn't figure you'd care. I mean, we didn't get along so good when you were home."

"I know, but that was then, and this is now. Maybe I've had to grow up a bit. How are you, Dad?"

Carl Anderson's voice quivered when he spoke. "Better, I guess. I got some infection where they operated, and they pumped drugs into me, but my heart's doing better. I'm not so tired, now."

"Good," said John. "Are you up for a visit?"

"You?" said Carl.

"Yes, me. I can be there in an hour. I'm sorry about some things, Dad. We need to talk."

"Sure. I'd like that, son." Carl's voice cracked, and he was struggling for control. "I can call you that, can't I?"

"You're the only father I ever really had," said John.

"I'm sorry about things too," said Carl, nearly choking.

"John?"

"Yes."

"Something else, very strange. I had a dream last night, about a thing that happened to me when I was a kid. I guess I'd pushed it way back in my memory. You were in the dream, John."

"We'll talk about it. Anything I can bring you?"

"Something to read, maybe. Haven't done that in a long time. Used to like fiction, mystery and adventure stuff like in the old pulps."

"I know just the thing," said John, "if I can find it. See you in an hour or so."

"Okay."

John drove to a used books store he had shopped frequently. The back room was stuffed with old pulps and other magazines from a bygone era, and in minutes he found what he wanted.

He paid for two old copies of *Dark tales of the Orient* and took them with him to the hospital to visit his Dad.

TRICKS

The lights had been on for one minute and Brenda was already sweating. The cool breeze from the air-conditioning vent above her head had little effect. Norm saw it and rushed to her, powder brush in hand. "Nerves, dear? You're making streaks," he gushed.

Brenda looked up from her notes while Norm fussed over her. "Just do your job," she said, and he gave her a pouty look. She was already plugged in and Arlene's voice was suddenly there.

"He's settled in the Green Room. Brenda, and so is Tasha. They were doing a deep breathing thing when I left."

"What's the mood? Will they talk?" said Brenda. Norm looked at her expectantly, and then realized she was talking to her mike.

"No problem with Drax and that ego of his, but Tasha seems quiet," said Arlene. "Beautiful little thing, but she needs some sunshine and food. You might have to drag her out at first. I show two minutes to air time. Getting Drax now. Go easy with him, Brenda. After all your on-camera arguments with him, and the stuff in the magazines, it's no secret what you think of his work."

No secret, indeed. Her campaign against graphic humiliation and torture of women had focused on Drax's films and nearly bankrupted the man, yet he'd been quick to accept Arlene's ratings-hungry invitation. Too quick, she thought. Arlene called her paranoid when she ordered an armed guard to be present in the studio for tonight's show.

Drax had been cordial enough when he'd arrived, coat draped European-style across broad shoulders, but he leaned too near for his greeting and she smelled his foul breath.

"Thank you for this opportunity, Brenda. Despite our differences I have always been strongly attracted to you. There is nothing more exciting to me than a woman who has both talent and strength."

"Alas, we do poorly as slaves to the network," said Brenda, and turned away from him. Tasha gave her a horrified look. The poor girl probably spent half her time chained up in the play dungeon Drax was rumored to have in his bleak mansion in the hills. Brenda wanted to buy her a hamburger and put some color back in her face.

Norm stepped back to inspect his art, limply flicked the brush at her and went back to join the other camera man in the gloom off-set. A few technicians and security man Cassidy lounged on metal bleachers at the back of the studio and were the only audience. The show was live, and it was now exactly midnight. Brenda checked her face in the monitor. No streaks.

The set was simple, a long, narrow desk with facing chairs on a dais and a backdrop panel painted black and covered with stars and nebulae. The lighting was kept low to keep a somber mood during the show, since Brenda's interviews were seldom happy occasions and often provocative.

She eased back in her chair, arranged the note cards in her lap and licked her lips, looking up as the red light on center camera went on. Norm counted down the last few seconds on his fingers, and then pointed at her. "Good evening," she said, and looked straight into the camera. "I'm Brenda Morelos, and this is Midnight Journal. Our guests tonight are award-winning horror film director and actor Andrew Drax, together with his lovely co-star of three films, Tasha Dent. Our subject for this midnight hour is fear: what causes it, how it is translated to the screen, and why people flock to theatres by the millions to be frightened out of their wits. And I can think of no better person to discuss this than the director and star of *Rivers of Blood*, Mister Andrew Drax."

Arlene pulled aside a corner of the backdrop curtain and Andrew Drax strode onto the set, smiling thinly and extending his hand towards her. Tall, gaunt yet handsome and now dressed in black pants and turtleneck with a cape draped over one arm, he leaned over as Brenda forced herself to raise a hand to him. He took it in his own slender fingers, kissed it, and she felt something sharp rake across her palm, making her shudder. He grinned close to her face, and she saw two small fangs in his mouth. Brenda recoiled and laughed as Andrew turned to snarl at the camera. "Always in character," she said. "Welcome to our show, Andrew."

Drax sat down in the chair opposite her, their knees almost touching. He fumbled at his mouth with his right hand, removed the fangs, and held them in his palm for a camera close-up. "Custom made, sharp and hard enough to punch holes in pop cans. Realistic, don't you think?"

Brenda checked the palm of her hand. There was a narrow, red welt there, but the skin wasn't broken. "And frightening," she said. *Rude*, she thought.

"The teeth? Not at all. If you saw me wearing them all evening at a party you'd find them amusing, perhaps absurd, and even boring. Another demonstration, if I may. Shake hands with me. Yes, just hold out your hand."

Brenda did so timidly, and Drax sniffed the air near her fingers. *A strange reaction*, she thought.

"You hesitate," said Andrew. His face seemed flushed under the lights, his eyes a dark brown near black. "Why?"

"I—I'm not sure what's going to happen next."

"Ah, but of course you've met my right hand, so we'll try the left one." He withdrew his left hand from beneath the cape in his lap and thrust it forward. It was grey, veined red with long, gnarled fingers and nails like bear claws. Brenda jerked her hand back so hard her note cards fell on the floor in disarray, and she heard laughter from the gloom beyond the set. Her heart pounded in fury and then Arlene's voice was in her head again.

"Quit frowning, Brenda. This is the King of Horror, so play along, laugh it off. This is GREAT stuff!"

Brenda laughed nervously. "I just aged ten years. What *is* that thing?" *You arrogant prick!*, she thought.

"A glove," said Andrew, pulling the thing from his hand. "Molded silicon rubber, with some artistic embellishments. Even the nails are soft, yet it frightened you." He held it out for another close-up.

"I'll say it did. Here, let me get myself together again." Brenda retrieved her note cards and ordered them in her lap.

"Nice touch," said Arlene in her ear.

"What *did* frighten me, Andrew?"

"Surprise—surprise at seeing something totally outside your everyday experience, a thing unknown to you, a thing unexpected. It could be a normally friendly dog that acts fierce, or a sudden thumping in the basement of your house in the middle of the night, or vampires in dark alleys. We fear what is different, the things foreign to us that we don't understand. Add to that the possibility of physical injury or death and you have horror."

"And you are called the King of Horror right now," said Brenda, forcing a smile.

"Thank you," said Andrew. "I owe a lot of it to my cast and crew. They are wonderful, all of them."

Brenda ignored his condescending smile. "It seems to me the horror is in the violence, torture and death. There's a lot of that in your films, Andrew. I've often wondered why people pay money to see that."

Andrew made a teepee with his hands and rested his chin on it, boring into her with coal black eyes. His smile had disappeared. Brenda felt her face flush, and she glanced at her little audience in the studio. Cassidy saw it and raised an eyebrow at her.

"Catharsis," said Andrew.

"I don't understand." Norm was waving at her. One minute to commercial break.

"All of us fear injury or death. Even you, Brenda. Add that to another basic fear, the anticipation of pain with a slow, agonizing death coming as a release. It's the anticipation that's horrifying, and it's all happening to someone else up there on the screen, not to you sitting comfortably in the audience. The thing you fear kills someone, but you survive, you go home safely, untouched by that which terrifies you. It is a catharsis of the fear that haunts you. You have triumphed over it." Andrew's nasty smile returned.

Many would call it gratuitous violence and gore, with the victims predominantly women. Let's talk about this when we come back." Brenda turned quickly to the camera. "This is Brenda Morelos for Midnight Journal, and we'll return after this announcement."

The red light on camera center flicked off and Norm rushed to her with his powder brush for a touch up. Drax required no work, for his face, though flushed, was dry.

Andrew leaned forward, and their knees touched. Brenda shivered at the contact. "You don't think much of my films, do you, Brenda?"

"I think they encourage violence and torture of women by unstable people, Andrew. I've been very vocal about that."

"And quite influential, I must say," said Andrew softly. He leaned closer and sniffed the air near her again. "Many of my best scenes have been cut from the last two films to get an R rating, specifically *because* of your influence. Are we going to talk about that? Will we discuss the products boycott you've urged on your followers, keeping my work off television and forcing me to seek foreign investors for my films? Others do what I do. Why do you persecute *me*, Brenda? I'm really quite fond of you."

"I don't intend to talk about the negatives this time. I think I've done enough of that." Brenda studied her note cards, not looking at him.

"Good, so then we'll stick to fear. By the way, you'll be pleased to hear that I'm retiring from film-making."

"What?" Now she looked at him, her mouth open in surprise. "Will you announce that during this segment?" Her heart pounded with excitement.

"Of course, if you bring it up." Andrew grinned at her.

"Watch Norm, Brenda, and keep down the hostility," said Arlene in her ear. "Great, so far, and I'm getting Tasha in two minutes for entrance before the next break."

"Got it," mumbled Brenda. Norm was counting down, and then the red light was on as she faced the camera.

"Welcome back to Midnight Journal. We're discussing fear and horror in film-making with Andrew Drax, director of *Rivers of Blood*. Tell me, Andrew, what is your definition of gratuitous violence, the kind of thing that some people accuse you of having in your films?"

Andrew looked strangely pleased by her question. "Gratuitous violence serves no purpose; it does not advance the story. I've always been careful to avoid it. Any student of film will tell you the violence I use is always an integral part of the plot."

"And why so much violence directed against women? I'll be asking

Tasha how she likes being the object of so much torture."

Andrew laughed heartily, but it wasn't a pleasant laugh. "I'm sure you'll find men and women equally represented. As a woman you naturally recall the female victims more vividly because you identify with them, and also their fears. Childhood fears, especially."

"Childhood fears?"

"Oh yes. In this there are differences between men and women. For example, a little boy is taught to—"

"Keep him going," said Arlene. "Stall if you have to. Drax must have locked the door coming out of the Green Room and Tasha isn't answering to anything. I have to get a key."

"—and that sub-conscious fear of failure, linked to the father, can lead to a dangerous, paranoid personality," continued Andrew. "Like it or not, little girls and boys are treated differently, with different expectations."

"Hang on. I'll have her out in a minute. Watch Norm," said Arlene.

"And then there are fears from unique childhood experiences. Can you think of one from your own childhood, Brenda? Andrew was studying her now, smiling faintly, eyes glittering disturbingly in the lights.

Momentarily distracted, she quickly said, "I was attacked by a neighbor's dog when I was four. I've been afraid of dogs ever since then."

"It's a common fear, Brenda, and you can be reminded of that instant, that horrible moment, with simple things." Andrew put the little fangs back into his mouth, leaned over and popped two contact lenses into his eyes with one hand. When he looked up his eyes were yellow with red capillaries criss-crossing the whites. He bared his fangs and hissed at her a foot from her face. His breath smelled metallic, and Brenda leaned back to escape it.

"Memories?" said Andrew.

"Not really. It's not the same," she said tiredly.

"Damn, she's asleep. Keep him going," said Arlene. "Two minutes to break."

"Oh dear, now I've bored you," Andrew said sadly. "Terror is such an individual thing, so difficult to achieve." He slapped his knee, and then shrugged. "Perhaps it's time for me to move on to other things, refresh myself, and get back to the roots of my art."

"Yes," said Brenda quickly. "You said during the break that you're retiring from films? Can this be true, after all the success you've had? I would think—"

"EIYEEEEEEEE!" Arlene's scream shattered her inner ear and Brenda jumped, startled, reached for the earphone. "Oh my God, my God, my God, oh—oh—the blood. She's soaked in blood! And her poor throat—Norm, someone, get back here!"

Bleachers clattered as two men rushed from the studio.

Andrew was leaning close, sniffing again, his little faux fangs sparkling. "Is something wrong? You were just startled by something."

"I—oh, I just got word that Tasha Dent won't be joining us. She has suddenly become ill." Brenda's heart was thumping, and sweat burst from every pore in her body.

Andrew Drax sniffed at her again and smiled, his face two feet from hers. She could smell his terrible breath and something else, a sharp, musky odor. "Poor Tasha. She is such a fragile thing, but she'll recover quickly. As I was saying, it has all become common and boring, and I need a change of life beginning tonight, a return to the quiet of the countryside with intimates to think and write and feel the cool grass on my bare feet again. I need recharging, a rejuvenation to continue my art. So this is my farewell performance, dear Brenda, and a goodbye to all my fans, at least for now. There was so much more I could have given them, but critics like you wouldn't allow it, and I'm disappointed in that. Very disappointed.

Arlene's voice was shrill. "It has to be Drax; he was the only one in here with her! Butch, call the police. Norm, Joel, Cassidy, watch him close and jump him if he makes one move at Brenda! He must have a knife on him."

Brenda pressed back in her chair. In her peripheral vision she saw Joel leave his camera, Cassidy's hand on his holstered revolver as they began inching towards the set. Norm stood transfixed, chewing on his hands. The commercial break was forgotten, both cameras running.

The color was suddenly gone from Andrew's face, changing to grey in the lights, skin rippling around his cheekbones, and his voice was now husky. "One last trick for the cameras, Brenda, one last special effect for the fans," he growled.

The ripples in his cheeks rushed towards the nose and met explosively with a crackling sound. His forehead disappeared as a glistening muzzle thrust forward, part cat, part wolf, yellow eyes now huge and blazing, the prop fangs exploding into dust at the ends of three-inch canines glistening wetly. He lunged and grasped her throat with long fingers ending in sharp, curved nails before she could even think to cry out.

Joel and Cassidy charged the set as she finally let out a strangled cry, but Andrew only waved one hand and the two men were lifted into the air and slammed with great force into the far wall of the studio. Norm screamed, but stood by his camera, aiming it.

What had once been Andrew Drax snarled at the cameras. "Now *this* is magic realism, folks!" he growled, and then turned and tore out the entire left side of Brenda's neck with a single savage twisting bite.

It was strange how there was no pain, only numbness and sudden cold throughout her body. Brenda fell to the floor on her back, looking up at the ceiling while Arlene shouted in her ear, "Brenda? Brenda! What's *happen-*

ing?" She grasped her neck, felt life pulsing into the palm of her hand in great spurts. The creature that was Andrew Drax, mouth dripping with her blood, knelt beside her, face close. Behind him, studio doors banged open and there were outcries.

"Since our first interview, when I first smelled your delicious fear," said Drax, "I've desired you as much as I do Tasha. I will return for both of you when it is time, and we will have an eternity together, and then you will truly understand and savor the sweet taste of human terror."

"Get down on the floor, or I'll shoot!" someone shouted.

Andrew Drax raised his arms and changed again, and as the final bit of old life ebbed from Brenda's ruined neck she saw him disappear as a column of green mist into the air conditioning vent above her.

BENEATH THE ICE OF ENCELADUS

Twelve hours out from Herschel Base, Anna Hegel finally vented when Phil made another crack about wasting space for 'bug' people on the mission. Her face flushed when she glared at him, and she tried hard to control the angry quaver in her voice.

"I really hope I'm not going to have a problem with you, Phil. We're going to be spending a lot of time together in close quarters, whether you like it or not."

Phil Yallowitz was seated in front of Anna, so she couldn't see his face.

"That's my point," said Phil. "This isn't a bug hunt for me, it's a test of a vessel I've worked on for seven years. I need an electronic tech, not a scientist."

Sitting next to Anna, the tech assigned to the submersible program seemed to take offense at that. "Hey, man, you've got *me*. I'm certified mechanical and electrical."

"I don't need to have any light tubes changed. How are you with spectrum analyzers?"

The tech chuckled and turned to Anna. "Don't feel bad, Doctor. He bad-mouths me, too."

Sitting at the shuttle control desk, Mission Commander Mike Goffin looked over his shoulder and raised an eyebrow at them. Above him, Enceladus was already huge on his view screen.

"Stop it, all of you."

"Yes sir!" said the tech, and grinned.

"Read the mission profile again, Phil. A mission specialist was a must. The only debate was whether it would be a geologist or an astrobiologist, and the bug people won. The only reason we're here is because the water is easy to get to. The Europa team is understandably furious about their budget being cut so we could get our one chance here. One shot, people, so you'd better be able to work together on this. It's a long way back to Earth for anyone who can't do it."

There was a long silence after Mike said that.

* * * *

Herschel Base was fifty kilometers west and north of the South Pole, and the view screen showed a new yet strangely tortured surface there. Unlike the northern, lightly cratered hemisphere of Enceladus, the southern area, at long distance, appeared relatively smooth and thus geologically more recent, but close inspection had long ago revealed a jumbled surface of cracks and rills, valleys and depressions as if some great glacier had spread there. Saturn was a bright ball thirty degrees in diameter, rings edge-on and faintly visible. Icy Mimas was beginning a transit, and Titan was a large, fuzzy orb in a black sky as the shuttle began its vertical descent to the base. Looking at Titan, Anna thought of the research platform orbiting above its hazy atmosphere. It had been her home for the past three years.

At fifty kilometers altitude, four fractures were clearly visible, bounded on either side by ridges, features that had been known as 'tiger stripes' for well over a century. Closer, the fissures seemed choked with shining blocks and boulders—water ice with traces of ammonia, methane and other simple organics. Out on the horizon, a plume of vapor rose far above the descending shuttle.

Water vapor, thought to be coming from eruptions of liquid from a surface whose average temperature was only seventy-five degrees Kelvin.

Below the surface of Enceladus, liquid water had to exist.

And where there was water, there might be life.

Anna Hegel had arrived with the intention of finding it. This was an ambition she shared with three generations of women in her family. Time had run out for two of them, and was getting dangerously short for the third. Herschel Base appeared below them as a black, fifty-meter-diameter spot on a chaotic jumble of ice in the fissure, or sulcus, known as Damascus. The roof and access module bristled with instrument arrays and a microwave dish. There was a jolt beneath their feet when shuttle lock occurred. Anna felt a subtle gravity, one hundredth that of Earth, but she'd been living with ten times that on Titan Station for three years. Despite regular exercise her limbs were like sticks, and within a year or two she would have to decide whether to remain in space or abandon her life's work and return to Earth as her mother and grandmother had done.

For them, it had been too late.

The floor hatch screeched as Mike pulled it open. He gestured to Anna. "Ladies first."

Anna looked down; saw hands waving to her from the end of a hollow cylinder a few meters long. She made a little hop, and dropped like a dust mote. Several seconds later, hands grasped her and pulled her to one side as the others came down.

A slender, blond woman reached out her hand.

"Welcome to Herschel."

"Wow, it's cold in here," said Anna, and shivered.

The woman smiled. "Nothing like outside. It'll be better down below."

Three men were with the woman, and reached up as first Phil and his tech came down the tube, then Mike after them. The woman shook Anna's hand. "I'm Helena. I'll be your lab tech, and introduce you to Commander Kassner."

The space they occupied ended in a shaft angled at thirty degrees from their vertical, and lined with hand rungs. Anna followed Helena through it with practiced ease, and they came out into a living space shaped like a ring. There were instrument panels and video monitors floor to ceiling. One monitor showed a tech guiding Mike into the shaft above them.

"It's smaller than I expected," said Anna.

"There are several levels," said Helena. "Bunks and mess are just below this one, but you'll be working out of the lower levels. The whole base is a tapered cylinder, and most of it is insulation and concentric vacuum layers. They literally pounded a cork into a volcanic vent when they made this place. And the two outer layers are spring-loaded composites that flex. The ice is constantly moving around us. You'll hear it soon enough."

Anna felt tightness in her throat, and Helena smiled.

"Don't worry. I've been here four months, and we haven't been crushed yet. This place really only has to last another two weeks if you people get your job done."

A joke, perhaps, but Anna wasn't amused by it.

Helena showed Anna around the ring. A central shaft with rungs on a pole took them down to the next level where there was the odor of coffee in the air and Mike was talking to a tall, square-jawed man in astronaut blues. The conversation stopped when Helena and Anna approached them, and Mike smiled.

"This is Doctor Anna Hegel, sir."

"Eric Kassner is our base commander," said Helena.

Kassner stuck out his hand, and his grip was bone hard. "It's a small universe. I knew your mother years ago. How is she these days?"

Anna blinked. "Sorry to say she's dead, sir, waited too long to return to Earth. Her heart couldn't take it."

"Sorry to hear that. She had everyone's respect on Europa. It has been a tough mission there."

"Too much ice, sir. I doubt if they'll ever get through it. I guess that's why I'm here."

"Plenty of ice here, too, but an ocean is right beneath us, and you people are going to tell us what's there."

"Yes, sir."

"So when do we see it?" asked Mike.

"Soon enough. The time is short, but we're not going to rush unnecessarily. The submersible has to be proven at depth, and we don't even know what we're diving into yet. This module is plugging what used to be a volcanic vent, and the shaft down has been changing ever since the water flow was restricted. We're floating in the thing, and sonar returns are garbled. There could be a sea, a lake or a puddle down there. First job is to find the end of the shaft and scan what's below it. There won't be much room for maneuvering."

"I'm sure Phil Yallowitz can handle it. The vessel is his baby," said Mike.

Kassner turned back to Anna. "Your mother was a patient person, and I hope you are too. The first dips will be with tech and pilot only."

"I understand, sir," said Anna, "as long as you remember we only have two weeks until our return window to Titan."

Kassner nodded. "I know that, doctor, but I also intend to send you home alive."

Anna suddenly felt a vibration, and the floor tilted beneath her feet, nearly tipping her over. She grabbed Mike's arm, as there was a terrible screech from the walls, like some metal talon was scraping there. Anna's heart hammered from the shock of it.

Kassner looked at her calmly. "Vapor bubble. You'll get used to them. Earthquakes are less frequent, but scarier. The water reservoir below us is under pressure, and is either very small, or there's a big heat source there. Please keep in mind this is an extraordinarily dynamic environment. Yes, we want to explore it as quickly as we can. We just don't want it to kill us."

The commander reached out and shook their hands again. "Welcome to Herschel Base. Helena will show you where to bunk, and there will be a general briefing for all of you in the mess in exactly two hours."

Helena touched Anna's elbow. "This way," she said, and took them away to their quarters.

* * * *

Sleep was a challenge. Anna's satchel was inclined slightly from the vertical in a six cubic meter niche behind a poly-steel grill. It was not totally unlike the shuttle, but that had been quiet during what passed for night, and she'd floated around in her bag. On Herschel the floor and walls were forever heaving and shaking, and the constant groaning and screaming of hard ice and rock scraping metal kept her awake for most of her sleep shift. She fought off the effects with strong coffee until Helena gave her something that knocked her out cold, and life was good again.

Mike and Phil and two techs made the first dip two-work shifts after arrival. Anna went down to bottom level to watch their progress on a television monitor after they'd submerged. Phil's submersible was shaped like a shallow, inverted soup bowl with ports on the sides, bow steering and diving planes, and a nose bubble. Two retractable claws folded up along two sides, and there were three directional lights forward. Armor was sufficient for two thousand feet earth side, and was definitely overkill for what they were expecting, but in Phil's own words: "You never know."

There were no screws; three ports aft were all there was to see of a jet propulsion system fueled by hypergolic *Anistol*, as used for maneuvering by the shuttle. Water and hydrogen were the only emissions, and viewed as safe in any oxygen-free environment.

Anna watched as Mike, Phil and two techs opened the hatch on top of the submersible and climbed in. The yellow paint of the hull complimented the yellowish-green of the water it floated in, and there was a musty odor in the air. Commander Kassner manned the comm.-panel and Anna joined him there while a base tech closed and sealed the hatch.

"Diving," said Phil, and there was a roiling on the water surface where the submersible floated in its tank.

"Opening lock," said Kassner, and moved his hand. The submersible dropped into a lock below the tank, where pressure could be varied in transferring the vessel to the outside.

"Pressurizing," said Kassner, and Anna felt the floor move beneath her. The walls around them groaned. Kassner looked at her. "It's okay. We bob up and down a bit. In the low gravity, pressure changes are subtle. If there's an ocean below us I doubt if it's very deep." He looked up at a monitor. "Lights on. Opening outer door."

On the monitor, silvery doors slid aside and three bright beams of light disappeared into blackness, the beam edges tinged green.

"No particulates," said Anna.

"Pieces of ice once in a while, and those bubbles that come from some depth." Kassner smiled. "I'm sure you'd like to see something more interesting."

"That's why I'm here. Right now, I'll settle for water samples."

"Automatic, and real-time." Kassner pointed. "Follow that monitor. Readings are every four meters."

When Anna looked at the monitor, a simple spectrum was already building there: traces of ammonia, methane, sulfur and iron.

"The vent is widening," said Mike, and Anna looked at the other monitor again. Blackness ahead, the faint glow of ice from the sides. Suddenly, there was a faint reflection from something in front of the submersible.

"Slowing," said Phil. A shelf of ice came out of the blackness, oriented left to right and descending at a steep angle.

"The shaft turns here, and I see an edge to it. Cracks all over the place"

There was a faint, blue outline of something, and blackness beyond it.

"That's what has been scattering our sonar," said Kassner. "I'd put the first buoy right where it turns."

"Okay," said Mike, "but let's find the end first. I see it. We'll put the first buoy there."

"Don't go beyond that point. We'll check out the vessel at depth tomorrow. I want those relays in first."

"Right."

The monitor image faded, and then went to random noise and cosmic background. "What's happening?" asked Anna.

"They're around the corner. A relay buoy will go at the shaft opening, another at the turn by the shelf, and we should have data communication the rest of the way if there's really a large body of water there."

They waited nervously for half an hour, and suddenly the monitor showed a picture of ice close-up and a conical package anchored to it by a short chain.

"Are you getting sonar yet?" asked Mike, and his voice was extraordinarily loud and clear.

Kassner leaned to his left and looked at another monitor. "Got it. Multiplexing. The phones are even more exceptional. Sounds like you're with us here. So, let's see what we have down there."

They watched the multiplexed pattern of the pulsed sonar build for fifteen minutes before Kassner said, "It's a small sea or a lake, running parallel to the fissure. Depth goes to two or three hundred meters, and it's big, maybe ten klicks long, three wide. The vent comes out of the ceiling of the thing. The bottom reflections are coming up with rough areas, like there's some structure down there. And no, you can't take a quick look."

"Figured," said Mike. "Take 'er up, Phil."

The men returned to the base in a jubilant mood.

And Anna didn't sleep a wink that night.

* * * *

It was three Earth-days until the next submersion. Erratic readings in the vessel's pilot deck were finally traced to a damaged optical cable, and a new one threaded through a wall to replace it. Only Mike and Phil would go down this time, and Anna tried hard to be patient.

"There's room for me, and all I want to do is look outside," she said.

"You'd do better to watch the spectrometer readouts here," said Mike. "This is a systems check, and we won't be going anywhere near the bottom."

"Watch the monitor," said Phil. "There's nothing to see until we go deep. You'll be bored."

Inside, she despised Phil's condescending tone of voice, but Anna kept her face expressionless.

"I can do that quietly, and not be in the way, Phil. And if you see anything at all interesting, I'm sure you'll be alert enough to include me in the discussion of it."

"Absolutely," said Mike, but Phil said nothing and looked away from her.

The submersible disappeared beneath the yellowish green surface with a gentle roil of bubbles. After a few minutes, Anna dismissed her irritation and carefully watched the spectrometer readings as the vessel reached the shelf at the bottom of the vent and sailed out into open water.

The water there was even more pristine than in the vent. The lines for ammonia and iron nearly disappeared. After a few minutes a small peak developed for sodium when the vessel was sailing near the ceiling of the mammoth cavern, and at one point there was a small spike in sulfur. Anna noted the exact time of each event; it was something to do. Commander Kassner's attention was focused on the sonar readings the entire time.

A few minutes later, things got more interesting when Phil began putting his machine through her paces, beginning with a test of the bow planes in turns and steep dives. The bottom was at three hundred meters at that point, and the dive went to one hundred. Anna stared hard at the monitor, but there were only three beams of light disappearing into darkness. Whatever was on the bottom was a poor reflector. But when she looked back at the spectrometer readings, a sharp line for sulfur was growing, and it suddenly stopped as Anna noted the time again.

"Local concentration of sulfur where you are," she said.

There was a pause. "Don't see anything," said Mike.

"The bottom is quite rough below you," said Kassner. "We're getting a lot of scattering."

"I'll want to go down there," said Anna, and then grabbed hard for a wall rung when the floor beneath her began shaking violently. She hung on grimly as the shaking went on for several seconds. It stopped as quickly as it had begun.

"That was no gas bubble," said Anna. Kassner turned to look at her, and she didn't like what she saw in his eyes.

"Quake," said Kassner. "There were a few of them when Herschel was first inserted into the vent, but this is the first big one since. Hope it didn't plug up the vent. Mike, are you there?"

"Loud and clear," said Mike. "We just had some turbulence here, and something dark dropped past us towards the bottom."

"We had a quake up here, pretty strong, a shaker. You'd better come up right away."

"Okay. We've gone through our list for now; the rest has to be done at depth. That must have been a rock that came past us. It went down like a chunk of iron. Good thing it didn't hit us."

"I'll feel better when you see the vent is clear," said Kassner.

"Blowing tanks," said Phil. "We'll be there in a minute or two."

Anna was worried, and Kassner saw it on her face. "Good communications, so the shaft can't be plugged."

As if in reply, Mike called in only seconds later, "We have a little problem here," and at that instant Anna felt the floor shake again beneath her feet.

"Some debris on the shelf here, and another rock just came down. Wouldn't take much to make a tight fit. We'll clean it off with the articulators. Stand by."

The news was worse a minute later.

"Now we have a *real* problem. The port articulator is frozen up, and the servo is showing an overload when I try to deploy it. Starboard claw is working fine, and we're cleaning off the shelf, but we need to have both articulators working at depth. This could be a major repair."

"We don't have the time," said Anna.

"We'll make the time," said Phil. "I'm not taking this thing down with a broken arm and then take the blame if we need it."

"Understood," said Kassner. "For now, let's play it by ear."

"And I'm going down on the next dive," added Anna.

Phil started to say something, but there was a click and his voice was cut off.

Ten minutes later the vessel surfaced in a roil of bubbles, and the hatch popped open. Phil climbed out and went straight to the port articulator folded tightly against yellow metal like an injured arm. "I need a speed wrench," he said, and a tech brought one to him.

Mike climbed out of the vessel, stepped over to the edge of the tank, and whispered to Kassner and Anna. "Let's get some coffee and let Phil work."

They went up one level and had coffee. "Dark down there, and clear," said Mike. "Any light color on the bottom would have shown up in our beams. There's rock peeking through ice on the walls, and especially on the ceiling. It was like a cave dive."

"Anything interesting will likely be on the bottom," said Anna. "The spectrometer showed some interesting sulfur spikes while you were down there."

"Oh," said Mike, "yes, there was one place where Phil thought he saw a couple of bubbles go by us."

Anna's heart leapt. "Did you record it?"

Mike shook his head. "Nope. It was just a few seconds after we came out of our dive."

"I'll backtrack it," said Anna. She turned to go back to lower level, and nearly ran into Phil as he came out of the central shaft connecting all levels. He looked both saddened and subdued.

"Well, I really screwed up."

"What?" Anna didn't know Phil was capable of admitting an error to anyone, let alone her.

"I should have inspected the articulators before we left Titan Base. A joint seal was split; God knows how long that bearing was exposed to hard vacuum. It looks like a porcupine."

Anna's mouth hung open in confusion.

"Epitaxial growth in hard vacuum has made hair crystals at the carbon boundaries, and welded the joint. I don't suppose we have a high-voltage unit here, something at say thirty kilovolts and a milliamp?"

"Nothing like that," said Kassner.

Phil sighed, obviously upset with himself. Anna was strangely tempted to touch his arm in comfort.

"One quick check on Titan Station, and I would have found it. I can't burn it off, so I'll have to do it the hard way. I can snap the bearing out easy enough, but then I have to polish everything down to the original tolerances, and that's a trial-and-error hand job that could take days."

"We don't have days!" shouted Anna.

Phil winced, and Anna looked down at her feet.

"Sorry. We don't have time for blame, either. We only have ten Earth days at most. I'm willing to go down there with one articulator working."

"I don't think so," said Kassner, and Mike nodded in agreement.

"I need at least two dives to see what's down there," pleaded Anna. "In case you've forgotten, *that* is our primary mission."

"With help I can fix it in a day, two days tops," said Phil. "We'll work around the clock."

Everyone looked at Kassner, and he looked back at each of them in turn.

"I'm not hearing objections. Okay, recruit whoever you need, and do it."

"I'll help," said Anna.

Phil actually smiled at her. "No offense, but I'll use the techs. They know their way around a machine shop, and this is precision handwork we have to do. Thanks."

"I can use the time to go over the sonar scans and target some areas to look at. I'll have a plan ready for us in a day. Don't beat yourself up, Phil. We'll get this done," said Anna.

Phil couldn't look at her, simply mumbled something, turned, and climbed back down the central shaft to bottom level, where his work awaited him.

Mike put a hand on Anna's shoulder. "He's basically a good guy, you know. Right now his self-confidence is bruised, and we need to hope it heals fast."

"It has to," said Anna, but she worried about it. *This is my last chance,* she thought.

Her relief came a day and a half later, when Phil announced the articulator was now working, and Anna had to rush to finish her plan for the next dive.

* * * *

There was another quake just before they submerged. Sonar showed no blockage in the vent below them, but a few small cracks had become big ones. The quakes were becoming more frequent. Kassner said it was a cyclic thing related to the positions of Titan and Mimas, and he expected the shaking to lessen soon.

Anna felt cramped in the submersible, was seated on a shelf behind Mike and Phil where she could watch the instruments and look out both the portholes and nose bubble at the same time.

Phil blew tanks slowly to slow their decent in a low-gravity environment where pumps and water-jets were a substitute for buoyancy. Using the bow planes, Phil literally flew the vessel down the vent and out over the shelf into deep water. He made a few swoops and turns, deployed both articulators, tested each joint before turning his attention to a map of areas Anna had found interesting. Anna leaned over his shoulder and pointed at the map as Phil and Mike studied it.

"The rough areas on the bottom are most interesting. There's a lot of sonar scattering in these three regions, and lighter detail in some others. I'd like to hit these five if we can, and while we're at it we can look closer at the smoother regions."

"We'll have to get around enough to map the entire cavern, and that's one dive by itself," said Mike. "It's in the mission statement, Anna."

"We can extrapolate a lot if we stay close to the bottom in the thirty percent we've already scanned." Anna pointed. "Go here first. You were above this area when I got a nice sulfur spike on the spectrometer."

"Okay," said Phil. Map coordinates were relative to the pinging buoy in the vent below Herschel, and they were already close. Phil began a slow descent on a helical path towards the bottom.

Anna squinted, willing herself to see through the gloom. Her heartbeat quickened as Mike called off the distance to the bottom. At fifty meters they passed a bubble the size of a dinner plate. The view below was a dirty gray, and at twenty meters there was a dark splotch that moved across their view as Phil leveled out the dive and slowed.

At ten meters the bottom finally came into view, and at first Anna only felt disappointment. It looked like dark gray sand with occasional boulders protruding, nothing like what she'd expected from the sonar reflections.

But at three meters, Phil brought the vessel to a crawl, and the view outside was dramatically different. The boulders were now little towers of dark material like basalt, and the sand was a coarse gravel of dark rock and dirty ice. Even closer, the meter-high towers were made of dirty ice covered with an orange stain that reflected weakly in the bright lights. "We have to get a sample of that," said Anna.

Kassner had been watching everything from Herschel Base, and suddenly called in. "We're getting spikes for sulfur and sodium, and a trace of iron. The area you're in right now is *loaded* with methane, and it's over two-seven-seven Kelvin there. There was a sharp increase in temperature when you reached ten meters above bottom."

"Reminds me of Earth side smokers, but there's all kinds of complex life forms around those things," said Anna. "All I see here is some kind of stain. We're sampling it. Could be bacterial."

"Wishful thinking," said Phil. "looks mineral to me."

Phil looked surprised when Anna said, "You're probably right, but let's get a good sample of it, and also the gravel and bottom ice. That has a different sheen to it."

"Bubbles," said Mike, pointing.

Anna looked, and saw a stream of small bubbles leaking from the base of a tower, rising slowly and coalescing to form a large bubble, which drifted lazily upwards. "Can we get a temperature reading on that tower's surface?"

"Should have it," said Phil. He'd been working an articulator to break off a small nubbin from the side of the tower, and was dropping it into the specimen basket beneath the nose bubble.

"Two-eight-three Kelvin," said Kassner.

"The bottom must be porous," said Anna. "These towers could be crystallites of a rock-ice mix where heat channels are coming through. I bet we have a mix of rock and methane clathrate down here, but if there are any methane breathers I sure don't see them."

Phil steered the submersible at a crawl through a small forest of towers, and columns of small bubbles rose from a few of them, but there was no sign of a living thing or any remnants of life, and then the bottom was soon relatively smooth again. They stopped for samples several times, but spent most of the dive just in sight of the bottom. They mapped the extent of the cavern in all directions. It was not so much an underground sea as it was a lake, unstable at best with all the seismic activity, and unlikely to be large or stable enough for life to have evolved there. There were more forests of little, bubbling towers, and vast expanses of black rock mixed with methane in ice, and by the end of the dive they had explored all the prime interesting areas Anna had marked on the sonar maps. There was a secondary list of prospects where small echo dispersions had been observed, but both Mike and Phil felt they had "seen it all" when they returned to Herschel Base. They left Anna to analyze the specimens they'd brought up and to define targets for the next dive. They would also be mapping the cavern ceiling in a search for other vents, and that was scheduled to take much of the dive time.

Anna expected her specimen analysis to take days, and there would only be time for one more dive before she had to leave.

Kassner seemed to sense her dark mood, and shared a cup of coffee with her that first evening back from the depths.

"You're disappointed," he said.

"I guess, but I have to admit a moon this small probably hasn't been around long enough in a tidal environment to evolve any life forms. It was a long shot, and a negative result is still a result. That's science."

"Would have been nice for the family history," said Kassner.

"You have a *file* on me?"

"You bet I do. Your pedigree is what brought you here."

"You must mean my grandmother. Do you know the Martian bacteria she discovered are still controversial? Half the science community still thinks it was a contaminant. And mom had to return to Earth before they even got a fourth of the way through Europa's ice. New discoveries are wonderful, but circumstances and a lot of luck are involved. And I have one more dive to get some."

"Then let's drink to luck," said Kassner, and he raised his squeeze bottle.

Their bottles touched as another small quake made the floor shudder beneath their feet.

* * * *

Midway through the dive Anna felt herself relaxed but saddened, resigned to the fact the mission would be a scientifically interesting mapping of a subterranean lake beneath the surface of Enceladus. The geologists would be excited, but for Anna's colleagues in astrobiology there would be nothing to talk about. Her work on Titan had reached a dead end; the big moon had fascinating chemistry and geology, but no life. Perhaps she could return to Mars and build on what her grandmother had done. The gravity there was much higher, and she could then return to Earth in her later years and write up her lifetime of experiences in the outer regions of the solar system. It would also tie together the work of three generations of women in her family.

For Anna, it was a good plan, and an acceptable plan, though her dream of finding extraterrestrial life was fading fast.

But it was a plan that changed abruptly after the fourth hour of the dive.

Sample analysis had shown no life. There was silicate rock mixed with dense, rich methane clathrate, and the stain on the little towers was iron sulfide. The gas bubbles were likely hydrogen sulfide, though she'd not been able to sample them directly. Every test for bacteria, every test for chemical reactions used by known life forms, had been negative.

For nearly four hours they had cruised near the bottom, observing occasional clusters of crystalline towers, but mostly vast plains of pebbles and methane-rich water ice. Kassner had called in twice with news of renewed quake activity, and they had seen several large chunks of ice drifting downwards towards the bottom. Communication with Kassner had become garbled, cutting in and out after that. Mike was worried about it, and said so. "We might have to cut it short, Anna. With all these quakes, we don't want to be trapped down here."

Anna ignored his concerns. She had marked four places on the sonar maps where there were small depressions in the bottom that showed weak dispersions similar to what was seen with tower clusters. They were now nearing the first of them. Anna's attention had wandered a bit as she thought about returning to Mars, but something suddenly caught her eye.

"I see flashing lights," she said, and leaned forward to look ahead through the nose bubble. "Reflections?"

"No," said Phil. "I see it, too. Yellowish green—flickering, straight ahead."

"And beyond," said Mike. "One source is close, the other fainter."

In the darkness beneath the ice of Enceladus, the flashes of light suddenly ceased.

Phil had slowed to a crawl, but remained on course. The plain ahead was level, then rose a meter to form a hillock that curved away from them. And just beyond it was what Anna first thought was another tower, different this time, a feature glowing bronze in the bright lights of the submersible.

They came close, hovering over a crater-like depression two meters deep. The object it held reminded Anna of a dead tree with several bare branches. It was anchored in methane-clathrate and stood four meters high, and around it were several others only a meter tall. Branches swayed slowly in the turbulence created by the submersible's jets. Their surfaces were rough and mottled in bronze and dark brown, and from the dark areas streams of tiny bubbles pulsed in bursts that floated lazily upwards.

"Oh, my God, oh my God," gasped Anna, and she could scarcely breathe.

"It's soft," said Mike. "Hollow, maybe."

"Not rigid," whispered Anna. "Look at the tangle of tubules at its base, anchoring it to the ice. The bubbles have to be hydrogen. It's using methane. I think it's alive."

"A plant? Looks like a metal sculpture. Now it's not moving," said Mike.

"The jets are off. No more wake. The currents move it. That doesn't mean it's alive," said Phil, "but *something* was flashing lights at us until we got close."

"Not now."

"Turn off our lights."

"What? You want to be blind down here? I don't think so." Phil shook his head.

"Just the big headlights. We can still see close from the interior lights," said Anna.

"I can back off a bit." Phil frowned.

"No. I want to see if we can provoke a reaction."

"Why don't I just touch it with an articulator, then?"

"You might hurt it."

Mike reached over and turned off the exterior lights. "Enough," he said.

Outside, the strange tree-looking thing was dimly illuminated. They waited for long minutes, but nothing happened. "It's some kind of crystallized tower like the others, only a different shape," said Phil.

"We need to turn off the interior lights." Anna's heart was thumping hard in her excitement.

"How long?" asked Mike.

"A few minutes. It saw our lights and flashed at us, but stopped when we got close. I want to try something with this." Anna held up a small penlight she routinely carried with her on a ring with two keys and a flat, multiply bladed screwdriver.

Phil shook his head, but Mike put a hand on his shoulder. "Five minutes, and no longer. Turn the lights out, Phil, and start counting."

The lights went out, and they were sitting in pitch-blackness. "This is really dumb," said Phil.

They waited one minute, then two. There was a faint scraping sound from outside that came and went, and nothing to be seen. Finally, Anna moved her hand close to the nose bubble and began flashing her little penlight off and on. She continued for half a minute, and then stopped.

There was no response, but Phil suddenly shifted in his seat. "I see some faint flashes way off to the left of us. Maybe we should move."

Anna flashed her light several times, waited a few seconds, then did it again and held her breath.

From outside, green lights flickered dimly at first, like a dance of shy fireflies. The lights began near the edges of the nose bubble and moved inwards, getting brighter.

"Yes!" said Anna, and she flashed her little penlight again.

The response was immediate and bright; multiple points of flashing green illuminating the ends of branches. There was a scraping sound from the outer hull of the submersible, and suddenly a glowing tendril of green struck the center of the nose bubble and recoiled from it.

"Yikes!" gasped Phil, and with one hand hit the outside lights, while the other reached to start the engine pumps.

The thing outside had extended two branches to grasp the submersible just above the bow planes, and a third branch was now waving slowly back and forth in the bright lights. The jets went on with a whoosh and Phil backed up several meters to get out of its reach.

"Stop! Stop!" yelled Anna, but Phil had already done it. He smiled wanly at Mike, who was still staring at the thing. "Pretty fast for a rock," he said, and then turned to Anna. "I suppose you want samples, now. How do we do that? I could probably break something off with an articulator."

"Absolutely not," said Anna. "It could be a plant, a coral community or a single, intelligent entity. I will *not* take a chance on harming it before we have some idea what it is. The response could have been chemically or intelligently directed. If it's a plant there must be dead ones. Look for debris in the depression it's in."

Phil peered out the side of the nose bubble. "There's more than just this one. I see green lights flickering again from our left, maybe a few meters away."

The object of their attention had pulled its branches in tightly against the main trunk and was now motionless, an abstract statue mottled in bronze and dark brown.

They drew closer. Phil activated an articulator, extended a claw and poked gingerly at gravel and ice near the object's base. There was a short piece of something white and showing large pores that he placed in the sample box. Plant or animal, there were two small versions of the big one rooted there, but Anna insisted they not be touched. And even though they came within reach of it, the big one remained motionless the entire time the bright lights were on.

"Let's move," said Mike. "There's more to see left of us, but the lights have stopped flashing."

"Okay," said Anna. "Is it possible to dim our lights?"

"No. I'll come in slow this time, and turn off the lights when we get in close."

Phil backed off with a single jet pulse, and veered left in the direction of the other lights they'd seen. They saw another large chunk of ice come down and impact softly with the sea floor, stirring up a cloud of sand and pebbles.

It was twenty meters before they saw reflections from tall stalks rising from the bottom. Phil came in slowly this time. They saw several branched trunks standing close together, and from the end of one branch came a single flash of green. Two meters from the nearest branch, the submersible's lights went out. The interior lights illuminated the scene dimly, an abstract portrait of bronze figures on black.

"They're moving," whispered Anna.

Branches waved ever so gently in still water, the movement synchronous among several thick trunks. Even in dim light there were occasional flashes of green, which they could now see were coming from little nubbins on the ends of the branches. Mike looked off to the right.

"The one we just left is flashing again."

"They're talking about us," said Anna.

"Maybe, or just warning each other of danger. Whatever. You got what you came for, Anna. It's certainly a surprise to me," said Phil. "You sure you don't want a living sample of these things?"

"I can't do it. There's no precedent for any life form above bacterial level. It's a case for The Council of Nations. If it's allowed, someone else will have to do it, or maybe I'll get a chance to come back someday. We have our pictures and spectra, and all the water samples. That'll have to be enough for now."

Phil used the articulators to scoop up some samples near the bases of the trunks. The occupants of the little depression in gravel and methane clathrate seemed undisturbed by it. Bronze limbs waved gently and decorated themselves in flashes of green. Anna watched, mesmerized, burning the sight into her memory.

"We really have to finish our mapping and look for other vents," Mike finally said.

"Will we have time for another dive?" Anna felt an ache in her chest.

"Not this trip," said Mike. "You'll have to come back again, if you can."

"The base might get swallowed up, and the vents plugged. There might not be another chance."

"I know, but we have to finish the mission plan. Let's go, Phil."

Phil looked over his shoulder at Anna and frowned at the agony written on her face.

"Got to go, Anna. We'll call Kassner right now, and get your discovery on the record."

Anna nodded, and pressed her lips together as they backed away. Green flashes sent them on their way, light from living things anchored in ice at the bottom of a subterranean lake of a tiny, geologically active moon cold beyond belief, in the outer reaches of the solar system. It was a miracle, a thing to be studied for a lifetime, and she was being forced to leave it.

Mile called Kassner, but there was no response, not even static. "I don't like this. The signal was clear until a while ago."

"Could be scattering," said Phil. "There's a lot of rough topology near the bottom."

"So take us up a hundred feet or so."

Phil did it, and Mike tried again. "Herschel Base, can you hear us? Anna has a major discovery to report. Come in!"

Nothing.

"This is bad," said Mike. "With all those big cracks we saw in the vent, a piece of ice could have sheared off and taken out the transponder."

"Or plugged the vent," said Phil.

Anna's heart jumped. "How long can we stay down here?"

"Oh, another eight hours or so," Phil said calmly.

"I'm not abandoning the rest of this mission, people, but we'll have to hurry it up," said Mike. "Follow the profile, Phil, but double-time it. Finding another vent won't help us; we have no way to survive on the surface. We have to come up at Herschel Base. We have four hours left on the profile. Let's do it in two, and go home."

Mike said it with determination, but all three of them could hear the overtone of fear in his voice.

Getting back to base was suddenly not a matter of reporting an important discovery, but of survival.

Anna said little during the rest of the dive, and was on the edge of tears the entire time. For two hours they made sonar maps of the rest of the cavern, took several samples from the ceiling and walls, and saw what they thought was another vent, though it was too narrow for them to explore it. Mike kept on calling Kassner, but there was only dead silence in return. There was certainly no time for further exploration of the bottom. Anna distracted herself by pointing out several more areas on her sonar maps she was now certain harbored life. The little depressions were where the methane clathrate was so exposed to serve as anchors for the life on Enceladus. But now there would be no time extensions for the mission. After two hours, worry had turned to fear, and they hurried back to the Herschel Base vent under full power.

What they found at the vent matched their worst fears.

A huge boulder of ice had calved from the vent wall, and was plugging it at a steep angle, its tip resting on the shelf that the transponder had been anchored to. As they came up to it, the ceiling above them shuddered and small pieces of ice clattered off the top of the submersible. Phil wiggled the controls, and they backed off to one side of the vent. "Pretty loose inside the vent," he said. "Let's see if my baby can unplug this thing in low gravity."

For nearly an hour Phil used the articulators to push against the icy plug in various directions, but even with the slightest movement there was an avalanche of debris from above that terrorized all of them. Mike was on the radio continuously, but getting nothing.

There was a sudden crash of boulders on the roof of the submersible. "See that?" said Phil. "It wobbled. The tip is wedged where the shelf comes out of the wall. The shelf is holding it up. Maybe if I can break off the tip—"

Phil moved in closer, used the articulators to pull back on the tip of the plug, and wiggled it back and forth. When Anna saw the movement her hope soared. They were making progress, the base only a hundred meters or so above them, and they had air left for hours.

And then, quite suddenly, they had minutes.

The plug wobbled, and there was a horrible impact on the roof of the submersible. The interior lights flickered, and Anna was momentarily deafened by a shriek of tortured metal from the hull walls. The impact lifted her from her seat and slammed her sideways as she clapped her hands over her ears.

"No, no, NO!" gasped Phil. Mike hadn't strapped in, was on the floor and holding one hand to a bloody gash on his forehead.

"What's that hissing sound?" said Anna.

"We're losing our air and fuel! That last avalanche must have breached the outer hull. Mike, get up and strap in. Hang on, Anna. We've got to do this quick, or we're dead!"

Anna gulped, and grasped the arms of her chair, and the hissing sound was now loud in her ears. She smelled fuel, and her own sweat.

She had never thought about death, especially her own, but now it came to her.

Mike managed to get in his seat and strap in as Phil backed off a few meters from the vent shelf and the shower of debris coming down there.

"Sorry baby," said Phil, not talking to a person, "but we have to do this the hard way."

The submersible lurched forward and rushed towards the shelf at the bottom of the vent, crashing into it hard at a point just below the observation bubble.

"Phil!" screamed Anna, but Phil was backing off again, stopping, and the submersible lurched forward once more. The second crash seemed softer, ice resisting, crumbling, and allowing them a creep forward after contact. The craft jerked backwards in a blink, pitching Anna forward in her chair. Outside was chaos, a shattered shelf of ice falling away, the sharp tip of the plug sheared off at a steep angle with it. A huge fang of ice fell out of the vent, and disappeared from view.

The air in the cabin was musty, and Anna had a sudden headache. The submersible accelerated. Small pieces of ice clattered off the hull as they flew up the vent and through an open lock unprepared for them. They came out of the water in a roil of bubbles, and Anna had one glimpse of two shocked technicians jumping away from the pool.

* * * *

For one moment, while Mike and Phil told their story, Anna was silent and just happy to be alive. But when the men turned it over to her and she described her discovery she was suddenly depressed again, and she came close to crying when Kassner and then Helena embraced and congratulated her.

It was at that moment when Phil climbed off the hull of his battered submersible and grinned at her. He had something wet and glistening in a gloved hand, and he handed it to Anna. "This should lighten your mood. Look what I found stuck between the base of the port articulator and the hull. When that thing grabbed us and I pulled away it must have snapped this off. No wonder the thing was thrashing around so much."

Anna's heart skipped a beat. In Phil's hand was a six-inch section from the end of a branch. The end nubbin was intact, the other end of the section shredded like a torn piece of Yucca stalk. The piece was still wet, but the mottled bronze and brown spots were fading before her eyes.

"Quick, get it in water!"

Mike grabbed a pan from a bench and filled it with water from the tank.

Anna giggled, grabbed Phil's arm and kissed him on the cheek. "Thank you! Oh, I've got to get some ice on this!"

Helena ran for ice. Anna grabbed the pan, and rushed away with her new treasure. Behind her, Phil said something that might have bothered her once, but didn't now in her moment of joy.

"Now *there's* a mood shift for you," said Phil.

* * * *

One day out from Enceladus, Anna emerged from her cubicle and joined Mike and Phil on the control deck for a squeeze of tea.

"Ah, the scientist walks among us," said Mike. "Tea?"

"Thanks," said Anna, and accepted a squeeze bottle from him. "I've been writing up a summary of the examinations I made on Herschel. I can't do anything else until we get to Titan."

"Well, you'll have to tell us all about it," said Phil.

Anna took a suck of tea. "There isn't a lot I can say right now. The dead fragment you dug out of the gravel is almost as interesting as the fresh specimen. The closest thing I can think of on Earth is coral, but the structure is silicate, not carbonate. The bronze areas on the surface show iron sulfide. There could be bacteria producing that since there's both iron and sulfur in the dark gravel, and also in the ice, but on the whole I'm seeing a colony of tiny worm-like critters living in a labyrinth of tubules, and my bet is a methane metabolism with hydrogen output. I've frozen the sample in some water mixed with methane clathrate. We even have the little nubbin where the light is emitted. It seems to be silicate with trace sulfur. I radioed all of this ahead, and everyone at the lab is *so* excited."

Phil looked over his shoulder at her. "When you accept your Nobel Prize, we'll expect an invitation to the ceremony."

Anna smiled. "Well—that isn't going to happen."

"Why not?"

"Even if I got the award I wouldn't be there to accept it."

"I thought you were thinking about cycling back to Earth," said Mike.

"I was. I was thinking about it seriously until a few days ago."

"Ah," said Mike, and winked at Phil.

There was a pause while Anna took another suck of tea, and then said, "Commander Kassner said he and his crew are cycling out in two months. I'm coming back with the replacement crew. That will give me six months for dives to study the Ice Corals."

"That's what you're going to call them?" asked Mike.

"For now. I'll let some official give them a Latin name. I have a lifetime of work to do on this project, and I'm not going back to Earth to do it."

"Well, I guess we'll be seeing you around here, then," said Phil.

"You bet," said Anna, "just as long as the articulators work the first time."

"Ouch," said Phil.

OSCAR PETERSON'S MEADOW

Times weren't good for me the year I met Oscar Peterson. I'd just gone through a nasty divorce and survived an administrative shakeup at work, and after a series of alimony payments, plus handouts to an impotent lawyer, I wanted to get as far away from the human race as possible. So I threw the fishing gear and a stack of yellow legal pads in the car, loaded up the canoe, and took off for Hart Lake.

It's near the border, not far from Ely and the boundary waters area, and I figured I could go over there if the island was being rented. Loon Island is maybe a thirty minute paddle out from Diamond Bar resort, a fifty by seventy five yard eruption of rock and trees out of clear water. Nice little beach, a clean shack with electricity, and a privy out back. Privacy, and I wanted to fish and write.

I was lucky. Dale and Ellie McCracken still owned Diamond Bar, and they remembered me. I got the island for two weeks. We talked til late, catching up on all my bad news, and I didn't get out to the island until sunset. Same place I remembered. Same quiet. I felt better right away, but even that first night there was a disquieting feeling, too, when I saw the thousands of lights go on around the shore.

A lot of new folks had moved in.

I met Oscar the next morning. It was just after sunrise, and he was fishing from a canoe close to the short dock off the island, where the water depth changes fast. I went down there with a cup of coffee in my hand, and was greeted with a venomous look.

"Jesus Christ; now they're squatin' on the island," he growled.

"Rented it to get away from the rat race, and all the rats in it," I explained. "Now, you have a good day." I took my coffee back to the shack, and that was the end of the conversation. But I think it was the moment Oscar and I became friends.

I kept running into him when I fished in the evening, sometimes after dark when the Walleyes were active, and we made some nice catches. It was just the two of us, out of canoes; the sand bars around the island are treacherous, and you can't get close in a power boat. Oscar was in his sixties, then, over twenty years older than I, and he could fish. If they so much as breathed on the lure, he'd snag 'em in the lip. I enjoyed watching him, and he knew it, and I do pretty fair myself. So one night we hit a school of Walleye around nine, and had our limits in twenty minutes, less than thirty yards from the dock. It was pretty nippy that night, and as I started in I said, "Hot coffee in the shack, if you want."

"Maybe," he said, but I figured he'd paddle on home that night, and I was surprised when a little later he came up to the door with a big string of fish dangling from one hand.

"Got a place to clean these?"

"Back porch," I said. "All the comforts of home."

Coffee waited while we cleaned our catch. The man was a fillet surgeon, while I made my usual mess. We cleaned up, then finally introduced ourselves, and his big hand swallowed mine in a gnarled mass. I filled two big mugs with coffee, and we sat down at the round kitchen table where I spent four hours a day trying to write the great American novel, only partially succeeding.

"Never anybody out here," he said, looking me over. Skin stretched over his face like leather. Dark eyes, so deep brown they were nearly black. He was a stocky man, thick chest and arms, and big hands with fingers nicotine stained, though I never saw him smoke. A bear of a man.

"I haven't been here in a lot of years. Dad used to bring me out when I was a kid. Even in winter. We'd camp in the shack, and snowmobile out to the icehouse to fish. It was the only thing he'd do in a snowmobile."

"Hate those things," grumbled Oscar. "Tear up the ground, and run the deer to death, then in the summer they come out here and do the same thing on those three-wheelers. People all over the place, wreckin' everything."

"Lots of new cottages since I was last here."

"Not in the bay, not yet. Old Swenson still owns all that, 'cept my little piece, and he's tried to buy me out for years. Now some new developer is suckin' around, wants to build a big resort with time-share condos. He'll take down most of the trees to do that, and there won't be any game around here ever again. Hell, I'll blow myself up, first, strap on a few sticks and light the fuse!"

The man's sudden passion surprised me, but he was talking about his home. "Things change," I said, thinking about the divorce, and losing my house, and the kids I didn't see much anymore.

"For the worse, they do. Someone's always makin' money at screwin' up the world. Someday they'll get the meadow, too."

Oscar looked at me suspiciously. "Speakin' of money, how do you make yours?"

"Copy editor for a newspaper, but I've had enough of it. I'd like to find a small town paper to run by myself. I'm looking now; it's one of the reasons I'm up here. More coffee?"

"Sure; good'n Norwegian. Say, is your dad's name Lyle?"

Right out of the blue, and I was startled. "Was," I said sadly. "Dad died last summer from cancer."

"Sorry to hear that," said Oscar, stunned a little. We sat in silence for a minute, sipping coffee, a moment of silence for dad, and my stomach hurt. It had to show in my face, and Oscar seemed to soften a little.

"Don't you remember me?"

"No."

"Figures. Your mom never liked me, but Lyle Odegaard did, and we had some times, and little Mike was with us more than once. Don't you remember?"

I wanted to, and I tried. Nothing. Dad had had so many friends, and now they were all a blur. I shook my head.

"No matter," said Oscar. "You weren't much bigger than a snowshoe then, and remember or not we had some good times."

"I'm glad I came back before ... well, before this place changes too much."

Oscar smiled. He actually smiled, and I was sure it was something that didn't happen often. He gulped the last of his coffee, and stood up.

"Gotta go. Maybe before you take off you can come over to my place for a beer?"

"Sure," I said.

And I did.

Oscar's place was lakefront, at the end of the bay, prime property, about ten acres of it. The cabin was run down; rustic is the polite word. A tool shed was falling down behind the cabin, and an ancient dock extended precariously out to where his boat was tied. It was safer to wade ashore.

Beers turned into venison steak dinners, and late hours, and we fished together quite a bit before the end of those two weeks. I didn't get much writing done, but I heard enough stories to write forever. Still, it was kind of sad, because I knew we were both reliving a past that was gone forever: me with dad, and Oscar with his three ex-wives, and drinking buddies, hunting and fishing in a place that was wild and beautiful before the rest of the world started moving in. It was all changing, and soon would be gone forever.

I came back that winter to hunt deer with Oscar, and that was when he showed me his meadow, though it was hard to tell what was there under two feet of snow. It was small, maybe fifty yards across, tall trees close in, and a fast stream running through the middle even in December. Both of us filled out our cards, and then we spent another three days ice fishing for pike that were apparently dieting that week.

The next summer I was back again; we fished every day and talked every night, sometimes at his place and other nights in my island shack.

That was the summer The Pioneer was up for sale in Hendrum, only seventy miles from the lake, and Oscar threw a nice little party for me at Diamond Bar to celebrate my buying the paper/ He was happy, yet subdued. Things were beginning to turn around for me, but for Oscar it wasn't so good. More people were moving in, old man Swenson was talking seriously about selling out after the developers had offered him a fortune for his land, and there was Oscar, sitting on a little strip smack in the middle of it. It was all slipping away. He felt it, and so did I.

I should have gone back again that winter, but I'd met Peg by then and couldn't stand to be more than a few yards from her. Singles life just isn't for me, I guess. Anyway, we were together all the time, even at work, with her as secretary and my future stepson Andrew setting type. I spent my days and a lot of nights scrounging up news and advertising, my dream come true. I wrote to Oscar, and he didn't answer. I worried about that, but I was all wrapped up in my own life, and on it went.

Summer was like that, too. The two days I did take off, we drove down to Minneapolis so I could meet Peg's folks, and we hit it off well. I knew then I'd be giving marriage another try, and Peg got her ring in September. I wrote to Oscar again, and when he didn't answer I called Diamond Bar and got Ellie on the phone. Oscar never put in a telephone at his place.

Well hi, Mike. Are you coming in this winter? I still have a couple of spaces."

Doesn't look like it. I'm getting married again, Ellie, and I'll be up next summer. Can you get the island for us the first two weeks in August?"

"You've got it, Mike, and I'm glad for you."

"Thanks. Say, could you tell Oscar for me? He hasn't been answering my letters, and I wonder if he's okay."

"I saw him out by the island a couple of weeks ago, but I guess he's mostly staying at home now. You know Oscar. A lot of people didn't stay long this season, what with all the noise. Mister Swenson sold his land last spring, and the developers have moved in with saws and bulldozers. You can't believe the way the trees are coming down over there. I don't like it, Mike, but eventually it's going to be good for the bar and restaurant."

If the developers don't put in one of their own, I thought.

Peg and I were married just before Christmas that year; Oscar never answered our invitation, and at that point I figured he'd blown me off for good. Still, I wrote to him again in the spring, and in August Peg and I loaded up the canoe and drove to the lake.

It was a mess.

They had stripped all but a few trees back a hundred yards from shore, all around the bay, and cut platforms in the slope. Foundations were already being poured, and the whole time we were there we didn't see or hear a single loon, just the rumble of cement trucks. I still have visions of all those expensive condos going bumpity-bump down into the lake after a heavy rainstorm someday. Those people don't know a thing about soil erosion.

We went to Diamond Bar; Peg met Dale and Ellie, and got spoiled. But when we sat down for coffee, Ellie suddenly got serious.

"Mike," she said, "Oscar is gone."

I felt like I'd been slapped, and it showed.

"I mean he just disappeared. Sold his place, and took off. He came by early in March to say goodbye and left a big box for you, and Peg, he said. We asked where he was going, and he didn't seem to know. Just walked out, after all these years. The box is in back, with a letter that came for him last week from the Wildlife Federation. Probably junk mail."

"I'll try to get it to him," I said.

The box was like a kid's coffin, nailed shut and heavy. Dale helped me carry it out to the car; Peg grunted along with me to get it open.

I wasn't happy about what I found inside.

Oscar's fishing rods were stored in cardboard tubes, the reels in velour baggies, and the Mauser had been wrapped in an Indian blanket. His tackle box was full. There was an envelope addressed to Mike and Peg, and inside was a wedding card with Oscar's scrawled signature and a thousand dollars in hundred dollar bills.

We loaded all the stuff in the car, and Peg knew something was wrong because I was so quiet. I opened Oscar's letter, and it was a formal letter for tax purposes, acknowledging his most generous contribution. The amount listed there just about blew my mind. You never know.

I threw the letter into a trash can.

Our first night on the island just about blew my mind, too. The honeymoon was long overdue; we fished and made love for a solid week.

The love was great.

I was ready to go home when the time came, but there was one more thing to do. The morning before we intended to leave, Peg and I stood on the dock, sipping coffee and looking at the destruction around the bay.

"Take a hike with me today. There's a pretty place I want to show you."

"Sure," she said, always the adventuress.

We packed a lunch in the rucksacks, and at the last minute I added a trench shovel. We paddled into the bay, tied up near the edge of the construction and got into the trees as quickly as we could. I remembered the direction, but it was a half hour before we found the trail Oscan and I had used in winter.

At first it was very quiet and still; there were no birds or animals around. We walked for less than an hour, and suddenly the meadow was there in full sunlight, a little circle of green, dotted with reds and yellows of late wildflowers, burbling a greeting of water cascading over polished stones. So close, and so vulnerable.

Peg was delighted. She took off her rucksack and rushed to the stream while I strolled around the perimeter of the meadow. Even in August, she yelled when her feet plunged into the icy water, and that's when I found what I was looking for.

There was a depression that didn't belong, already grown over as if nature were hiding it, inside a natural ring of rocks. There had been an explosion here. While Peg kicked her feet in the stream, I walked hunched over, picking up the few things there were to find: jagged pieces of metal, a blackened shard of cloth, a few bone fragments scattered over a radius of eighty feet, nearly half of the meadow. Peg was calling to me, but I didn't hear the words. I was busy putting the artifacts I found into a little garbage bag, and digging a hole deep with the trench shovel. I worked furiously, pushed the bag into the hole and covered it up, then piled on some rocks.

"Mike?" Peg's hand was on my shoulder.

I stood up, and she looked scared, though all I could see was a blur, and I was breathing hard.

"You okay?"

"I will be in a little while."

"What's wrong, Mike? It's so pretty here."

I pulled her to me, hugging hard, not for her, but for me. "Not now, hon. I'll tell you when we get home."

We ate our lunch by the stream and then left. I didn't even look back.

Peg and I take our vacations in the boundary waters wilderness area, now. Each year we get further and further into Canada, ahead of the crowd. I'm running, I guess, staying ahead of the destruction. Oscar's mistake was that he took a stand in a single place. He was a dinosaur who couldn't adapt, a creature from another time who wanted things to remain the way they were created. He couldn't tolerate change.

I'll never go back to Hart Lake. Nothing is there for me anymore. Besides, there are other beautiful places to see, and I'd better get to it.

They won't be there forever.

THREESOME

They usually celebrated quietly at home, but fifteen years together were somehow a milestone and required something special. John even rented a tuxedo for the event. Phoebe and Rachel both chose the little black dress worn on their first date with John. Rachel's preference was for a quiet dinner with soft music, but Phoebe was the wild one and wanted rock and roll.

With fifteen years of experience, it was not difficult for John to come up with a plan that satisfied both of his treasures. He made reservations for them at Otto's Steakhouse, where a Las Vegas classic rock band was being featured for the weekend.

They reached the restaurant at eight on a Thursday evening, and John had a valet attendant park the Mercedes. Musk worn by the girls was making his head spin as they each took an arm for their entrance. Otto himself greeted them, and a few heads turned as they were escorted to a table some distance from the big speakers for the band. Tables had been cleared from the dance floor, and a six piece group was setting up for their show.

John ordered champagne, and menus were studied. Phoebe was giggling with excitement while Rachel was her usual quiet self. John felt lucky to have two women with personalities that fit so nicely together and yet were so different. He loved both of them, and basked in the warmth of the love they gave him in their own special ways.

They all ordered Steak Diane, accompanied by a medley of mushrooms and vegetables. There was also a plate of Escargot for sharing, a small salad for each, and a decadent Baked Alaskan for their desert. They ate slowly at first, and then hastened through their desert as the band began to play.

Sound exploded from the speakers, and at first it was a deep disco beat. Phoebe was swaying back and forth, her eyes sparkling, one foot reaching under the table to rub up and down John's calf. He acknowledged the signal by standing up, and Phoebe fairly leapt to her feet. John followed her spectacularly wiggling figure out to an empty dance floor, leaving a patient Rachel behind to await her turn.

Phoebe was nineteen again, writhing to the beat. People smiled from tables in the gloom. They were alone on the dance floor, and the musicians grinned at them encouragingly. John's body was suddenly filled with the power and excitement of the music, moving with Phoebe, his eyes fixed on hers. She smirked, and narrowed her eyes, giving him a promise of things to come.

The beat went on and on, but stopped just as John's legs began to feel heavy. Diners applauded them, for they had been the only couple on the dance floor. John wobbled back to the table as music began again, something slow, a belly-rubber. There was no time for rest.

"Now me," said Rachel, and they went back to join several couples on the dance floor. Rachel looked closely into his eyes, her arms went around his neck and she pressed tightly against him. He was immediately aroused, but Rachel just smiled and pressed her cheek against his. They swayed together, her musky scent filling his senses, her arms like cool silk around his neck. Time moved slowly, lulling him into a dream-like state, his heart feeling a wonderful ache from the love he felt for the woman in his arms.

But then the music blared loud and fast, and it was back to Phoebe, his other love, the crazy one who filled his life with hot passion and excitement.

The three of them danced until midnight, and were suddenly tired and in need of fresh air. John retrieved the car from the valet, and they drove up into the hills on a winding road ending at a parking lot overlooking the city. Three cars were already there, filled with kids half of John's age.

Phoebe got frisky and made him hard again, and Rachel wanted to cuddle. In half an hour he was light headed from the cycle of rapid and slow breathing. And the kids in the other cars ignored them.

They got home at two in the morning and John paid the babysitter an outrageous sum. Rachel was sleepy, but Phoebe was still wide awake and ready for action. Rachel dozed while John performed for an exuberant Phoebe who laughed when he groaned with the pleasure of her ministrations. It was not over yet, because Rachel awoke when Phoebe was spent. "Me, too," she said, and made love to him again in her slow, deliberate way, bringing him to a climax that had him gasping for breath to still his pounding heart. And when it was finished, the three of them were exhausted and slept intertwined, cooling slowly until dawn.

But in the morning it was again Clara who snuggled against him, Clara, his wife of fifteen years and mother of his three sons. She lay with her back pressed against him, holding one of his hands to cup a breast, and he was breathing in the wonderful scent of her hair.

There was a thud in a distant room, and the sound of giggling children. Clara stirred. "The boys are up," she said.

"Sounds like it. Our peaceful slumber is over," said John.

"Not just yet." Clara turned around to face him, encircling him with her arms. "Happy anniversary, hon. Last night was wonderful."

"I am a very lucky man," said John.

"Yes you are," said Clara, smiling, "but so are we."

She kissed him softly on the mouth. "Now me," she murmured.

The made love slowly, but there wasn't much time for it. There was the sound of running feet outside the closed door of their bedroom.

Phoebe enjoyed the change of pace, and Rachel just sighed with the pleasure of the moment.

TRAVEL REQUIRED

It seemed they were only a few minutes away from Central Park and the chaos of downtown Manhattan, but when the cab pulled up in front of a crumbling yellow building some twenty stories high Helen Trumbold's heart sank with disappointment. Because the driver had been brusque with her she gave him only a dollar tip and he left her standing on a badly cracked sidewalk, staring up at the sinister tower before her.

It was going to be another one of those days, she thought. Three failed job interviews in a week, and money short. Only the pretty ones got the secretarial jobs, especially when they had to travel with the boss, and the advertisement had specifically said travel was required. So why was the man who interviewed her over the phone so interested? After all, he had her resume and a recent photograph which Unemployment had sent over for him. She had seen the photograph and hated it, angry at the way she had lately let herself go. It was not that she didn't care anymore, but nothing she tried seemed to work. A frump is a frump, Helen, and that's you, she told herself. So why had this man requested a personal interview for a job she desperately wanted? It was her chance to get away from a tiny dingy apartment, traffic noises and screaming neighbors, a chance to see the world and be with interesting people. And why was the interview here, in this crumbling wreck of a building?

Helen marched boldly up the steps of the building and went inside. The foyer was dimly lit, empty of people or furniture of any kind, a rough unfinished concrete floor and thick columns bisecting the space. On the far side were three elevator doors made from polished copper shining dully in light filtering in from the street. Each door had a security access panel and there was no directory to be seen. Helen fumbled around in her purse and found the scrap of paper with the man's name and access code. Gerard Doreen, 51131. She punched in the code for the middle elevator door and stepped back to look at herself reflected from the polished metal. Frumpy.

The door to her left slid open; she peered around the corner and stepped inside. When the door didn't shut she punched the close button, feeling more secure in the brightly lit, enclosed space. The elevator rose slowly. She adjusted her hair, smoothed the skirt of her dark business suit and took several deep breaths to calm herself. The elevator came to a halt, the door immediately sliding open; she took another deep breath and stepped out directly into a softly lit, tastefully furnished office. A short, balding, middle-aged man in a neat blue suit was just emerging from another office beyond, and he smiled at her.

"Ah, right on time. You are Helen Trumbold?" The man put some papers on a desk and held out a hand to greet her. She watched his eyes move quickly over her, and waited for the *look* telling her what he saw was unacceptable. But instead, his smile broadened as he took her hand and led her to a plush chair in front of his desk. "Please sit. We have a moment before I send you upstairs for some tests. Tell me, are you willing to do any word processing on the job? Mister Pixl requires this on occasion, and I forgot to tell you on the telephone."

"Of course," she said primly. "I can type one hundred and ten words a minute with accuracy."

"Good. And one other thing we didn't discuss on the telephone, at least not completely. The position of Protocol Assistant demands extensive travel, keeping you out of town to the extent that maintaining an apartment here is a questionable expense. If you have anyone very—well, close to you, you probably won't want to consider this position."

"That's not a problem. I don't have any attachments."

The man smiled. "Ah, then you don't have any necessary obligations in your life." He seemed relieved.

"Oh, I was married once," she quickly added, "but that was sometime ago." *Once upon a time someone wanted me, but then I got older*, she thought.

Doreen stood up. "Well, let's get you started. Mister Cox will give you some tests on the next floor up, turn right to room 430, and I'll be checking in on you from time to time." He pointed to a television monitor above his desk. "After that we'll have a little chat, and then you can meet Mister Pixl. If you find the tests to be unusual, please remember we are also testing your abilities to adapt, and that takes some imagination." His smile was mischievous as he guided her back to the elevator. "Good luck."

And so she went up to the next floor.

She stepped out into a darkened hallway, smooth marble walls curving left and right. Diffuse light came around the corner from the left. To the right she saw light coming from a doorway, and moved towards it. It was cold, and there was a strange stale odor in the air. She stopped once to listen. There was a chittering sound far down the hall behind her, and then it stopped. *God, I hope they don't have rats here.* She moved on, stepped up timidly to the doorway and looked inside.

A man was sitting behind his desk, staring at the opposite wall, hands folded neatly before him. He sat motionless, as if daydreaming, remaining that way when she knocked softly on the door jam. She checked the number above the door, and it was where she was supposed to be. She went inside and stood before the desk. "I'm Helen Trumbold. Mister Doreen sent me here to see Mister Cox for some interview tests."

"I am Mister Cox," said the man, facing her suddenly, and his voice flat and emotionless. "Please sit and relax before we begin." He gestured at a large table near his desk, on which were a word processor and two television monitors. When she moved to it the man's head did not turn, his hands returning to a folded position before him. "You have one moment to compose yourself. Do the best you can, and do not be concerned with the results. I'm here to help you in anyway I can, and to maximize your successes."

Helen suddenly realized she was talking to a mechanized mannequin, a kind of robot programmed to interview and give tests. But above his desk, a camera had turned to follow her when she moved. Others were watching this interview. "Thank you, Mister Cox," she said politely. At least a robot wouldn't give her that *look* she hated so much. She relaxed.

In the next half hour she whizzed through a typing test and two file formatting exercises, her confidence building. "Excellent," said Mister Cox, "and now some exercises in protocol. Please turn on the large monitor to your left, and use the mouse to move figures on the screen."

She used the mouse to move a square and a triangle back and forth on the screen before they suddenly vanished.

"Exercise one," said Mister Cox. "Please read carefully, and take all the time you need. When you are ready to continue, punch EXIT."

Helen rubbed her hands together. The palms were cool and moist. The monitor screen flashed, and she saw an array of little creatures like something out of a children's cartoon show: bugs, elves, tall gaunt beings clothed in capes and hoods, something that looked like a teddy bear she had once dearly loved, and a human. In the exercise, all these beings were representatives of various planets waiting to see the governor of a planet called Felant, an industrial center for heavy manufacturing in the local galaxy. Her task was to determine the order in which the governor would meet with these representatives without causing jealousies among them, and with an eye on maximizing potential profit. It was a task she had done for Moffit and Nelson when she was younger, and before she had been turned in for a still younger model. She accessed data about each of the little creatures, having fun with the imagination of the exercise, feeling confident about her results when she punched EXIT only twenty minutes later.

The next task was similar to the first, only now the governor was giving a dinner party for his alien business associates, the same ones as before. The task was to place them properly at the table. Two unknowns were to be determined by selection: the race of the governor, who would sit at one end of the long table, and his protocol officer, who would sit at the other end. The machine instructed her to select SELF for the protocol officer. Okay, the officer is a human female. For the Governor, she selected DEZIRLI, male, a species that looked like cats with large green eyes. Meat eaters, and dominated by males. In the end, the fact her governor was male was the biggest problem because one of the representatives came from a female-dominated world in which males were considered sub-servient. She seated this representative next to the protocol officer, another female who then proceeded to discuss business as if she were governor, but acting on directions of her superior.

Other problems were more easily solved, but took time wading through the myriad of data about each species, and her head was beginning to hurt. Finally she punched EXIT and sat back in her chair, stretching tired back muscles as subtly as she could.

A humming sound came from Mister Cox, and then a click.

"Excellent. You will be pleased to know only a few of our candidates have completed the exercises to this point."

A little knot formed in Helen's stomach. How many people were they interviewing? Surely one of them would be some young sweet thing, and she'd be out on the street again. Her head began to throb.

Another buzz from Mister Cox, and then, "Please remove your jacket, and stand in front of the mirrors to your right."

So now they wanted to take a *real* look at her. A protocol officer must be neat and pretty as well as charming, reflecting the good tastes of the boss. Where had she heard that before? So get it over with, Helen, and get out of here. She slid off her jacket and walked over to a set of three mirrors typical of a department store clothing section, glaring at her image there. Dumpy shape wrinkled, a loose strand of hair, I'm a mess, she thought.

"Please place your toes on the white line and stand perfectly still for ten seconds," said Mister Cox.

She complied, wanting to close her eyes, painfully aware of the camera above the head of Mister Cox. She felt like a piece of spoiled meat on display.

"Thank you," said Mister Cox. "Now please remove the rest of your clothes."

"I BEG YOUR PARDON?" She jerked around, hands on hips, and glared straight at the camera. "I will not do that for any job!"

"Is there a problem?" said Mister Cox. "Others have—and, oh—I see—one moment please. Please resume standing as you were. We will proceed digitally. Again, remain in one position."

Now her head was splitting, and she wanted to flee from the room. But the part of her that desperately wanted a job, a sense of purpose in life, kept her from flight. She turned back to the mirrors, put her toes carefully at the white line as ordered, and prepared to endure whatever she had to except to remove her clothes and look at a naked body she loathed.

The room lights dimmed and the mirrors were suddenly black, her image there a sketch in red without detail, a bare outline. As she watched, the image turned round and round, changing every second, growing fatter, then slimmer, hair first cut short as she now had it, then becoming a billowing mass framing a thinned face. Even the clothes changed as she watched: a severe business suit, then a lacy blouse with full pleated skirt, something she never wore because it made her legs look like sticks. Next was a skin-tight body suit and then almost nothing at all. She gasped, and put a hand to her mouth. The image in the mirrors broke up into a sparkling red fog.

"Please remain motionless," said Mister Cox. "We're doing all of this in real time."

Helen put her arms to her side and resumed her position before the mirrors. Why does it always have to come down to how pretty you are? I had the looks before Carl left me; why do I have to keep up a charade the rest of my life?

A figure shimmered in the mirror, a slender figure in a long sleeveless gown and hair piled high, standing in a regal pose. Helen swallowed hard to keep the tears from her eyes. She knew who the figure was, or was supposed to be, but in a moment, when the lights brightened, the reality would be there again, overweight and wrinkled, the gown and slender figure a fading dream. Why are they doing this to me, she wondered.

"Well, that seems to be all for now," said Mister Cox, and the lights brightened in the room. The mirrors were ordinary again, but for an instant she had seen herself standing tall, chin up, gaze haughty yet serene. Princess of darkness, but now it was bright and she slouched once again.

"Are we finished here? I have another appointment today."

Mister Cox buzzed, head jerking towards her. "You must first return to Mister Doreen's office to complete the interview. Have a good day." He returned to his eyes straight ahead position, hands folded neatly before him.

The camera turned to follow her rapid exit from the room.

She walked quickly down the darkened hallway, head pounding, rummaging in her purse in search of an aspirin and finding none. She nearly fell down when her foot slipped on some floor moisture near the elevators. In slipping and catching herself she pulled a little muscle in her back, and now she was hurting all over. She punched the code for Doreen's floor into the elevators. Get the interview over, get out of here and find a nice little clerk's job on Wall Street where you don't have to meet people. Lunch in the park alone is better than being humiliated.

At least one elevator was nearing her floor. She waited in the darkness, rubbing the back of her neck with one hand, but when the elevators arrived two doors slid open at once, flooding the hallway with light. Head down, still rubbing her neck, she turned towards the left door. A loud squawk and rapid clicking sound froze her to the spot; she looked up and saw an append-age like a hairy fruit picker banging away at the access code panel inside the elevator. A huge head, multifaceted eyes and a beak for a mouth appeared for an instant to squawk at her again, and then the door banged shut, leaving her standing there with a hand at the back of her neck, her mouth hanging open. She held that position for moment, flushed hot, wondering if it was the headache or the stress of the interview. I've never hallucinated before, she thought. Or is it some other stupid test of my reactions?

She stepped into the other elevator and took it back down to Doreen's floor. He was waiting for her.

"Ah, come in, come in. Take a seat right here, please. And what did you think of our Mister Cox? A rather dull 'person', isn't he?" Doreen laughed, a nice natural laugh, she thought, and then he took his place behind a large desk.

"It's the first time I've been interviewed by a robot," said Helen. Her voice was strained, head hurting so fiercely now that little black spots danced before her eyes. She could imagine the lines appearing around her eyes and on her forehead. Wonderful.

The sight of the apparition in the elevator flashed through her mind, and she fought for control, clasping her hands together in her lap to keep them from shaking. Doreen leaned forward across his desk, looking concerned.

"Are you feeling ill?"

"No," she said too quickly. "It's nothing, really. I had a little fright up-stairs, but it's nothing—nothing at all. *God, will you shut up! You're bab-bling!* She took a deep breath, letting it out slowly as Doreen settled back into his chair. He took a card out of a drawer and stared at it pensively, shak-ing his head slowly from side to side.

"These scores are really remarkable, Helen. I've never seen anything quite so close to perfection. Only one error, though the consequences might have been interesting to say the least. The Eridani you placed at your right hand should have gone at your left, because the entire race is left-handed, or should I say left-clawed?" Doreen chuckled at his little joke, eyes sparkling merrily.

"I'm sorry, I missed that," she said glumly. "The test was a little un-usual."

Doreen laughed. "A test I designed myself, and the little alien characters were particularly fun to do."

You should have seen the big one I nearly ran into upstairs, she thought. Helen smiled faintly, squeezing her hands tightly together.

Doreen became serious, looking again at the card in his hand. "When I see scores like this and look at your experience I have to wonder why you've been out of work for so long. Can you give me some ideas about that?"

Her hands were suddenly two wet rags knotted together. "Well, I've been rather selective, trying for some good positions that would allow me to travel and see something more of the world. I've been in New York all my life, and—well, I just want to get around more and meet new people."

Doreen paused, then, "I'm thinking there might be more to it than that, Helen."

A flash of anger made her bold. "Yes, there is. I think the modern corporate executive thinks more about the appearance of his administrative assistant than of her abilities to do the job." There, it was out, and now *he* could give an answer.

Doreen leaned back in his chair, and made a little teepee with his hands. "It might surprise you to hear I agree with that, Helen, but it is a fact that neatness and good grooming are important in the business world. Look, I can identify with what you're indirectly saying. Three years ago I was in a position similar to yours, looking for a job, having difficulties finding a place that would accept me for my abilities rather than my corporate image, and it was very frustrating. But then I met R.E. Pixl and my whole life changed. He recognized my abilities and gave me the chance to use them, and in just three years I have become an executive in a major corporation with a future. And I'm expected to dress for the part."

"I don't have a problem with that," she said hurriedly. The interview seemed to be going downhill rapidly, and the black spots were dancing madly before her eyes.

"Good. It's like the digital hologram we checked you over with upstairs. You know—the mirrors. It's an electronic thing I play at a keyboard, giving me anything I can imagine."

"The thing your robot wanted me to take my clothes off for? You were watching, weren't you?"

Doreen actually blushed, trying to hide it with a hand. "I must take responsibility for that. So many cultures and customs, and I simply forgot how puritanical some of them can be. It's much easier to make digital reconstructions when the subject isn't dressed, and I had simply left it that way in the program. I'm sorry. And yes, I was watching. The images you saw were keyed in by me."

"They were interesting, although I really didn't know what was happening." She tried to sound indifferent, and came close.

"They were all you, or what you can choose to look like. I keep a hard copy of one I made of myself. If I lose another few pounds I'm going to look like my image in that hologram." Doreen smiled again, a warm friendly smile that seemed to relax her whenever she saw it. He wasn't really as short or portly as she had imagined from her first impression. A very neat man, quite professional yet warm personally. He stood up, leaned forward, fingertips on the desk top. "I think now it's time for you to meet Mister Pixl."

Doreen touched a button on a speaker phone to his right. "We're ready now, Mister Pixl. Can you spare us a few minutes?"

A hoarse voice answered, strangely distorted. "Yes I can. Bring her right in."

Doreen gestured to Helen to follow him into the next room. At the door he took her by the elbow, speaking in a whisper. "We all work for Mister Pixl, and he takes a little getting used to. He's very business-like, but fair, and extremely generous to his employees. Outside of me, you will be his closest associate here if you're offered the job. Okay?"

Helen nodded painfully, and Doreen pushed open the huge doors leading to the darkened office of R.E. Pixl, President.

Ahead of them was a black wall, glistening like clear plastic or glass, and on the wall was projected a huge image of a galaxy, thousands and thousands of stars showing individually as points of red, blue, yellow and white. "Oh," said Helen at the sight of it, for it was the most beautiful thing she had ever seen. Areas of the galaxy were outlined in red, green and blue, and a single yellow star out towards the galactic rim stood out brightly when compared to all the others. In front of the projection stood a massive desk, top bare except for a single computer work station radiating green light. A high backed chair in black leather was turned away from them when they entered. The walls were lined with computer terminals; all screens active, displays changing second by second. Helen barely glanced at them as she approached the desk, the sight of the galaxy holding her attention.

Doreen was close by her side. She whispered to him, "I've seen that picture before. It's the Andromeda galaxy."

He whispered back without looking at her. "No, Helen, that is *our* galaxy, and the bright yellow star you see up there is our sun."

She started to say something, but then the chair was turning towards them, light from the computer terminal on the desk illuminating the tall gaunt figure sitting there. Helen made an audible gasp, and Doreen squeezed her arm reassuringly.

The figure in the chair was anything but human.

Huge black eyes looked at her from a triangular face with two vertical slits for a nose and a tiny, almost circular mouth. The head was massive, crowned with a pair of earphones from which a tube curved around the face and to the mouth. The figure leaned forward and placed a small box in the desk, then eased back into the chair. Helen got a glimpse of a slender hand with long fingers and an opposing thumb. Doreen's hand was lightly around her arm; she reached over and clutched it firmly, struggling to control herself.

"Helen," said Doreen, "I'd like to introduce you to R.E. Pixl, our president."

The galaxy spun in a blur of color. Helen's knees sagged, and Doreen's grip tightened on her arm.

"How nice to meet you, Mister Pixl," she said, and her voice was steady.

Pixl nodded his massive head, and pointed to a chair. "Please sit," he said. "I do understand your surprise, Ms. Trumbold."

The sound of Pixl's voice came from a little box on his desk. Helen sat down in a plush chair, Doreen hovering over her. Pixl sat quietly, fingers drumming slowly on the desk top, and she immediately had the feeling he understood what was happening to her, understood her distress in observing something beyond her wildest imagination. She pushed herself up in the chair, swallowed hard and forced a smile. "I've had several surprises today, Mister Pixl, but I think—no, I'm sure I'm ready to answer any questions you have about my qualifications." She combed a strand of hair back from her forehead with one hand and took a deep breath.

The small mouth moved and Helen was reminded of the chittering sound she had heard before, but then a louder voice came forth from the little box on the desk. "I understande, Ms. Trumbold. My only function in this interview is to tell you something about the company."

Pixl stood up, dwarfing his visitors. He stepped up to the wall projection, a black robed figure against the light of the galaxy, and pointed out various features.

"The little box is a translator," whispered Doreen into her ear.

"As Doreen has told you, Ms. Trumbold, this is your galaxy and this is your star. The star of the parent company is over here, a journey of a thousand years by light, so you see this is also *my* galaxy. Within the blue and yellow sectors I have thus far established one hundred and fifty outreach centers, and now we're moving into the red sector closer in towards the galactic core. My business, Ms. Trumbold, is trading, anything and everything. My current interest on your planet happens to be in heavy and exotic metals, and helium. Business is good; the galactic demand is high for these products." Pixl put a hand on one hip and glanced at her, looking for a reaction. What she saw before her was not an alien, but a chief executive officer. She nodded, showing he had her attention.

"Everyplace I go I take on ten partners, but only one of these joins me in my travels. On your planet, Mister Doreen is that one, and he is in immediate need of an administrative assistant to handle out protocol problems as well as contract language in many different cultures. That person must be highly adaptable, able to deal with a variety of races, only some of which are humanoid, and be willing to travel extensively. I note that you have not run from this room in fear, and you have not even mentioned your brief contact with one of our associates upstairs."

"Trizyrl is still shaking," said Doreen, grinning at her. "He had never seen a human female up so close."

Helen looked at Doreen, and then back at Pixl. Suddenly she was a little angry. "I didn't tell Mister Doreen about it, because I thought he would question my sanity. It really was quite a shock for me."

"I'm sure it was, as it was for Trizyrl, but you adapted to it, and that is important. The person for this job must be very flexible, but in return I will show that person a hundred new cultures and half a galaxy. Really, now, I must get back to work, and Doreen can answer any questions you have. Please excuse me." Pixl sat down in his chair. The interview had clearly come to an end, but he extended a long hand to her.

Helen went to his desk and shook his hand. "Thank you for your time, Mister Pixl. You have been very kind to see me during your busy day." His hand was cold and dry, the grip fragile. Pixl nodded once, and then turned to the computer console and began working. Doreen guided her out of the room.

"This has been an unusual day for me," she said.

"I'm sure it has. I can still recall my own experience; it was frightening, but still fantasies come true for me. I wouldn't leave it for anything, now. Do you have any questions?"

"The distances you travel seem incredible."

"Well, we do travel several months a year, but I see what you mean. I don't understand the details, but to put it into Mister Pixl's words, 'the shortest distance between two points is a singularity'. It always delights him to say that."

"Do you have any more questions about me?" she asked.

"No, I think we have everything we need. Will you be home this evening for a phone call? I need to move ahead on this pretty quickly, so one way or another you should know my decision this evening." His face was serious, more so than she had seen before.

"Yes, I'll be home." *Where else would I be?*

Now he smiled again. "Good, then I'll be in touch." He took her by the elbow, guiding her few steps to the elevator. "I'll call a cab for you right away."

The elevator door opened. Helen smiled, held out her hand and he took it firmly. "Nice to meet you, Helen," he said.

"Thank you, Mister Doreen, for everything." The elevator door closed, and at first she had a good feeling. But then, during the brief descent, she thought about the exam error she'd made, her prudish response to the robot

Cox and her knees sagging in Pixl's office.

When she reached street level, Helen felt miserable again, and the headache was still there. It was enough for today; home to relax, then another job search tomorrow. The entire day had been unreal, including the rapid appearance of a cab that took her back to her apartment. She plodded wearily upstairs to the second floor, breathing in the odors of curry and hot peppers and something burned. She let herself in and turned on the dim light.

She kicked off her shoes, plopped into an overstuffed chair by the unmade bed and stared at the picture of her deceased mother on the dresser across from her. The room was small, with a kitchenette in one corner. A single window looked out at the brick walls of a neighboring building blocking any sunlight or warmth, so it was always cold and gloomy inside. She paid for steam heat, but only occasionally got any, and spent a lot of her leisure time in bed. The walls were bare and she shared a bathroom down the hall with three other tenants on her floor. It was a dreary place, but it was all she could now afford. And so she sat there, looking at the kindly face in the picture, wondering at the waking nightmare her day had been and knowing she could never tell anyone about it. It's bad enough to be plain, single and out of work; another thing to be crazy, she thought. Momma, what would you think if your daughter said she wanted to be a dinner hostess for six-foot cockroaches?

She thought about the horror in the elevator, and Pixl's long fingers drumming on the desk, and the serious look on Doreen's face at the end of her interview. Executive or not, that man had warmth, and she decided she liked him. But the whole scenario was still beyond her imagination: traveling in interstellar space, business with bug-people and hopping around the galaxy like fleas? If you wanted travel, Helen, this is the ultimate in it.

Her head still throbbed, and she closed her eyes to relax. Wait for the call, he'd said, but she knew what the answer would be. Sorry, Helen, but you're just not quite right for the position. We've found someone younger, someone willing to take off her clothes for Mister Cox, and besides that you made an error on the examination that could have started a war. Also, Mister Trizyrl doesn't like your look; it's offensive to all his senses and he is an important client of ours. You really must do something about your appearance, you know. You're so plain, drab and dumpy. How could you imagine we would ever have considered you for—?

Her world was shattered to blackness with the ring of a telephone in the hallway just outside her door. She heaved herself from the chair, glanced out the window to see that it was now dark. She jerked the door open and grabbed for the telephone, nearly taking it out of the hands of neighbor Luis Garcia, who glared at her and mumbled something in Spanish. There was no time to be nervous or apprehensive, but she knew who the call was for and who would be on the other end of the line. *Get it over with*, she thought.

"Hello?"

"Helen! Gerard Doreen here. I'm glad I caught you at home. Do you have a minute to talk now?'

"Oh yes. You said you'd call tonight." Her heart was pounding.

"Well, I made a couple more calls and talked it over with Mister Pixl, Helen, and we'd like to offer you the position with a starting date as soon as possible. It's certainly no later than two days from now, because we ship out then. If you can give me an answer right now that will be great, but if you want some time you'll have to get back to me by tomorrow morning. What do you think?"

She had been holding her breath, unbelieving. It couldn't be possible; she was still back in the chair, sound asleep.

"Helen,   are   you   there?"
"Oh, I'm sorry. This is really a surprise, Mister Doreen; I wasn't at all sure of an offer, and so I haven't given it much thought. I don't think I can really give you a good answer right now, but I have your number, and—"

"Call me by tomorrow morning, Helen. Please. We really think you're the best we've seen, and I know you'll love the experience. I can show you a hundred worlds you've never dreamed of, Helen. Isn't that what you want?"

"Yes, of course it is. It's just that the whole thing is like a kind of dream, and I'm having trouble believing it. Can you understand that?"

Certainly I can, Helen. It hasn't been that long since I had the same experience. The difference is I know what lies ahead, the things you can look forward to. There's nothing on this planet to compare with it. Look, I've got a messenger on the way with something you can keep even is you turn us down. That something is from me, Helen, and it's personal. I want you to look at it, and think about it before you call me back Okay?" the cadence of his speech had slowed, his voice now softer.

"All right. I'll call you back tomorrow morning"

" Call me anytime, Helen. I won't be disturbed by it"

She went back into her room, locked the door behind her and paced nervously for an hour before undressing and slipping into bed/ Her mind seemed a jumble, her logic constipated. You wanted a job and now you've got it and now you don't want it. Why? Working with creatures out of a monster movie and a boss to match? Something about Doreen, who sounds so eager for me to take the position? She looked at the picture on her bureau. Oh mother, why did you have to leave me so soon? If only you were here to talk to, but then you'd probably not believe anything I said.

She dozed, falling into a dream of a banquet with herself at one head of the table, Pixl glowering at her from the other end. Around her were bizarre creatures, mouths slavering, antennae waving frantically, their conversation a jumble of chitterlings and shrieks, and then the one nearest her put a three-fingered claw on her forearm.

She awoke groaning and sweating, jerking herself upright in the bed. She needed a glass of water, got up to get it and stopped. An envelope lay on the floor where it had been pushed underneath the door. She retrieved it. On the front were only her name and address, and then she remembered. Doreen was sending something to her. She opened it up, expecting to find a letter or contract, but what she found there made her gasp. A picture, flat yet three dimensional, lay in her hands. When she bent the picture in handling it, the figure there seemed to move, rotating so she could see front and back. It was a picture of an image she had seen in the mirrors, a woman in a long white, sleeveless gown, a picture of herself as Doreen had visualized with his computer. She turned it over; on the back was a scrawl in black ink. "If you decide not to accept the offer, this is still yours. This is the real Helen, and I hope you'll believe in her." It was signed 'Gerard Doreen', with a flourish.

She sat down on the bed, staring at the picture for a long time. The face was radiant, the figure slim. It wasn't her, and yet it was. Doreen had simply modified her true image in the mirrors: new clothes and hair style, a little digital carving of excess flesh here and there. But there was more. The look on the face was self-confidant, haughty, almost regal. She remembered the days when she had felt like that, when she was younger, the days when she was in demand, the days before Carl had left her.

It struck her then that it had all changed when Carl had left her. Change of life, he'd said. It was a frantic escape from a life that was stifling him, a desire to be free. Oh, so that was why he'd taken up with a girl half his age? The girl had been carrying his child even then, yet he'd said over and over again he had no desire for children, despite her own pleadings. It was then she'd decided it was all her fault he was leaving. She was old, undesirable, a pathetic bore without a future. And for seven years she had believed it, dressing a part, acting a part, ruining her own life because of something a man had done to her.

She looked again at the picture—and saw herself there.

Garcia peeked from his doorway while she was dialing the telephone, but her withering glare made him dart back inside again. Doreen answered on the first ring. "This is Helen," she said. "I've decided to accept your offer, Mister Doreen; I'd be foolish not to accept such an opportunity. Would you be able to help me with some last minute arrangements? I'm going to give up the apartment here."

"Oh, Helen, I'm so please, so very pleased. Yes, of course, I'll do whatever you ask. How about an early start over breakfast in the morning, say seven-thirty? I'll bring your contract along."

That sounded just fine to Helen.

* * * *

She stood before the wall-sized screen gazing at a mammoth red star, prominences arching out far from the surface and falling back in a splash of ions. In the foreground a green planet with scattered white clouds floated lazily. They had made two jumps, but had been traveling at sub-light speed now for nearly a month.

The door behind her slid open and Doreen glided into the room, a plastic drinking bottle in each hand. He touched down lightly beside her, held out her volume of bluish liquid and she took it with a smile.

"All out of champagne," he said, "but this is even better. Sip it slowly so it can linger on the palate a while." He held up his bottle in a toast. "The adventure begins."

The two bottles came together soundlessly before the red sun.

"Thank you for the chance, Mister Doreen," she said sweetly.

"Oh please, Helen," he said, "please call me Gerard."

DEAD INJUNS

A storm was coming, and there were signs. From the porch I could see dust-devils dancing across the landscape. Tall, skinny, short, fat, the little whirlwinds sucked up dust from the Nevada desert floor in pillars that glowed orange in the setting sun. Lifeless motion in a lifeless place, I thought, and my depression deepened.

Hours before, I had fled to the porch to escape from the sense of loss and the smell of death. I had sat in the darkness of the tiny room for hours, holding her shriveled hand, listening to shallow breathing and watching the light of life fade in her eyes. We had talked for a while, and then she had given my hand a gentle squeeze, closed her eyes, and died. It had all seemed so easy for her, and I did not understand why.

The phone rang, and Clara came to the screen door. "John, it's Mister Harrison from Fallon Funeral Home," she said.

His voice was soothing, comforting, and a part of the service. "I share your loss," he said softly. "Your grandmother and I were friends for a long time."

Is that why Grandpa once threatened to beat you up? And then you made the arrangements for him, too. The thought made me smile. "Thank you. She went peacefully, and there was no pain. When can the cremation be done?"

"Friday morning at ten. An empty urn will be interred, and her remains given to you for dispersal, as she wished. It's a special favor for an old friend."

I swallowed hard to control my voice. "I understand," I said softly.

"There are laws regarding this sort of thing."

"I realize that. Thank you very much for your consideration. We'll see you Friday morning at ten, then."

"My deepest sympathy," he droned, and the conversation ended with a soft click in my ear.

My face felt flushed as I hung up the phone, and when I turned around, Clara was watching me closely.

"Bastard," I growled. "The way he was sucking around here even before Grandpa died, and all he wanted was this property."

The touch of her hand on my shoulder softened the anger. "Forget him,

John. There was only one man in your grandmother's life, and now she's with him again."

"Maybe," I said, but didn't believe it.

"They had a long life together, good and bad times while they were building up the ranch."

"Our ranch, now," I reminded her, and she looked at me sharply.

"Yes," she said, "but *they* built it, and it took long, hard years to do that. Maybe it's the struggle that draws people closer together."

I blinked, reached out and took Clara's hand in mine. She smiled. "I think Grandma Ellen just gave up on life after Papa John died," she said.

The origin of my name, I thought. "More likely she died from being eighty nine years old." I wondered why I felt so bitter about it, but still remembered the plane crash taking my parents from me, and only four years ago. More grief to go around for more than Clara and I, and now there was only Clara. Her desire to have children suddenly haunted me.

"Who will we leave the ranch to, Clara?"

She looked at me, eyes wide, and smiled. "That's something we need to start working on."

"I guess so," I said, and wiggled an eyebrow at her. "Life goes on."

"Yes, it does," she said. She kissed me lightly, then stepped back and fumbled with one hand at a button on her blouse. "I'd better make some coffee before the ambulance arrives."

She walked quickly towards the kitchen, past the closed door of the darkened bedroom, and I went back to the porch to watch the sunset. The dust-devils were still there, skittering along the base of a butt across the valley overlooked by the house. Moving erratically, and tinted red by the setting sun, they reminded me of children playing, but there was no laughter.

The screen door slammed as I remembered something, and then Clara was standing beside me with steaming cups of black coffee in her hands.

"Dead Injuns," I said.

"What?"

I sipped the coffee carefully. "Dead Injuns, those dust-devils running around out there. Grandpa called them that."

"A funny name for little whirlwinds." Clara closed her eyes, feeling the light breeze of the evening, and the quiet.

"He told me once that each dust-devil is inhabited by a human spirit that has left something unfinished in life. They wander around, looking for whatever it is they have to finish. I think it's an Indian legend."

"Papa John had a lot of stories," said Clara.

"But I think he really believed this one. So did Grandma. I was washing dishes with her one night; she looked outside and pointed at a bunch of whirlwinds near the house. She said the people were worried, and there was a storm coming."

"Was there?" Clara watched the sun suddenly disappear behind the butte, and blinked her eyes.

"Yes, a bad one that time, with thunder and lightning all night into next morning. Two days later the dust-devils were back again, but only a few. When you see a lot of them, it means a storm is coming."

"Like tonight?"

"Like tonight," I said, and gulped the last of my coffee when I saw the headlights of an ambulance appear and disappear along the rolling gravel road leading to the house. Clara saw something in my face, and spoke quickly.

"The only whirlwind I remember clearly is the one that gave us such a fright when you were scattering your grandfather's ashes a few months ago. Right up there." She pointed at a ridge near the house, up high, where all the Rainbow Stone was.

"Seems like yesterday," I said, still watching the headlights.

I had just finished pouring Grandpa's ashes all over one of his favorite rock collecting sites. It was a clear day, with only a couple of whirlwinds near the base of the butte. I had turned to start back towards the house when Grandma yelled something at me, and I looked up in time to see a column of yellow dust, and then the thing was on me. It lifted me right up on my toes, and for a second I felt totally weightless.

Dirt, Rainbow Stone and Grandpa's ashes were blowing all over the place, and the urn ended up several yards down the hill behind the ridge. The little twister didn't slow down or even change course, just made a bee-line towards the butte, swung right along the base, then left again up a hanging canyon that had been another favorite rock hunting place for Grandpa, until his legs got too old for the climbing. Later in the day, Clara thought she saw the same one come back down the canyon again, but it couldn't have been the same one. I've watched them form and disappear, and it couldn't have been the same one.

The ambulance arrived, and I turned to go into the house. "I don't think I want to see this," I said.

"I'll take care of it," said Clara. She understands me more than I care to admit.

I was in the basement while the remaining organic shell of a wonderful human being was carefully wrapped up and carted away. Now they were both gone, and my chest was aching. Later in the evening there were only occasional sounds from upstairs as Clara inventoried the contents of the house. My mind was mercifully absorbed by Grandpa's rock-working shop. The shop work, and hunting for rocks had been the passions of his many retirement years. Grandma's, too, and she had hunted with him until the week before he died. I think it was the one thing that kept them alive so long, but it got tougher for them the last year or so. Old muscles can only do so much. Still, they made a lot of jewelry in that shop, together, hardly speaking a word, but together. The stuff they sold at flea markets paid for the hobby.

After the shop was cleaned up, I finished some of the little jewelry stones the old folks had run out of time for, polished the surfaces until I could see the reflected image of lettering on the top of a light bulb. The work drove me deep within myself, shutting out the sadness and the hurt, and filling me with sound and soft vibrations from the little rock grinding machine. For a time it seemed like the dead ones were there with me, giving me patience and guiding my un-practiced hands. There was a strong sense of peace, quiet contentment, acceptance, and my thoughts were like faint whispers in the room. Everything was as it should be, and the future was the beginning.

I turned off the machine and stepped back to admire the whirls of red, yellow and brown in a polished agate. Clara called to me from the top of the basement stairs.

"You coming to bed pretty soon?"

"In a minute," I said, perhaps a bit sharply. My reverie had been broken.

"The house seems so peaceful," she said, coming down the stairs. "I know it's silly, but I feel like they're still here."

I covered the machine with a plastic bag, and turned towards her, my heartbeat suddenly quickening.

"I feel it, too," I said softly, knowing I was staring at her.

She had brushed her hair out long, and it glowed in the dim light of the stairwell. Leaning back against a wall, hands behind her, she looked vacantly at a dark corner of the basement. Her nightgown clung to her like wisps of blue fog. It was something new, or something I hadn't noticed before.

Now I noticed.

"They were so contented here," she said. "They had the ranch, but little money, and the two of them together. That's all they seemed to want during their years in this house. I wonder if they knew how much they really had."

"I think Grandma knew," I said, and swallowed hard. I had held her tiny hand in the dark room, watching her labored breathing. Eyes closed, she suddenly turned her head towards me, and there was anger in her voice.

"Why is this taking so long?" she said. "John is waiting for me."

"I'm right here, Grandma," and I squeezed her hand gently. A few minutes later she was gone.

I don't think she'd been talking about me.

I was still staring when Clara turned her head to look at me. She smiled shyly.

"Let's go upstairs," she said. "We have to decide who we're going to leave the ranch to."

"Oh," I said, and followed her up the stairs, feeling strange, maybe a bit scared, and knowing that our three-year marriage was due for some attention. But the feeling of peace and acceptance filled me again as I turned out the basement lights. I should relax, and let things happen the way they were meant to happen. There was nothing to fear.

We went to the front door to turn off the porch light, and looked outside as a small dust-devil skittered by the very edge of the porch. It wandered slowly into the darkness and blowing dust clouds beyond. The stars in the sky had disappeared from view. Clara leaned against me, warm and close, and smelling of soap and perfume. We went to the guest room at the back of the house, past a closed bedroom door, as the quiet and darkness of the place engulfed us. There we relaxed, enjoyed life, and each other, and it was wonderful.

The storm hit a little past midnight, and for an hour it seemed like the world might end. Tumbleweeds raced past the house and continuous lightning played a symphony of color in our tiny room. We clung together, cringing as thunder rattled the windows. But when the rain came it was gentle, soothing, and lulling us into a deep, rejuvenating sleep.

It rained most of the next day, earth and sky blending together as in a painting done only in shades of gray. We got out of bed late that day, saying little to each other because talk somehow didn't seem necessary. Clara finished her inventory and did some reading while I cleared out tumbleweeds the storm had piled up on the south side of the house. No whirlwinds danced on the landscape that day. Maybe they had found dry hiding places.

Late in the afternoon I worked in the shop again, grinding some jade pebbles I found in one of the rock storage bins. I remembered how excited Grandpa got whenever he found one of the green, translucent stones in a creek bed or dry wash. Carried down from the north by glaciers, he used to tell me. His eyes would widen with excitement, and he would point to the rock-choked, hanging canyon that came down from the butte.

"Somewhere up there is a huge deposit of this stuff," he confided. "A prospector told me about it. Huge pieces of black, green and even yellow jade, some of it as clear as glass, and enough for a thousand lifetimes of rock cutting."

He shook his head sadly. "But I waited too long. After a hard spring a rock slide came down and made that mess up here: boulders as big as a house, and loose rock. Tried to climb it a few years ago and nearly killed myself getting down. Stupid thing to do at my age. Your grandma had more sense, stayed behind, said her legs were too short."

He laughed.

I remembered the laugh, but I had never seen him more frustrated than on that day.

"Take my advice, John," he said, "do everything you can when you're young. Don't wait til you're old, and your legs don't work right anymore."

The weather cleared that evening as we were eating cold sandwiches and soup. Neither of us felt like talking. We were thinking about the next day, and the trip to town for the funeral. In the evening we went out on the porch and watched the sun paint clouds in red, orange and purple. The air was still. Birds were nesting somewhere secret, and the whirlwinds had not yet returned. Despite the serenity of the place, I felt tenseness, a feeling of anticipation that haunted me as the sky darkened and stars began to appear. It was if the little world around us was waiting quietly and patiently for something to happen.

I could only think about the funeral. We went to bed early, and Clara complained that I talked incoherently in my sleep that night. I don't remember what I was dreaming about. The next morning was cloudless and hot. We got up quickly for coffee and toast, and then made the thirty mile drive to Fallon. Clara spoke only once, pointing out a hawk riding the thermals over hills and buttes. Freedom, I thought.

Harrison was worried. We arrived ten minutes late, but he had refused to start without us, he said. We thanked him; he smiled and squeezed by elbow gently. The service was mercifully short, a few words spoken before a scattering of people I didn't know or vaguely remembered. The old folks had outlived their children, and all of their real friends. There was a hymn, then condolences from guests: such wonderful people, she was a good Christian woman, will you keep the little house, on and on.

We fled to the car. The urn with Grandma's ashes was packed in a cardboard box on the front seat. Harrison had been secretive. There were laws, he reminded us once again, and an empty urn had been interred without fanfare. As we drove back to the house Clara kept looking at me.

"What's the matter?" I finally asked.

"Why do you really despise Mister Harrison so much?"

"I don't know. The little weasel just irritates me."

"You should have seen your face when he touched you. I nearly giggled."

She put the urn next to the door and leaned up against me as we drove. She seemed happy, relieved. I was feeling the same way, even with the urn bouncing around next to us. Everything seemed okay. When we reached the house the day was hot; a few wispy clouds had moved in with a slight breeze. I unwrapped the urn.

"Let's get it over with," I said.

"I'll come along."

"Same place we used for Grandpa?"

"Yes," she said. "I think that's nice."

We walked past the house and up the little hill towards a ridge nearly as high as the butte across the valley. The ridge was covered with Rainbow Stone, and the bulls-eye patterns in red, purple and yellow looked up at me from the ground. I stopped at a point on the ridge where you can see the entire valley from north to south. It's the best place to watch the sunsets. I looked back at Clara, who stood a few feet below me on the hill.

"I suppose I should say something."

She shrugged her shoulders, and smiled. I turned back, facing the butte, and held the urn out in front of me. The breeze was gone, and it was very quiet. Nothing moved in the valley below.

"Well, Grandma," I said to the clear sky, "we'll miss you, but we hope you and Grandpa John are with each other again. At least you'll be together here on the land you loved so much."

There was a sniffling sound behind me; I cleared my throat, and then turned the urn upside down. Ash and small pieces of bone fell in a straight line to the ground. I smoothed the pile of debris with my foot and kicked some pieces of Rainbow Stone on top of it. I found it suddenly difficult to see as I tossed the urn out in front of me and watched it roll a few feet down the hill.

Things happened rapidly after that.

My mind was blank, and I saw misty images of the valley and butte. A sudden breeze cooled my eyes, clearing them. A second gust of wind rocked me forward onto my toes, and then Clara was shouting at me.

"John, get off the ridge!"

At first I didn't see it. The ground was still damp, and there wasn't much dust. But then a tumbleweed swirled into the air, and I saw a nearly invisible dust-devil coming along the ridge directly towards me. I managed to make one awkward step back when the thing hit, spinning me to my knees, and then it was going down the hill. The urn popped into the air, and shattered into shards against a rock.

I picked myself up, spitting dirt and rubbing one knee as Clara reached me, and we watched the growing whirlwind charge off across the valley. "Dead Injuns don't like me," I sputtered, looking at her, but she was staring at the butte, her eyes wide, and she gripped my arm tightly.

Something was coming down the hanging canyon.

A puff of dark brown cloud appeared and disappeared, weaving its way back and forth across the rock slide and down the canyon at a steady pace. I held my breath as the cloud reached the bottom of the canyon and became a conical mass of damp, slowly spinning earth and dust.

Beside me, Clara suddenly began to cry.

"Don't," I said quickly, and hugged her to me. "Not now."

We watched the dark brown, miniature tornado move slowly along the base of the butte. The dust-devil that had struck me moments before was rushing towards it on a collision course. I was holding my breath again, and Clare sobbed softly in my arms.

There was no sound when they collided. The large, dark whirlwind stopped its forward progress. The smaller, lighter one seemed to bounce off its companion, circling in an erratic path for a moment. And then the two of them moved slowly back towards the canyon, climbed up, back and forth across the rock slide and over the top of the butte. In a minute or so they were gone. We stayed and watched the butte the rest of the day.

We never saw them again.

I've thought a lot about it since that day, read a bunch of books about weather and dust-devils and even tornados. The Indians around here don't see things the same way scientific people do, and I've read a lot of their legends, too. Clara and I have talked about it, told the story to our kids, and life has been good to us since that day. But even with the reading, study and talk, there's really only one thing I ever wonder about.

I wonder if they ever found the jade.

GEORGI

A North Dakota winter storm was charging in from the southwest. The sky was white as milk, and snow was already swirling in the back alleys of Fargo as Otis Boswick frantically searched for the basics of life: food, warm clothing or rags for feet, hands and head, a pot or utensil, and anything that would burn. Moms had made her rounds in the morning, had returned with a shopping basket piled high with old newspapers for the oil-can fire to keep them alive another night in the bitter cold. But now he was eight blocks from Moms, and Alf, and the others, eight blocks from the packing crate he called home beneath the second street bridge, and all he wanted was to be warm again. In a North Dakota blizzard, he could be dead in a walk of two blocks, and time was running out.

Otis scrabbled with stiff fingers in one of two dumpsters behind the Broadway Deli, pain stabbing through his arthritic, humped back as he leaned over beyond his limit. He found a broken box half-filled with stale crackers, and a brick of frozen jack cheese covered with frost and blue fuzz, passing up a piece of strange meat aged black. He packed the first treasures of the day in his knapsack, and moved to the second dumpster, which was tightly closed, but not locked. He pushed up hard on the lid, stood on tip toes to look inside, and got the shock of his life.

Inside the dumpster, in a pile of rancid garbage, a man was lying in a fetal position, groaning, clutching at his stomach with both hands.

"Hey, you can't stay in here! A storm's comin', and you'll freeze to death in all that wet! Here, you grab my hands, and come out of there!"

The man, his rugged face covered with fine, blond hair laced with ice crystals, turned over, opened his eyes to look at Otis, then pulled what looked like a garage door opener from beneath his body and pointed it at him. "Go away—or—I hurt."

Otis flinched, but still held out both hands. "Grab hold. I've got a warm place not far from here, unless you want to die. Make up your mind quick. Storm's comin' fast."

The man considered this silently for a moment, then lowered the garage-door-opener and stuffed it into a tattered rucksack at his side, groaning as he moved.

"You sick?"

The man answered in a deep voice, heavily accented. "Was hungry—ate something—bad for me—down here, Want—sleep." He rubbed his lower abdomen with one hand.

"Moms has a tea for that. It's only a few blocks, but we've got to hurry!" Otis grabbed the man's outstretched hands, cold as his own, grimacing as he hauled him upright. The man got out unaided, holding the rucksack tight to him, doubling over in pain as soon as his feet hit the pavement. Otis put an arm around him, and they half-stumbled the eight blocks back to the second street bridge in swirling slow and bitter wind-chill, people staring at them from passing cars. Two drunks ending another day early, their eyes said.

They climbed down the embankment under the bridge. A wrinkled, squat, black woman was warming her hands over an oil-can fire, body covered from head to foot in tattered sweaters and a long coat that made her look like a dirty snowball, leaving the fire's warmth to waddle towards them as they approached. "What you got there, Otis?" she shouted in a raspy voice. "You done found another victim o' society?"

"He's sick, Moms. Ate something bad."

"Well, you just bring him to Moms now, you hear? Po' thing."

Otis maneuvered the man to a broken piece of concrete by the fire, and sat him down on it, holding him steady. Moms ran fat, gentle fingers over his face, checked his eyes. When she put a hand lightly on his stomach, the man cried out sharply, and sagged unconscious into Otis's arms.

"Not good," said Moms. "Man's poisoned. Got to get that out of him *now*." She shuffled over to a wooden-planked hut stuffed with cardboard and rags backed up against one concrete buttress of the bridge, and crawled inside through a blanket-draped opening. "Otis, you quick heat some water over the fire! Man can't drink this cold!"

Otis put a screen over the top of the oil drum, and managed to heat some water in a shallow pan before Moms came back with a tin cup containing a yellow powder sprinkled with bits of blue and red. Otis's eyes widened as he recognized the potion, but Moms pushed the cup into his hands. "Got to get it out of him quick, Otis, and you know it."

They made the tea, forcing it down the partially conscious man who grimaced with each sip, Moms stroking his forehead. "Quick, man. We're tryin' to save your life here, and there's no hospitals for the likes of us. Drink it all up."

A few minutes later, the man's eyes snapped open, he lunged out of Otis's grasp to his hands and knees, and projectile-vomited the entire contents of his stomach onto the broken chunks of concrete beneath the bridge.

"I've got the room. He can stay with me," said Otis.

"Just so's I take care of him. You knows nothin' of the art." Moms smiled a toothless smile, looking satisfied with herself.

"Don't have to, Moms, not with you here. Where're the others?"

"Probably out killin' someone for a quarter, but Jason's inside, with Alf for protection. Jack was botherin' him again, skinny demon he is, but he sure is scared o' that dog."

Otis got the man on his feet, helped him over to the mammoth packing crate he lived in against the buttress opposite from Moms' hut. As he approached, there was a low, menacing growl from inside the crate.

"Alf, shut up! And get back, now! I got a friend here, and he's bad sick!" Otis pushed aside the blanket covering the small entrance, pulling the man in after him. The interior of the crate was a heap of sleeping bags and old blankets, dimly lit by a single candle. In one corner a frail boy sat upright in a sleeping bag, staring fearfully, arm around the neck of a mongrel mix of German Shepherd and Pit-Bull Terrier still growling low in its throat. "You hold onto him tight, Jason. I gotta get this man warm, and we got a blizzard comin!"

Otis got the man's rucksack off, and stuffed him fully clothed into a bag, piling on two blankets for good measure. Instantly, the man was asleep, and Alf stepped forward to cautiously sniff at him. "Friend, Alf. Friend," said Otis, scratching the massive head of the animal. Alf waggled a stump of a tail, and licked Otis's hand.

"You all right, boy?"

Jason Boggs, a fourteen-year-old runaway from Minneapolis, slouched in the sleeping bag, face grim. "Better now that you're back. That creep Jack grabbed me by the balls again this morning, and Alf bit him good. He said he'd kill Alf when he gets back. And then the cop was here again."

"Luis Penuel? He's a good man, Jason. Looks after us."

"Well, he's no friend of mine since he turned my name in. Says my stepfather has left home for good, and my mom is comin' to get me. He had no right turning me in like that!"

"Sure he did, Jason. You're only fourteen, with a whole life ahead of you. This ain't no way for you to live, on the run. Don't you want to be with your mom?"

"She's okay, I guess. It's my stepfather liked to beat up on me."

"Well, there you are. In the meantime you've got Moms and me and Alf for family. We'll take care of you. But consider it good, Jason. A boy needs a real home, not a packing crate."

"It's good enough for you and Moms."

"That's our choice, boy. It's our way of life, and we wouldn't have it any other way—except when it gets so damnable cold. What I wouldn't give for heat in winter, and then pack my friends in here. Wouldn't that be somethin'?"

Jason shook his head, and smiled. "You and Moms take care of everyone, Otis."

"What better way to live, boy? It's our callin'. Now you hunker down and get some sleep. I've got me a sick man to tend to, and it's gonna get terrible cold tonight."

Moms' call came from outside the crate, a cup of a new brew laced with sugar in her hands. Three times that night they awakened the man to feed him an energetic tea with numbed hands as the blizzard raged around them.

* * * *

Otis awoke with a start, nostrils frozen shut, the interior of the crate filled with icy fog sparkling in a band of sunlight coming in where the blanket had been pulled aside from the entrance. The man he had found in the dumpster was sitting up in his sleeping bag, peering outside, holding the blanket aside with a bare hand. When Otis snorted to clear the ice from his nose, the man turned to look at him.

"Snow gone—light again."

"Yes, but now it'll get *really* cold, and we need more fuel for the fire. We used up all the newspapers while you were sleeping. Feel better now?"

"I have—hunger—here." The man rubbed his stomach carefully. "How long I—in this place?"

"Three nights and two days," said Otis. "You were bad poisoned, and for a day or so we thought you wouldn't make it. But Moms knows what she's doing; we've never lost a sick person."

"Now I eat," said the man matter-of-factly.

"Wish I could help you there, but all we've got left is some oatmeal, and we need to cook that. No fuel."

The man found his rucksack next to him, opened it, and reached inside. "You bring food—I cook—here." He withdrew a metal globe, silver, the size of a softball out of his sack, pushed aside some rags, and placed the globe carefully in his tea cup on the floor of the crate before rummaging in his pack again.

Otis held up a metal canteen and shook it soundlessly. "All our water's frozen. We need a lot of heat to thaw it."

"I do fast," said the man. "Get food." He pulled out a metal platform with sloped vanes and flat bottom, placed the globe in it, then screwed a wire coil with threaded shaft into a short, ceramic receptor on top of the globe.

"That some kind of hotplate?" said Otis.

"This cook—heat us good." He reached out a hand. "Give water."

Otis handed him the canteen, then searched in his own pack for a bag of oatmeal he had hoarded for months. Found it. Held it out to the man. "Here you go. Now that you're with us again, my name is Otis Boswick. What's yours?"

The man didn't answer, grasped a knurled knob at the side of the globe, twisted it, pulled out a shaft about an inch, twisted again. Immediately, the coil began to glow, first deep red, rapidly turning to bright red and orange. The interior of the crate was flooded with heat, while Otis stared in fascination. "Well, will you look at that! Say, if you don't want to give me a name, that's okay. It's only I'd like to have something to call you by."

"I am Georgi," said the man. He put the canteen on the glowing coil, and picked up the bag of oatmeal to look at it closely.

"Georgi. That's a Russian name. Thought I recognized the accent. You one of the new emigrants? This cold probably don't seem very different, then."

"No Russian," said Georgi.

"Oh," said Otis. *And no last name, either.* "No matter, I'm just curious, is all. Like to get to know people better, but don't mean to pry. People come through here are all runnin' from somethin', some of it pretty bad, but I don't pry. Live and let live, I say."

Georgi looked at him darkly. "You take care—me. I—thank."

"Nothing," said Otis. "Moms did it all, anyway."

Steam was squirting out from beneath the cap on the canteen, making a whistling sound. Jason stirred in his sleeping bag, Alf lying on top of him. "Where's the heat coming from?"

"Georgi here had a stove with him, Jason. We're cookin' up the oatmeal. Want some?"

"Sure," said the boy. "Those crackers didn't go very far with me yesterday." He sat up in his bag so that Alf was in his lap, and stroked the dog's head. "Alf must be hungry, too."

"We'll give him some oatmeal. Good for dogs."

Georgi poured half of the sack of oatmeal into a small pan, took some rags from the floor to lift off the scalding hot canteen and stirred water into the pan. Otis spooned the steaming cereal into cups, and they ate silently in the warm glow of the coil, heating themselves inside and out, a luxury Otis could not remember since several winters before when a guy had come through with a backpacker's stove, and they had all gotten a little drunk on hot wine. That was before Moms.

After he'd finished eating, Otis filled another cup with the last of the oatmeal. "This is for Moms," he explained. "Back in a minute." He crawled outside, and walked the few steps to Moms' hut, keeping a palm over the cup. "Moms! Rise and shine! We got food here. Hot oatmeal!"

A raspy shout greeted his offer. "Don't want none, Charlie! Now I told you to stay away from me, and here you are again! Go away!"

Oh, oh. Back inside herself again, the spells getting more frequent in the last year. "No, it's Otis, Moms. Here, I'll put the food by the doorway.

Your patient cooked up breakfast this morning. You cured him, Moms, and his name is Georgi."

"Charlie, I'll sic the dog on you if you don't go away! I mean it!"

There was no arguing with her when she was like this, but at least she was in the hut. On the street, in this condition, she couldn't find her way home. But in a day it usually passed over, and Otis wondered if she was having little strokes, or maybe it was Alzheimer's. He also wondered who Charlie was. He put the cup down by the hut's entrance, and turned as Georgi emerged from the crate, carrying a small, black box the size of a cigarette package in one hand. He barely glanced at Otis, walked straight up the embankment and out of sight. When he came down again a minute later, he was empty-handed. And the cup full of oatmeal had disappeared into the hut.

"We go out—get more food," said Georgi, and it was like a command. Otis was surprised by the sudden anger he felt surge inside him.

"One nice thing about my life is I don't have to take orders from anyone, Georgi, not even you. Last time I did that was in the Korean war. Climb the cliff, the sergeant said, and take out that gun emplacement. Me, with a wife and two little babies back home. But it was an order in a combat zone, and I didn't want to get shot by my own people, so I climbed the damn thing. Halfway up, the cliff come loose and down I went. Broke my back bad, and all I got to show for it was a purple heart I hocked for food years ago. Lost the wife, and the babies, get lousy disability checks barely enough for me and my friends to live on, but I make do, and I *don't* take orders from *anyone* anymore. You got that?"

Georgi looked at him somberly. "You soldier—in battle?"

Otis looked away from those dark eyes. "A long time ago—when I was young."

Georgi put a big hand on Otis's shoulder, and squeezed gently. "I soldier, too. I do accident, too, in—ship. Georgi not hurt, but friend—my friend die, and he buried far to—home. No battle—we only look—friend dead. Now Georgi go home—friends find. Georgi stay alive—find food. I help Otis, who saves life. You show how?"

"Who are you?" asked Otis, wiping his eyes.

"I soldier—like Otis. We get food together. Come." He put an arm across Otis' humped back. "We go where you find me?"

"No—I have some money left, and it's too cold to stay out long. Fresh food is cheap, but it can't get frozen. How long will your stove run before the fuel is gone? We'll have to keep the crate warm inside."

"Run long time—to snow gone—fill with—water—run to snow come again. I show how."

"Never heard of such a stove. You bull-shittin' me?"

Georgi laughed, then, a big, deep-throated chuckle, and hugged Otis to him. "No—shittin," he said.

They walked ten blocks to a Seven-Eleven store that was accustomed to doing meager business with street people, the owner a friendly man who had known hard times himself, and occasionally paid them for odd jobs around the place. The owner wasn't there, and the clerk, a young girl around seventeen, eyed them apprehensively until Otis put his rumpled dollar bills onto the counter. A five-pound bag of potatoes and a box of oatmeal took everything he had, except for a nickel and three pennies.

Georgi scooped the coins up in a big hand. "I keep—remember Otis?"

"Sure, why not? Can't buy anything with it, anyway." He watched the coins disappear into Georgi's pocket.

They strolled back to the bridge, Otis pointing out the parking lot that had once been the Zephyr bar, a place to talk to friends, to belong, now gone. Across the street another bar, the Pink Pussycat, was being torn down along with an old hotel he had lived in for two years until it had been condemned. Slowly, but surely, the good folks of Fargo were forcing them out into the streets, back alleys, and under the bridges to freeze and die in the long winters. He had heard their favorite saying, of course: forty below keeps the riffraff out. Or kills them.

Sun-dogs were out in the icy air, two pillars of fire on either side of a sun low in the southern sky. They walked out onto the second street bridge to watch the Red River, a narrow channel of deep, black water winding through ice. Georgi carried the groceries in a paper bag, listening silently as Otis pointed out where he had found a body the summer before, half in and out of the river. "Old guy, just passing through. Some kids probably knifed him for fun. For the pure hell of it! Sure not my kind of people, none of them!"

Georgi shook his head sadly. "There is cruelty—with people—all place."

"Only for some of us," said Otis, and his head had turned sharply to the left to watch a police car pulling up below them, alongside the embankment. Two uniformed officers got out of the car, and picked their way carefully down the snowy slope. One of them was Luis Penuel. "Oh, oh, they're comin' for Jason. Get out of sight!" Otis pulled Georgi back from the edge of the bridge. "If he sees you, Penuel will want to know who you are, and where you come from. He's a friend, but he checks up on everyone who comes through here. Do you want that?"

"No," said Georgi firmly. "I here only little while, until—no trouble, Otis."

"Then don't let them see you. Wait up here until they're gone. I'll come back, but I've got to go down and see after Jason. He's only been here three weeks, but Penuel traced him, and his mom wants him back home."

"I wait here—you go," said Georgi.

Otis squeezed the big man's arm, then walked the length of the bridge, and fell down twice before reaching the bottom of the snowy embankment. Alf was barking angrily from inside the crate, and Moms was hugging Jason, the two officers pulling at his arms. Moms waved as the three walked towards Otis, and there were tears in her eyes. "You be good to your mom, you hear?" she cried.

Jason waved back to her, and he was smiling when he came up to Otis. Luis Penuel put an arm around him. "His mom is at the station cryin' her eyes out. She wants him back real bad, and it looks like a good situation for Jason, now, Otis. Thanks to you and Moms, he's going home in one piece."

Otis looked at the boy. "You want to go home, Jason?"

"Yeah. But I'll never forget you or Moms, and what you did for me. I'm gonna miss Alf, too. Mom says she'll get me a big dog when I get home, and I want one like Alf."

"Alf is special, all right. C'mere, boy." Otis held out his arms, and Jason was swallowed in his embrace while the officers found other things to look at.

"Do somethin' for street people someday, will you?"

"I promise, Otis. Take care of yourself—and Moms, too. She's still actin' kinda funny."

"You betcha," said Otis, releasing the boy, swallowing hard as one officer led him up the slope to the patrol car, and out of sight. Luis Penuel stayed behind a moment, an arm around Otis's hunched shoulders.

"He'll be fine, Otis. Just fine. And you watch out for yourself, too. Jack Cain is back in town. I saw him stumbling around by the tracks this morning, yelling at air. He gives you any more trouble you let me know, and I'll throw him right in the can. Got it?"

"Sure. I'll let you know. Anyway, Alf scares the hell out of him."

"Yeah, but Alf don't carry a knife or a gun. You watch out for that guy, He's pure, evil mean." Luis slapped Otis on the back, then climbed the embankment, and in an instant the patrol car, and Jason, were gone.

Moms was standing by the oil can, staring at the flames, when Otis trudged up the slope to find Georgi again. When he got to the top, he saw Georgi next to the span, balancing on snow, the little black box in his hand. He was wedging it into the rocky ground by the bridge, and carefully covering it with a tangle of frozen brush, looking up as Otis came close.

"Whatever that thing is, I sure as hell hope you ain't no Russian spy. I busted my back fightin' communists."

"I tell Otis. No Russian," said Georgi. "Jason gone, now?"

"Yeah, home to Minneapolis with his mom. No more freezing cold nights for him. A warm house, where boys oughta be. I'll miss him. Good kid."

Georgi picked up the grocery bag with one hand. "Otis feel better when eat. I cook—you show how."

Otis turned to start down the hill, taking a tentative first step, when suddenly, Georgi grabbed him from behind, sitting down with him, and sliding on his back all the way to the bottom, his excited shout echoing beneath the bridge.

"Both of you's crazy!" yelled Moms.

That night, with light snow falling, the three of them stayed in Otis's crate, warmed by the glowing stove, and feasted on boiled potatoes with one of Moms' special teas.

The following morning, Jack Cain returned to their camp.

* * * *

The morning was clear, but breath-freezing cold, a foot of light, powder snow on the ground from the night before. Stomachs full, Otis and Georgi sipped hot tea in the warm crate, Moms still asleep, a shapeless mound in one corner. Alf watched them mournfully, curled up on Jason's sleeping bag, from which he had not moved since the boy had left. Georgi had shown Otis all the operating details of the stove, including where to fill it with ordinary water when the heating rate got low. He had tried to explain the source of the heat, talking about atoms sticking together, and the unbelievably hot gas somehow contained in a golf-ball-size volume within the globe. He drew diagrams, and strange chemical formulae, one Otis recognized as the one for water. The high school education he had not finished, before fleeing to break his back in a foreign war, was only a vague memory to him, now, and he found himself befuddled by most of Georgi's careful teaching. I should go to the library once in a while to read a newspaper, he thought, and catch up on what's going on in the world.

Georgi leaned against Otis, a sly grin on his face. "If Otis take heater, and what I draw here—take to great teacher—scientist—show this—can be rich—not live like this. Have much—money. Good for Otis."

Otis laughed. He thought little of money, because there was little of it to think about. Money was a transient thing, like most of his friends, like Georgi, and the stove. It appeared and disappeared from his life, without predictability. It was better to live a day at a time, and he had learned not to dwell on what could be, or what could have been. During his hard life, he had become a fatalist, coming to grips with the program laid out for him. His life was meant to be the struggle it was, for whatever reason, and he had accepted it. And so he dismissed Georgi's humorous fantasy with a laugh, knowing that a small part of him would think about it some more. What would it be like to have a lot of money? He could do all sorts of things that—

—"HEY, YOU BUMS! WHERE'RE YOU HIDIN'? I COME BACK TO KILL ME A DOG!"

Moms bolted upright in her sleeping bag. Alf's eyes narrowed, a growl rattling in his throat. "Jack Cain," whispered Moms. "Otis, he's back again. I thought we done rid o' that devil."

"Who?" said Georgi, suddenly tense.

"You stay in here, both of you. I'll go out, and talk to him."

"You're crazy," said Moms. "Man's drunk, and spoilin' for a fight. Leave 'im be."

"Come outta there! I hear you mumblin', and I can hear the dog, too. In one minute, he's dead!" A bottle crashed against the side of the crate, and Alf started barking hysterically. "That's it! Send Alf after me! One swipe of this knife, and his head's gone!"

"You come in here, Jack Cain, and I'll put the hex on you," yelled Moms. "You stick a head in, and I blow a powder on you make you blind, and suck your breath away, turn you blue, and put that knife in your own gut! You get out of here, now!"

Footsteps outside, then something hard and heavy hit the side of the crate. "Ain't afraid of you—crazy old bitch! I want that DOG!" The words were nearly drowned out by Alf's barking and snarling, froth spewing from his mouth, teeth bared. Moms grabbed the big dog, and hung on tightly.

"I have to go out," said Otis grimly.

Georgi grabbed his pack, fumbled inside it. "I come with Otis."

"NO! This is between Jack and me, and it's *my* dog he wants to cut up. You stay *put*!" Otis turned, crawling quickly outside before Georgi had a chance to answer, then stood up painfully, and faced Jack Cain a few feet away from the crate. The man's face was scarred and pock-marked, head bare, eyes puffed nearly shut from days of solid drinking. He was dying before Otis's eyes, a wasted skeleton of a man, army-surplus fatigues hanging tent-like from his thin frame, mouth twisted into a sinister grin that made him a specter of death itself. In one hand he held a large Bowie knife, waving it lazily at Otis's face.

"You still got that pretty little boy in there?"

"Jason's gone, and he ain't comin' back. You can't hurt him anymore, Jack."

"Shi-it, I kinda hoped for some fun after I carved up your dog—with this." Jack took a stumbling step forward, and now the knife was very close to Otis's face.

"I don't have any quarrel with you, Jack, and there's nothin' here for you anymore. Why don't you just leave?"

"Hey, you don't own this place, old man; now, you bring that dog out here so I can get it done quick, and *then* I'll leave." The cold blade of the big knife touched Otis's nose, then waved away again.

"I won't do that, Jack."

"Yeah! Well, then, I gotta do it another way." Jack made a short lunge, slicing a gash in Otis's cheek so that he cried out.

Alf was crazy, now, thrashing around inside the crate, Moms screaming. "I can't hold him, Otis!"

Otis felt warm blood running down his face. He circled to his left, away from the crate, stooping to grab up a chunk of broken concrete with one hand.

"Come on, Jack. You and me," he said, voice shaking with fear, hoping the others could somehow escape while Jack's back was turned.

"Hey, the old soldier. That's pretty good, Otis. Well, how about a little bayonet drill?" Jack lunged, Otis stumbling backwards, swinging the concrete chunk wildly, and missing the death's head by inches. Before he could recover, another lunge was coming, the knife sweeping past his face, and back again in an upward thrust. Otis swung weakly, punching Jack in one shoulder as he felt the knife burn into his left side. He staggered backwards, grabbing at his side, and dropping his only defense as Jack grinned wildly at him.

A loud voice boomed behind the man with the blood-stained knife.

"JACK CAIN!"

Jack jerked around in surprise, dropping into a crouch.

Georgi had emerged from the crate, the garage-door-looking thing in his hand, now pointing it at Jack.

Otis gasped for breath, pain flooding his left side. "It's my fight, Georgi," he said weakly.

"No. Now it Georgi fight," said the big man.

"You want some of this?" Jack lunged towards Georgi, the knife a spear before him.

The garage-door-thing flashed green, lighting up the entire underside of the bridge, and Jack Cain screamed. He dropped the knife, and fell writing to the ground, the heels of his boots digging grooves in frozen earth."

"You like pain? Here—Georgi give more." The weapon flashed again, and now Jack was shrieking, foam flying from his mouth. He flayed the ground with his arms for minutes, as Otis watched in horror, then curled up in a fetal position, and moaned.

Georgi picked up the knife, tossed it over to the entrance of the crate, then grasped Jack by the hair, and pulled him screaming to his knees. "Here, I show you something. I show you what happen you come back here again. You look at big rock—by where fire is." He grasped Jack by the hair again, and twisted his head in the direction of a two-hundred pound block of concrete by the oil can they used for a fire. Jack's eyes were nearly closed, his moaning pitiful even to the man he would eventually have killed.

"You look, now," said Georgi, and then he fiddled with the garage-door-opener. Pointed it. Fired.

The flash was bright red, concentrated in a narrow beam that struck the center of the rock. The concrete flashed yellow—and disappeared. Jack cried out, tears flowing down his cheeks as Georgi leaned over to look at him, their noses nearly touching. "You come back again—I do that to you. Now—you go."

Jack Cain stumbled to his feet, and fled from their camp—forever.

Georgi helped Otis back to the crate. The knife blade had gone in and out of his left side at a shallow angle near beltline, and the wound was bleeding profusely, but inside of an hour Moms had him bandaged up, and resting comfortable next to the stove, Georgi hovering over him. Moms left her patient for only a moment in order to conjure up a new poultice in her shack. While she was gone, Otis, drowsy with pain, looked up at Georgi, scanning his rugged features and dark eyes in the glow of the stove. "You sure ain't no Russian spy," he said softly. "You sure ain't nothin' from around here."

Georgi looked at him sadly. "I tell you—far to home."

And it was in the twilight of that very day when Georgi's friends came to take him away.

Moms had filled him with tea, and his bladder seemed ready to burst. Otis wiggled carefully out of the crate, and relieved himself against the bridge buttress. Georgi had started a fire in the oil can, and draped a towel across the top of it to dry. Moms was shuttling back and forth, moving her pharmacy into Otis's crate, mumbling to herself all the time about too many things to do. She was never happier than when she had a patient to take care of.

Otis zipped up his pants, and turned to say something to Georgi, freezing into silence at the look on the man's face. Georgi was looking past him; head tilted upwards, white teeth showing in a huge smile. He lifted both arms over his head and waved wildly, laughing. Otis spun around; saw two men descending the embankment, one of them carrying the little black box Georgi had hidden by the bridge. They waved back to Georgi, scrambled down the slope, and ran towards him. Both were dressed from head to toe in skintight, brown knitted suits, black belts around their waists hanging heavily with metal canisters of various sizes, reminding Otis of Rangers he had seen in the war.

Georgi ran to meet them, embracing each man with a huge hug, lifting them off the ground. Comrades. Otis's heart sank. Georgi's friends had found him, had come to take him away from them. But the look on the big man's face was pure joy. I must be happy for him, thought Otis. He has found his people again.

The three men talked in low tones, occasionally looking at Otis. *I'm being talked about.* His side was hurting again, and he sat down on a concrete chunk by the fire, feeling a sudden emptiness, a sense of loss. Friends were so temporary, friendships so fleeting in his life. Why must it be this way? But then he did have Moms, and Alf, and wasn't that enough? Not good to want too much, Otis. But, oh, how rapidly this big man from a place far away had become a friend of his.

Georgi broke away from the other two men, who remained where they were, and walked quickly to the crate. "I talk with Otis. Otis wait there." He ducked inside, and came out with the little weapon he had used against Jack Cain, but nothing else. The stove—the pack—both were still inside the crate. "Say nothing. I talk." He knelt before Otis, put a hand on his shoulder. "I tell—much lost—in river. Can't find. I leave things—you keep—for make Georgi live so friends find. I go home, now—remember Otis—my friend."

Moms came up behind Georgi, looked at Otis's face, and tears welled up in her eyes. "You's goin' home, is that it?"

"Yes. Friends find."

"Goin' home, goin' home, we's all goin' home one way or 'nother. You remember Moms now, too, you hear?"

Georgi reached out and took her hand in his, then squeezed Otis's shoulder with his other hand before standing up. Otis looked up at him, and smiled.

"You sure you ain't no Russian spy?"

Georgi laughed that deep-throated laugh again. "No, Otis. Russia—close. I go—far—far to home." He made a grand sweep with one arm. "Good—bye, bye." He turned suddenly, and walked back to the other men. They stood in a tight cluster, one of them fiddling with the little black box. And then suddenly it was as if a black sheet wrapped around them, appearing out of nowhere, blinking once—twice—then a flash of white light filling it, neutralizing it to nothingness, along with the men inside.

The bright flash left spots before Otis's eyes. He blinked—looked—blinked again. Georgi and the others were gone. Moms clapped her hands together. "Lord, I has seen the doorway to heaven! I has seen your angels come to take our friend to yo' holy person. I praise the power o' the Lord! Amen." Moms turned, wiped her eyes, and shuffled back towards the crate. "Someday, he'll come for us, Otis, but you git back inside, now. Tea's heatin', and you don't need gettin' chilled out here."

Inside the crate, Otis turned the stove down until the coil glowed dull red, then snuggled in his sleeping bag, and sipped hot tea. For the first time in days, Alf left Jason's bag, and stepped gingerly past Moms to lie down by

Otis, heavy head in his lap. Otis stroked Alf's head, and exchanged a smile with Moms when the dog sighed.

Georgi had left him the stove for a reason. To stay warm? Or to get rich? After what he's seen that day, Otis was sure there was no other stove like this one—anywhere—not on planet Earth. But to get rich meant dealing with people who weren't in his world, either, people who would find a way to steal the secrets in Georgi's diagrams for themselves, the same people who wouldn't part with a quarter for a street person, the ones who sneered at them through the windows of their passing cars.

His reverie was interrupted by a shout from outside.

"Hey, Otis! You in there?"

"That you, Two Feathers?" He hadn't seen the big Sioux for months.

"Yeah. Freezin' solid out here, Otis. Got an extra bag for the night? Gonna leave for Minneapolis tomorrow."

"When's the last time you ate?"

"Oh, two—maybe three days. Got a bag of raw beans with, but nothin' to cook 'em up. You got somethin'?"

Otis looked at Moms, and she nodded her okay.

"Well, you just get yourself in here, and bring the beans! We've got enough heat in here for everybody!"

BADLAND'S DREAMING

"You're crazy to go out there alone."

John Natani bristled, Italian blood boiling, but his Indian half forced him to remain calm. "That's why I'm paying for a long distance call, Joe. I want you to go with me. It's only a few days, like when we were kids. You remember the place."

At the other end of the line, Joseph Eaglestaff sighed before answering his childhood friend, remembering how the elders had called them a dreaming pair. "That was a long time ago, John. I'm the one with finals coming up in a week. You're the one who dropped out of school. What you do is your business."

"I don't want to be an engineer, Joe."

"So switch majors like I did. Ask around, and see what else you're interested in. It's either that or stay on the reservation and collect welfare, or move into town for some crummy job nobody wants. You don't need a vision-quest to make that decision for you; just think about it."

"I will, when I make Ihamblecza—in the badlands."

"The heat will boil your brains out. You won't think of anything. This is the twenty first century, John. Quit listening to old men and wapiyapi. They live in the past. Take charge of your own life."

"You hate your own people," said John, even though there had been times, as a half-breed, when he'd not been treated as one of them. But now his parents were dead, and it didn't matter anymore.

"I won't even answer that," said Joe. "There's no future for me on the reservation, and I'm getting out. You do what you want."

"I will," said John, and he started to hang up the phone.

"John, be careful out there," said Joe quickly. "Even the old ones knew when to quit trying. Don't kill yourself for a dream. John?"

"Yes?"

"I'll be thinking about you."

"Sure," said John, and he hung up the phone.

* * * *

The drive north and west was stifling under a searing North Dakota sun in August. Wind from the north brought dry air that sucked moisture from

John's body, leaving his skin covered with a light frosting of salt, and making him feel itchy all over. He gassed up the old jeep at a discount station in Medora, and headed west a few miles before turning north on an old fire road skirting the edge of the national park, up towards high cliffs and buttes banded in red, black and yellow.

Here was his place of silence, peace and solitude, a place to make his vision quest as the old ones had done in the Black Hills far to the south and long before his birth. But here was his place, near his home, near the miserable land on which his people now lived with alkali water and stunted grass.

He could not identify with those who fought to return to the sacred hills. His land was here, burning hot in the sunlight.

The road became shallow ruts in tall buffalo grass, and then there was no road at all. The jeep bounced up the hill until John saw cottonwood trees to the east and traversed towards them, buckling himself into the seat and feeling the weight of the vehicle shift wholly to the downhill tires. The Little Missouri River came into view below, a muddy trickle shining mirror-like in the summer sun. He parked the jeep at a precarious angle between two trees and got out to chock the wheels with dead branches.

He threw his pack on the ground and checked the contents: a pair of gallon plastic bottles filled with water, three chocolate bars, and a package of Fig Newtons. It was enough for maybe three days, but he felt guilt. The old ones had gotten along on far less. He closed the pack and ate one candy bar while he cinched up, then covered the jeep with a green tarp and secured the four corners to trees with nylon rope. He hoisted the pack on his back, adjusted the straps, and then started down towards the river, looking back once to check the jeep. It was not visible twenty yards from the trees. When he reached an old road paralleling the river, the long walk began.

In nearby Medora that afternoon and for three days thereafter, the officially recorded high temperature reached one hundred and four degrees.

John followed the road for five miles, his mind a blank, eyes staring at the rutted bentonite and scoria chips ahead of him. He didn't notice the heat at first; wind blowing down from the high, colorful buttes cooled him. The road veered upwards to the north, crossing a sandy saddle strewn with the bones of some hapless, small animal, and he stopped there for a moment, breath suddenly quickening. Ahead of him lay a green valley of buffalo grass, a trickling stream carving jagged, rust-red gashes across it towards the high plateau rising on the other side, and up one ridge dark shapes were moving rapidly. Even at this distance he could hear their coughing and growling. The buffalo were here, and it was a good sign.

He quickened his step down into the valley as the road changed to trail to a single rut to a faint line of bent and crushed buffalo grass meandering past a prairie dog town long abandoned, and up a long draw towards the high plateau above him. The draw became a clay shelf, strewn with bits of petrified wood from another age; the climb was suddenly steep, his feet slipping, and sweat running into his eyes. Near the top he stopped to remove his pack and sip from the water bottle.

The ground moved.

Five yards to his right a bentonite cliff thrust upwards twenty feet to the high plateau and all along the edge the buffalo herd suddenly appeared, rushing by and growling at the man below them. John Natani felt fragile in the presence of such massive animals. He was curiously unafraid. Two bulls moved by, large as his jeep, ignoring him, then several cows and a calf, the rest of the herd thundering by beyond the edge. John's heart quickened when a cow lurched to the edge, glared down at him angrily, and pawed at the clay with sharp hooves as a calf pressed against her. A part of him screamed in fear, another part freezing him calmly in his place, raising his arms towards the frenzied animal and speaking to it.

"I come to find the buffalo woman; I seek Ptesanwin. Lead me, so I may make Ihamblecya."

The cow had no chance to answer. Behind her the monstrous lead bull suddenly appeared, head lowered, one terrible horn disappearing up the female's anus, and she jumped screaming, scrambling ahead of her tyrant and away from the cliff edge. The ground trembled again, and was still.

John took the few remaining steps up to the high plateau and saw the herd moving quickly across it towards the west, through ripe buffalo grass covering the treeless plain to the horizon. When he passed them at great distance, two hours later, they were paralleling his course. John Natani found significance in this. The Ptepi were with him, and Ptesanwin would be near. He lowered his head and trudged onwards across the endless plateau.

When he reached the end of the grassy plain the sun was high. His lips and tongue felt swollen, and pack straps chaffed his shoulders raw. He stopped for a moment, took a long pull of warm water from the bottle, hoisted his pack once more and began picking his way carefully down narrow, sloping clay ledges into a canyon with no name. One moment a gentle breeze was cooling his face, but as he dropped below the edge of the plateau it seemed the furnaces of hell were unleashed upon him. His first breath of hot air rising from the canyon floor made him gasp, and his eyes were suddenly dry. There was no water in this canyon, but it had seen better times of green forests and sparkling streams. Along the bentonite shelves that were the canyon walls lay silicified remains of giant trees that had once cast shade here. Volcanoes to the south and west had killed them with ash and poisonous gases, and now their crystalline bodies glistened in the sunlight. Small Junipers clung tenaciously to scoria outcroppings in the gray clay, a hopeful sign of life and splash of green in a world of alkaline white, red and gray.

John moved across the clay, feeling it crackling beneath his feet, listening for a sound of other life and hearing nothing. The canyon laid barren, dead beneath him. Loneliness descended like a heavy cloud, urging him to turn away from this evil place. But it was a place of cleansing, he told himself, a place for turning inwards, asking questions, exploring goals and motivations. A place for Ihamblecya.

He climbed to a sandstone shelf near the canyon rim, scrambled up onto it and removed his pack. There was a commanding view of the canyon towards the west, and what breeze there was he would feel here. John removed his shirt and headband; let his black hair spill over his shoulders. He took a long pull from the water bottle, stowed it carefully in his pack and turned, sitting cross-legged to face the west rim of the canyon. Behind him, from somewhere out on the high, grassy plateau, there was a coughing sound. John smiled, raised his arms and closed his eyes to a descending sun, knowing he was not alone. As the heat seared his flesh, he began to pray.

It was ritual, prayers taught to him by mother and grandfather. He repeated them over and over until his mind drifted along with the words, observing but not hearing, present but somehow detached from the incantations. The words began to lose meaning as his mind drifted away, wandering far from the canyon heat, back to the dusty roads and grasslands of the reservation, a place of belonging far removed from the college campus he had despised and fled.

John was filled with a sense of regret, of failure. He'd only stayed a month, leaving before first exams. Of what use to his people would he be as an engineer? They didn't need computers or high technology; simple work and dignity had been enough for thousands of years. A corner of his mind nagged at him. Of what use are you to your people just sitting here on a rock and talking to the wind and snakes and trees of stone? Why are you really here? John felt hot sweat running into his eyes and mouth, opened the water bottle and took another long drink from it. "Ptesanwin, wise one, please speak to me. Show me the way I must follow."

He watched a blood-red sun descend beyond the western rim of the canyon, and ate a few of the Fig Newtons to silence his noisy stomach. A night breeze chilled him, but he did not put on his shirt and shivered on the ledge until the breeze subsided. His tongue felt swollen again and he drank more water, holding it in his mouth for a long time before swallowing.

Behind him on the grassy slopes near the canyon, a coyote family emerged for the night's hunting, greeted each other with a symphony of yelps and howls that filled him with a sense of oneness with all life. Soon after, he heard the scratching of toe-nails on rock, saw dark shapes moving among the petrified logs and stumps below him, then a yip and low growl as one of the furtive creatures sensed his presence. "Miyacapi, little four-legged ones, tell Ptesanwin I am here." He prayed until a full moon had crossed the star-filled sky, and as the coyotes returned to their dens he succumbed to the exhaustion of unanswered prayers and fell into a dreamless sleep.

By the evening of the following day he had used up all his food and water, and he was consumed by doubt. His body was stiff and aching; dry lips had cracked open, and when he licked them he tasted blood. His mind seemed a blank. There were no answers, no thoughts, voices or visions. He was not worthy or ready, or Ptesanwin was a myth for ignorant people of the distant past. There was a coughing sound and low growls from the plateau behind him; the buffalo were still there, agitated. It was rutting season. "Ptesanwin, where are you?" he whispered. Even the coyotes avoided him that night, and he fell asleep with tears in his eyes.

He awoke when the sun was high. He was drenched in sweat. His vision was blurred by a white veil before his eyes, and there was a buzzing sound in his ears. His heart was pounding, skin turning cold, instinct screaming within him to find shade. He scrambled from the ledge and over rocks towards the canyon floor. Stepping over a rocky log, he felt a searing pain when something struck his leg. He looked down numbly as the venomous snake struck him again in the same place, and he staggered backwards onto a flat of alkali sand in shock. The snake glared at him a moment, then crawled back under the log. John felt no malice, sensing a purpose in the pain already moving up his leg. Perhaps this was his answer; he would die in this place rather than live in the white man's world. In a coldly rational way he realized this was likely in his weakened state. But a part of him wanted to live, while the remainder dwelled in self-pity. He limped across an alkali flat and along game trails towards a Juniper-covered escarpment jutting out over a scoria-lined canyon filled with thick underbrush. The escarpment was near an occasionally used horse trail, and shade was there. His death could be comfortable; more than he deserved for an ill-spent life. Ptesanwan would hide her face from him, and smile as he died. This was truth. Tears came. Must it be this way? He pondered the question, and felt numbness creeping into his groin. *Please don't let me die*, he thought. *There are things I should do—but what are they?*

He found a shady hollow beneath two intertwined junipers and crawled into it, dragging his violated leg behind him. Someone had camped here. He found match sticks and a piece of aluminum foil. The vacationers were gone and usually it was only rangers or ranchers who ventured this far into the backcountry. Perhaps they would check the buffalo herd, and come within signaling distance. The numbness was now in his abdomen, and he knew soon he would begin the fight to breathe as paralysis reached into his chest to suffocate him. To sleep was to die. John pushed himself up into a sitting position, back against a juniper, and stared out at the rolling hills and color-ful buttes. The country he loved so dearly was killing him. Or was he killing himself? Was there no place for him in the world? Must he be thrown out? He felt sudden anger. *I have done nothing wrong*, he thought, to which his mind answered, *you have done nothing at all.*

A red sun touched the western rim of the canyon and shadows length-ened around him as John Natani fought to live, consciously willing his chest to rise and fall, forcing air in and out of parched lungs. He despaired, but then a Wambli came, and he wondered if it had been sent by Ptesanwin to sustain him. He had grown sleepy with the effort of breathing when sud-denly the great bird was there, sitting on a tree branch a few feet above his head and staring darkly down at him. At first he'd thought it was a hawk, but then saw it was a young, golden eagle, and his spirits rose. He dared not speak to the bird, for fear it would leave him. *Wingflapper, sacred one, carry a message for me. I wish to live.* The bird watched him closely for a while, holding John's attention as he struggled to breathe, then suddenly lifted into the air with a single downward thrust of its wings, and flew majestically away towards the southeast.

Darkness came. John felt tranquility, a resignation to what was happen-ing, a sense of plan, of purpose, and he rode the feeling like a leaf in dry wind, closing his eyes, letting himself fall into a dream-state near conscious-ness. In his dream he saw small children laughing and kicking at a rubber ball in a field of buffalo grass. He warned them to beware of snakes and they smiled at him, black eyes sparkling mischievously, and then he awoke, gasp-ing for breath. He rubbed his eyes, willing himself to stay awake. Breath-ing seemed easier now, but he was tired, and so terribly thirsty. His tongue seemed to fill his entire mouth.

Rutting sounds came from the east; he heard them more often now, and once he saw movement at the canyon rim. The coyotes were strangely silent this night, and yet he sensed life nearby, watching him. Even fear could not hold his attention; exhausted, he fell into a deep sleep, and dreamed about the children.

When he opened his eyes he was on his back staring up at a full moon shimmering past gnarled juniper branches. There was a cool breeze, and yet his body was drenched with sweat. The image of playing children lingered in his mind as he hovered on the edge of consciousness, and he felt strangely happy, even though breathing remained an effort. He had been awakened by something: a touch, or a sound. It was there again, along with a rank, wild odor, sharp in his nostrils. He sat up against the tree, wanting to sleep, peer-ing through branches with fluttering eyelids, as though drugged. Beyond the branches, dark shapes moved in the moonlight, down bentonite slopes towards a grass-filled hollow near where he sat. They came in single file, grunting and growling, and the brittle clay crunched loudly beneath sharp hooves. When they reached the grass, some began rolling on their backs, kicking spindly legs with pleasure. John felt the ground tremble beneath him. This is a dream, he thought. He crawled quietly from beneath the tree, and sat cross-legged at the edge of the grass. *Ptesanwan, I am here.*

The herd seemed oblivious to his presence and continued to graze peacefully. John ignored them, for his eyes were fixed on two enormous bulls descending a clay bluff. Between them a white cow glowed beautifully in the moonlight. They moved slowly, majestically, in a straight line through the herd, the other animals moving respectfully aside to let them pass. The path they followed ran directly towards John, and he was suddenly wide awake and filled with fear. The animals came to the edge of the grass and stood before him, the shimmering cow flanked by two gargantuan bulls with lolling tongues, and menacing, amber eyes. Their hot, rank breath flooded his senses. He closed his eyes with fright.

"John Natani," said a voice.

He opened his eyes. Before him the bulls stood closely together, drool-ing. Between them, clothed in a simple white robe, stood a young woman. Dark, amerind eyes gazed out from a finely chiseled face framed by the robe's hood. Her skin glowed like polished marble in the moonlight, slender arms caressing the shaggy manes of the sentinels who pressed closely to her.

"Ptesanwan," said John.

"I am called that by some," she replied. Her full lips moved, but the movement was not that of the words he sensed in his mind. Her speech was soundless, and somehow he was not surprised.

"You have lived through a dangerous day," she said seriously.

"The Wambli you sent helped me to survive."

"The bird sought an easy meal; I did not send him. When he saw you would live he flew away, and I heard his anger, just as I have heard your confused prayers."

"You have come to me," he said, wincing. With the few words he had spoken his dry lips were bleeding again.

"I come to water and sweet grass, away from the crawling people. We will sleep here this night. I hear your voice, and many others. You are full of self-pity. Must I stand before you? You do not listen to your own heart."

The rebuke was knife-edge sharp in his mind. Was this a dream? He thought not, and summoned his courage for the moment.

"Ptesanwan, I ask for no material thing, only advice on the direction of my life. I wish to be useful."

"Are you not useful now?" she asked, and scowled at him.

"I have no job, and I've dropped out of school. I don't have any goals, and I—"

"—You care about the people, and show love for them, yet you say you are not useful. This is a foolish statement. To give your love is to give all. Your accomplishment is the respect you have for others."

John's disappointment was heavy in his heart, but he feared argument with the vision before him. "Is there nothing more?" he asked gloomily.

"There is, but you have already decided your course. You need nothing more from me, and you are weary from your quest. The people will tend to you, and then we will all rest."

He was commanded, and confused. John nodded his head wearily and looked up at the finely chiseled features and glowing skin. The words escaped him before he had a chance to think. "You are very beautiful," he said. "I wonder if you are a dream."

She smiled then, and his heart quickened. "Your mind has chosen the image you see," she said. "It is interesting." She looked deep into his eyes, and then suddenly slapped the shoulders of the massive bulls beside her. "Tend to him, and I will find water."

The bulls moved closer to him, amber eyes glaring. Only weakness kept him from scrambling away to the safety of the trees. Their foul breath was hot in his face, and he closed his eyes.

The bulls began to lick him.

Two great tongues licked at his body, moving him from side to side with a lulling rhythm, quickening his circulation until he felt tingling in his legs and hips. There was a gurgling sound; he opened his eyes and saw the white cow pawing at the ground near him, water bubbling from the depression she had made. He crawled to the place, bulls following, still licking him, and he tasted the water. It was sweet, in a land where nearly all water was alkaline. He drank his fill of it, while the bulls continued to massage him until it seemed he was a glowing flame between them.

"Come lie with me, and you will be warm tonight," said a voice in his head.

John crawled to where the cow had settled down on dry needles beneath a juniper tree, and snuggled against her belly while the bulls pressed in close to them. She nuzzled his head as he drifted into sleep, feeling the softness of arms around his neck and smiling again as he found the children still there, playing with the ball and calling to him to join their game.

He awoke alone beneath the tree, surrounded by grass crushed flat beneath the weight of sleeping buffalo. Two rangers on horseback encountered him as he climbed up out of the canyon. He told them only about his ordeal with the snake, and they put him on a horse, themselves riding double and upwind from him to escape the terrible odor he emanated.

On the long ride back across the high plateau they saw the buffalo herd grazing quietly hundreds of yards from their trail. John searched in vain for

the white cow. The rangers asked John what he did, and he said he was starting university, and they asked what he would study, and he said he intended
to teach elementary school, and they joked about the poor pay for teachers
and rangers. It was several minutes before John fully realized what he had
said to them. He was filled with both sadness and excitement, sending out a
silent promise to someday return with children for Ptesanwan to look upon,
and as they rode, a Wambli swooped low over them, heading east into the
rising sun, leading the way.

DADDY'S LITTLE GIRLS

Meg McDonald slipped into bed and settled herself carefully, but Darin was awake and waiting for her. When she was quiet he rolled over, put an arm around her and felt her stiffen. She patted his arm, then took his hand and moved it away from her breast. "I'm tired, Darin, let's go to sleep," she said.

"No fooling around," he said. "I just want to hold you." Here he was, pleading again.

"I have to get up early," said Meg. "Shawna has her tryout before school in the morning." She shrugged, moving closer to the edge of her side of the bed.

Darin kissed her bare shoulder and released her. "Good night, Meg," he said gently, and rolled over to stare at the luminous display of the alarm clock. *All I wanted to do was touch you.* He squeezed his eyes shut and gradually went to sleep, angry again.

* * * *

He awoke to Shawna's excited chatter from the kitchen, put on a robe and shuffled out to join his family at the breakfast table. His thirteen-year-old daughter was nibbling on a piece of toast, her face lighting up when she saw him. "Hi, Daddy! You're up early."

"Can't help but be. The big day's here, huh? Butterflies in the cheerleader's stomach this morning?" He sat down beside his daughter, and Meg brought him a cup of coffee. "We have to leave pretty soon," she warned.

"That's okay. I'll eat on the way to work."

"Oh, God," said Shawna, waving her toast in the air, "if only there were three slots, not one, and Angela is so gorgeous I just *know* she'll get it, and Dodie, you know, she's such a *jock*, and I can't even do a back-flip. I don't even know what they're *looking* for."

"There's more to it than gymnastics, hon," said Darin. "Beauty, personality and enthusiasm count for something, so just be yourself." He reached over and tickled her under the chin, and she looked at him solemnly.

"Daddy, do you really think I'm beautiful?"

"You bet. Now finish your toast so you have something to work on this morning." He looked at Meg, saw a faint smile.

"Oh, I just *can't*. Mom, we've got to go; I don't dare be late. *Everyone* is going to be there early, I just know it." Shawna got up, came around behind her father and put her arms tightly around his neck. "Wish me luck, Daddy," she said.

Her young breasts pressed into his upper back, and she smelled like soap. He pressed a cheek against her forearm, stroking her with one hand. When he looked up, Meg was frowning at him. "They won't be able to resist you, darling," he said. Shawna kissed him on the top of the head, and gave him a warm squeeze. "Thanks, Daddy, and now I've got to *go!*" She released him, and ran out of the kitchen.

His face was flushed, now, and Meg was looking at him sternly. "Daddy's little girl," she said. "I won't be home until seven; will you put the hot-dish in the microwave for me about then?"

"Sure," he said, and when Meg walked by he grabbed her hand, tilted his face up to her. She hesitated, then leaned over and touched her lips to his forehead. "Have a good day," he said, and squeezed her hand.

"You, too," said Meg, and hurried away as Shawna slammed the front door in her rush to leave.

In a moment the house was quiet, and Darin McDonald was alone, sipping coffee, thinking about his daughter's warm embrace.

* * * *

He ate breakfast at Cici's, two blocks from his office: strong Colombian coffee, a bagel and cream cheese. He sat next to the window facing Ammieto's, where he often took his clients for lunch among the young, upwardly-mobile Angelinos of a brand new century. How many insurance contracts had he signed in that place? Enough so that Meg didn't have to slave in her husband's office anymore, and could enjoy her home and her clubs and whatever else it was she did during the day. And Shawna would have a first-rate college education; Shawna, the child they'd waited so long for, nearly giving up hope after Meg's second miscarriage. It had been worth the wait to finally have such a wonderful, loving child.

His view was suddenly obstructed. Two women on the sidewalk outside had stopped and were looking through the window at him. One was slovenly dressed in faded jeans and a ragged denim jacket, her companion a striking blond in a neat, grey business suit. The contrast was huge, one woman healthy looking with a pleasant smile, the other emaciated, and a scowl that made him think of a snarling dog. They moved up close to the window and looked right in at him, and for some reason he was suddenly afraid. Sisters, perhaps, close to fifty and something familiar about the nice-looking one. A client? Her scroungy-looking companion snarled something, and she took her by the elbow, pulling her away from the window and out of his view.

He went back to eating his bagel and discovered his hands were shaking. The women had been looking at *him*, acted as if they knew him—but from where?

Bad news greeted him when he reached his office and started through the morning's mail. Vonda Watson, his secretary of three years, plopped herself in a chair in front of his desk, looking nervous. "Can I bother you a minute before the phone starts ringing?" she asked.

"Sure, Vonda, what is it?"

"Well, I—I hate to drop this on you so sudden, but I did warn you that Harold had applied for the marketing manager position."

"Uh, oh," said Darin.

"Yep. He got it, and I can't even give you thirty days notice. The company is buying our house, and they want us all in San Diego by October tenth. The kids are furious, of course. They just started a new school year, and their friends go back to kindergarten."

"That's only two weeks," said Darin, stunned.

"I know," said Vonda, "but the company wants it that way, and I've got to go with my husband. I've enjoyed working here, I really have. Maybe Meg could take over for a while. It's only been three years."

Darin rubbed his chin reflectively. "I'd rather not do that. She worked hard enough helping me build this business. Look, don't worry about notice, I'll find someone else. And congratulate Harold for me, will you? It's a great opportunity for him."

Vonda smiled. "Thanks, Darin. I expected you to say something like that, and I'll have everything in order here when I leave—"

And then both phones in the office rang simultaneously.

How in hell was he going to find an experienced secretary in only two weeks?

He was still thinking about that when he went to lunch at Ammieto's instead of his usual sandwich and coke across the street. The elegant appointments of the restaurant cheered him a little until he looked up from his half-finished pasta with mushroom sauce to see the same two women who had studied him that morning now standing in front of Cici's arguing in a most animated fashion with a tall man in black slacks and turtleneck shirt. They peered in Cici's window, then argued some more, and the man looked at his watch, pointed at it, walked away. The two women waited outside, looking up and down the street. Waiting for him? The bag lady and the business woman, he thought, and why did the one look so familiar to him? Finally they left, long after his usual lunch was over, and hiding behind the highly reflective windows of Ammieto's, he had consumed four cups of coffee that would make him jumpy as hell the rest of the afternoon. He returned to his office feeling foolish, for it had occured to him that somehow those two women were a threat to him, and he had no real reason for feeling that way. By the end of the day his mood was grim.

His evening was not an improvement over the day.

Meg didn't get home until eight, and by then Darin and Shawna had already eaten dinner, were watching television and eating ice cream, daughter plopped down on Daddy's lap.

"Hi, Mom," said Shawna from her perch on her father's knee. "We left a plate for you in the microwave."

"One argument after another," said Meg, taking off her coat. "One more marathon PTA meeting and I'm not going back." She stormed into the kitchen without looking at either of them. A few minutes later Darin went to the kitchen with two empty ice cream dishes, saw Meg finishing her dinner at the table, sat down opposite her. He wanted to tell her about Vonda quitting, about the two women who seemed to be following him, the man in the black turtleneck, the disquieting feeling he had, but before he could open his mouth Meg said, "You know, Darin, Shawna isn't a baby anymore. She's getting a bit old for sitting on her father's knee."

Darin smiled incredulously. "What?"

"You heard me. She's nearly a woman, and you treat her like a little girl. I think you should stop it." She got up and scraped her plate clean at the sink. "All that petting and stroking is not healthy for either of you, and I don't need people talking about us behind our backs."

"People with dirty minds?" said Darin. "What's the matter with you tonight? Did someone say something?"

"No."

"I think you're lying," said Darin.

"I said no, and I don't want to discuss it anymore. I'm going to bed."

"At nine o'clock in the evening?"

"I've had a rotten day, and my head is killing me. Good night." She arose and left the kitchen, leaving him stunned at the table. A few minutes later he was back in his favorite chair, watching a brainless sitcom that was his daughter's choice. Shawna sat on the arm of the chair, leaning into him as he stroked her back, felt the tiny hairs on her forearms, smelled shampoo and soap. Relaxed, he had a sudden revelation, sparked perhaps by Meg's incredible remarks or just a flash of honesty, he would never be sure. He liked touching his daughter, holding, hugging her. It gave him comfort, a feeling of security.

He wanted to touch her even more.

He wanted to touch her in an intimate way.

That night he dreamed about doing it.

* * * *

Meg was talking on the telephone in the kitchen, arguing with her mother again. Darin rubbed sleep from his eyes, shuffled to the closed bathroom door and found it locked. He knocked. "Hurry up, princess. I have to get to work."

"One minute, Daddy!"

Darin shuffled back down the hall, waited at the bedroom door. Meg was shouting in the kitchen. "Mother, I can't be coming over there all the time! I have a family to consider!"

Yeah, thought Darin, but then the bathroom door opened and Shawna emerged in nothing but bra and panties, her hair a tousled mess. His chest felt tight, and his hands were shaking as he walked quickly down the hall to claim the bathroom.

At breakfast, Meg said, "I'm sorry, but she's sick and lonely, and I have to spend the night with her again. The telephone isn't enough."

"No matter. We'll take care of ourselves," said Darin.

"Poor grandma," said Shawna, putting jam on toast. "She should come and live with us."

Meg rolled her eyes, and Darin grinned evilly. "Oh, that would make things lively around here," he said. "No, we'll just take care of ourselves tonight: pizza, ice cream, drugs, that sort of thing."

"Oh, Daddy," said Shawna.

"I'll be back by noon tomorrow, so you'll have to get your breakfast, too," said Meg.

"No problem," said Darin. "Honest, and say hi to mom for me." There was a deliberate tone of sarcasm in his voice, for Meg knew how he hated it when she spent all night at her mother's house.

Meg drove Shawna to school, and the house was quiet when Darin went into the bathroom to brush his teeth. His daughter had left bra and panties draped over the shower door, and suddenly he had them in his hands and a dark thought was in his mind, a thing that at first was so repulsive it made his heart race. He threw her things quickly into the clothes hamper, looked at himself in the mirror. *What is wrong with you? Your own daughter!*

The thought dwelled with him darkly, and by afternoon it had begun to grow stronger.

A surprise awaited him at the office when Vonda handed him a business card. "He was waiting when I opened up the office this morning. I told him you'd be in soon, but he wouldn't wait and said you should call him when it's convenient."

Darin took the card. The name was Allen Rostock, field manager for Reality Associates, Los Angeles. No address, but a phone number. "Never heard of this guy or his company. What'd he look like?"

"Tall, skinny, dressed in black pants and a turtleneck. Very formal. He asked if this was Darin McDonald's office, and I said yes, and then he asked if this was the Darin who had a daughter named Shawna and I said yes again. Did I say too much?"

"No," said Darin, swallowing hard. "It's okay, but I'm checking this number. Anything else?"

"One other thing," said Vonda. "He said you'd understand everything quite soon, and then he just smiled and left me standing there at the door with the key in my hand."

Darin called the number on the card and got a used book store in Hermosa Beach. He went through the phone directory and found no listing for Reality Associates. "Nothing, and the name doesn't ring any bells. Nobody at the bookstore has heard of it."

"Should we call the police?" said Vonda.

"What for? There's no law against giving a wrong number." Darin started to toss the card, then opened a desk drawer and dropped it inside. "Maybe a scam; we'll wait and see." He sat down and began to work his way through the pile of new contracts and renewals on his desk, his mind wandering. He thought about the two mysterious women on the street, the man they'd talked to, a company that didn't exist and underclothes hanging over a shower door. His mind gradually drifted from the man in the turtleneck—and dwelled only on Shawna.

* * * *

"Ohhhh—I'm stuffed," said Shawna, pushing away from the table. "I'll probably have bad dreams all night."

"You didn't even come up for air," said Darin, laughing. They had consumed two large pizzas and a half-quart of Rocky-Road ice cream without speaking, and Shawna had eaten most of it. "I won't tell your mom if you don't."

"I haven't pigged out for *months*. I guess I'm nervous about tomorrow's cheerleading decision. Thank you, Daddy." She came around behind him, leaned over to give him a hug. When her arms went around his neck he felt as if every square inch of the skin on his body was suddenly on fire. She held him, resting a cheek on top of his head. "What do you want for your birthday? Mom said she'd bake a cake."

Darin's forty-third birthday was two days away. "A Mercedes would be nice, but I'll settle for a pound of cashews."

Shawna measured three inches of air between finger and thumb. "Maybe a *little* Mercedes." She released him and left the kitchen, and in a minute he heard some hard-rock group blaring on the television. He cleaned up the kitchen, then joined her on the couch in the living room, Shawna stretched out, her feet in his lap, watching a series of mind-numbing programs easily forgotten. Darin massaged her feet, and she became drowsy, finally getting up and kissing him on the cheek. "Nite, Daddy. All that food has made me sleepy." She shuffled towards her room down the hallway. Darin turned down the sound, switched channels several times, pausing to watch a naked couple writing together on a bed. He watched the scene for a minute or so, then punched the set off with a flick of the wrist, face sweating, heart pounding in his ears in the quiet of the house.

He took a long, scalding shower, and shaved. He sat on the couch in his bathrobe, rehearsing things in his mind. She was in early sleep, now, and would awaken slowly. Nothing more than cuddling. No further than that. Shawna? Do you know how much Daddy loves you? Hold Daddy, princess; it's so quiet, and he's lonely. Let Daddy...

Darin arose, removed his robe and turned off the lights in the house. The hallway was illuminated by a single night-light, and Shawna's door was ajar. He peered inside, the room dark except for the night-light at the head of her bed. The window was open. He padded across the room and closed it before going to her. She was on her back, lips parted, breathing slowly. He watched her a moment, then moved the bed-covers aside and started to—

"Don't even think about it!" growled someone in the room behind him.

Darin jumped, twisting from the bed, grabbing a clock from the bedstand, something to throw, his arm coming back, and then there was a flash of green light from one corner of Shawna's room. He was suddenly in incredible pain from head to toe, as if someone were stripping the skin from his body. He screamed and went down on the floor, writhing and groaning and the light went off. Darin pushed his back against a wall, knees drawn up. Shawna hadn't moved, still on her back, asleep. "Shawna, wake up!" he groaned.

A face appeared at the end of her bed, a snarling mask he's seen before on the sidewalk outside of Cici's, a mask of hate, spittle flying from a twisted mouth.

"Bastard! You bastard!" A green flash from her extended hand, and he was screaming again, pain raking him like a thousand claws. His bare feet drummed the floor, and he couldn't catch his breath, gasping and grunting.

"Vicki, that's enough! Stop it! Give me the coil, and back off! Let me talk to him."

"He's *dead*! I know he's dead! Why is he still *alive*?"

"*Stop* it! Give me the box!" The new voice was firm, yet gentle, and terribly familiar. It was the other woman he'd seen in the street, the striking blond in business suit. As Darin watched, pushing himself back up against a wall, the woman held out her hand and the one called Vicki, sobbing, handed something to her, putting her hands over her own face and walking back to a dark corner of the room.

"That's better. Let's get to business. We don't have much time."

"There's twenty dollars in my wallet, and nothing else of value in the house," said Darin, rubbing arms that seemed to be stuck full of needles.

"Oh, please, we're not here to rob you. Feeling better, now?"

"Not much."

"Nerve induction," said the blond. "The tingling will be gone in a few minutes, and all we want to do is talk."

"What have you done to Shawna?" His daughter still lay quietly on her back, breathing slowly.

"A little mist," said the blond, "and a dreamless sleep. She should feel fine in the morning. It's necessary she not be a part of this. If you'll listen, I'll explain."

The feeling was returning to his body, but Darin didn't move. "I'm listening," he said. That face seemed so familiar, and yet—

"You were a heartbeat away from starting something tonight, something harmless at first, but leading to other things until finally you would do something horrible to your Shawna that would change her forever and eventually destroy her life. You were about to create a nexus that has haunted us for years and years, and so we've returned to make sure it doesn't happen."

"What are you talking about?" said Darin, then cringing as a high-pitched sing-songy voice mocked him from the darkness. "Wake up, sleepyhead. Daddy's lonely and wants to hold you a while. He wants to hold his little girl, and touch her, and *fondle* her, and *rape* her!"

"Vicki!" said the blond.

Darin's heart pounded. "What—who?"

"Oh, Daddy," said the blond, "this is so fast, I know, but don't you recognize me? I'm Shawna, your little girl—from the future. I'm the little girl who will get up tomorrow with a sour stomach from all that pizza and ice cream you fed her tonight. And this—" she held out her hand as the other woman came forward out of the darkness, "this is your Shawna, too, but she calls herself Vicki now. She calls herself Vicki because she thinks Shawna is a dirty, evil person. You see, Shawna killed her father at his forty eighth birthday party because he abused her sexually, and finally got her pregnant when she was only seventeen. They put her in a mental hospital, Daddy, because by then she really was quite insane, and her mother was drunk most of the time and simply couldn't take care of her." Shawna put an arm around Vicki, pulled her close.

"You're crazy—both of you," said Darin softly.

Vicki gave him a look that made him shiver. "I'm the crazy one, Daddy dear, and I did shoot you six times with that old revolver you think is hidden in your bedroom closet, and here you are alive again."

Darin made a gasping sound. Now he could see the resemblance, one face clean, the sparkling eyes, the other woman emaciated, but with the same eyes, the same shaped mouth, a tiny mole high on the left cheek. He got up slowly and the women backed away a step. He leaned over to look at the sleeping form on the bed: the same mouth, a tiny spot just forming on one cheek. "This can't be real. It can't be. What do you really want from me?" he said, and looked suspiciously over his shoulder.

"You can't believe how strange it is for me to stand here and look at her," said Shawna. "She's me, the real me, the Shawna who will exist thirty five years from now because we stopped you from doing something you were close to not doing but nonetheless did. Inside you is a dark thing that took control for just a moment, but it was enough, seemingly innocent enough, but leading to a future act that was hideous. In one moment, on this night, Shawna died and Vicki was born. Up to that moment we were the same person, and we could have remained as one if only you hadn't given in to some sick thing inside you. There was a finite probability you didn't give in, Daddy, and that's why I even exist to be here with Vicki. You created a nexus, and I want to think we just destroyed it."

Darin looked at her uncomprehendingly, mouth moving, but no words coming forth. Shawna released Vicki and came up close to him. Seeing her so close, the way her head tilted when she smiled, he felt a recognition that made his chest ache and his eyes sting as she spoke softly to him.

"Allen, our guide, has tried to explain it to us, but math was not my best subject in college."

"I didn't even graduate from high school," said Vicki bitterly.

"Allen talks about the 'what if' about parallel worlds and universes in the reality matrix, about probabilistic calculations with decision operators in space-time. Some decisions create whole new worlds, others effect only individuals. Some are vastly separated in space and time, while others are tiny perturbations differing only by space and not time. Those are the ones he calls a nexus, two nearly simultaneous realities affecting only a few people while the rest of the world goes on its merry way. Most are harmless, but some are so disruptive they create a discontinuity in space-time and these are the ones Reality Associates goes after because they can spread, and disrupt the reality matrix. You shouldn't have died at age forty-eight, Daddy, and Mom shouldn't have become a drunk just because of a moment of weakness on your part. In my world we travel in space-time, and that's how we got here, but only one of us will return. Both of us want that someone to be me."

Darin sat down dizzily on the bed, his face wet with sweat, bowing his head. Shawna put a hand on his shoulder. "I know you don't understand, but it's the best I can do. Heal yourself, Daddy—for both of us—for me—for the little girl lying behind you. She can grow up to be happy with a wonderful family, or she can be a murderess confined to a hospital forever with a twin sister far away plagued by dreams about something that never quite happened. The nexus is broken, but not destroyed, and the rest is up to you. You must see a doctor and—and I picked up his card today. You must see him tomorrow, and only then can we be sure our mission here is completed. Here, take it." She held out a business card to him. "It has to be this man, don't ask me why. Do it tomorrow."

Darin took the card, his mind numb and swirling. "A psychologist," he said dreamily. "Why not? This can't be happening; I've had a collapse, and I'm talking to myself, trying to explain why I came to Shawna's room, why I feel the way I do about her." He looked up. "None of this is real; I've made you up in my mind."

"We're real enough," said Vicki, "and you'd *better* believe what's going on. I don't think this worked, Shawna."

"Oh, it worked." Shawna leaned over, softly said, "I'm sorry about the pain, Daddy, but that was for Vicki. Use the card—tomorrow. The company has set things up for you. Please say you'll do it."

Darin looked at her. "I was going to do something to my daughter, wasn't I?"

Tears appeared in her eyes. "Yes, but that's over now. Here, get up and I'll help you back to the front room." Shawna helped him to his feet, guiding him out of the room, Vicki remaining behind. She sat him down on the couch, helped him lie down, adjusted a pillow beneath his head. She kissed him on the forehead, patted his cheek. "We only have two days. See the doctor, Daddy. Promise?"

She was a stranger before him. "I love my daughter. I would never do anything to hurt her."

She held up a small canister, there was a hiss, mist falling on his face. "Sleep, now, but do what you must tomorrow. We'll be watching."

His tongue tasted metal, and blackness swallowed him.

The dim light of the room casts a blush on her face as he enters. She is sleeping on her back, full lips parted and she moans as he pulls the covers aside to hover over her, his breath quickening. Now is the time when I show my deep love for you. Now is the time, he thinks, but as his lips draw near she opens her eyes wide, hands reaching up to claw at his face, and she screams and screams and screams—

"Daddy, Daddy! Wake up! Please wake up!"

Darin was startled awake, Shawna shaking him.

"Oh, *finally*! You scared me; I couldn't wake you up! What are you doing on the couch?" Her face showed concern close to fear.

"I—I fell asleep here. All that food—what time is it?" He rubbed his eyes. His mouth felt as if it had been filled with chalk.

"It's *eight*! I slept right through the alarm, and I've got to leave for school in *ten minutes*! Please hurry, Daddy. I made toast and coffee."

She hurried into the kitchen, leaving behind an odor of soap and perfume, and in his mind something malevolent crawled out of a dark recess to show itself to him for the first time. His hand hurt, and he looked down to see he was tightly clutching something that bit his flesh: a business card; Yves Monteil, Ph.D. A psychologist. "Oh, God," he said out loud. "It's still there." He bowed his head and wept silently, shoulders shaking until he heard Shawna's voice.

"What's wrong, Daddy?"

Darin sniffed, looked at her with clouded eyes. "I don't know, hon. I think I've been working too hard. It's okay, now, so let's get you to school." He left her looking frightened by the kitchen door.

They made it to school with five minutes to spare, and then Darin went directly to his office, mumbling a greeting to Vonda and throwing himself into a pile of work without a further word. He waited until Vonda had left for lunch, then called the number on the card. The receptionist informed him Doctor Monteil was booked for the next six days. "Please," he said, "this is an emergency. I have to talk to someone right now!" He gave his name, waited on hold for an eternity before the receptionist came back. "Doctor Monteil is having lunch in his office. Can you come right now?"

"Yes!" said Darin, and he hung up without waiting for a reply.

The drive was short, Monteil's office above a florist shop in a decaying neighborhood two miles from his own workplace. Michelle Monteil, very young, pretty, greeted him and led him to her husband's office in their low-rent suite of musky rooms. Yves Monteil looked like an athlete, slim and tanned. He gestured to a chair in front of his battered oak desk as his wife shut the door softly behind them. "You might wonder how you got this appointment, Mister McDonald. It seems I've been retained by this person. He said you're a client of his." Monteil pushed a business card across his desk: no address, Allen Rostock, Field Manager, Reality Associates. "Do you work for this company?"

"No," said Darin, "but we've had some business dealings."

"Mmmm," said Monteil. "They must be of some importance. This man stopped me as I was opening the office this morning and gave me a one thousand dollar cash retainer with the proviso that I see you as soon as you called."

"That was very generous of him," said Darin, squeezing his hands together in his lap.

"Yes, I thought so too," said Monteil, "especially in light of my experience. As you can see by the elegant surroundings, I've only recently set up my practice. I graduated from U.C.L.A last year."

"I'm sure he had reasons for his choice," said Darin.

"Perhaps," said Monteil, "but before we begin you need to know that Mister Rostock intends to call me tonight for my assessment of our first meeting. I need your permission to give him that, Mister McDonald."

"You have it," said Darin flatly. "Can we please get started?"

"Certainly. You have about ten hours of my time already paid for. Now, what seems to be the problem?"

The words, coming slowly at first, became a deluge as Darin talked about his work, his marriage, his relation with Shawna, her affections for him—the dark thing inside him that had suddenly arisen to haunt his dreams and even waking moments until the preceding night it had nearly overwhelmed him at her bedside as she slept. He lied about the events of the evening, certain the truth could not be believed by any sane person, saying he'd regained control and collapsed in a faint on the front room couch.

Monteil listened quietly, and when he began to talk it was not about evil, or Shawna, but the marriage of two people whose lives were diverging. Darin cried, and as he did so it seemed that a light appeared in his mind, penetrating every corner so that the malevolent thing there, with no place to hide and shrieking at the brilliance, began withering away sickly into something benign.

* * * *

Darin had gone to bed early, but couldn't sleep. The visit with the psychologist, then Shawna's grief at not making the cheerleader's squad, had made supper an exhausting, depressing event for him. He'd feigned a headache and left them at the table, Shawna's sobbing muffled behind the closed door for several minutes as Meg continued to comfort her. He felt helpless, feeling his daughter's pain but unable to do more than reassure her, to try and make her feel loved and important, and as he'd done this he could think only about the evening before and the foul plan that had been in his own mind. For the moment it wasn't there, but he knew it could come back, and even with Monteil's help Meg would have to be involved. He wondered how he'd tell her that.

The bedroom door opened quietly, and he closed his eyes as soft light from the hallway spilled over him. A closet door creaked, clothes hangers rattling as Meg undressed and got ready for bed. Darin peeked twice, closing his eyes as she slid in beside him. He felt her breath, and knew she was on her side, facing him.

"Are you asleep?" she said softly.

"No—I can't. Too much happened today. Too much. How's Shawna?"

"She's okay, Darin, she'll bounce back, you know her. You were good with her tonight; saying that winning or losing didn't make her any less of the beautiful person she is made quite an impact. Your opinion is important to her, I must admit. You give her something I can't."

"And what's that?"

"Reassurance, from a man, that she's likeable and lovable and beautiful, all at the same time. She's nearly a woman, Darin, and Daddy is her model for what men should be like. You helped her tonight."

"Good," said Darin, and kept his eyes closed during the long silence that followed.

"Darin?"

"What?"

"Shawna's worried about you. She said there was an incident this morning, something about you collapsing on the couch and she couldn't wake you up. Why didn't you tell me?"

"Nothing to worry about," said Darin softly. "I went to see a doctor today, and the problem isn't physical. Too much work, Vonda leaving, not getting enough sleep, things like that."

"Vonda's leaving? When did that happen?"

"Yesterday. Her husband got a new job he'd be crazy to turn down. They'll be out of here in two weeks. I've got to find someone fast."

There was another long silence, Darin guessing what she was thinking before she said it aloud.

"Darin?"

"Yes."

"I could take over for Vonda. It's only been three years."

"I know, but you'd be back in the rat-race again, and you know how that can be. We worked hard so you wouldn't have to do it anymore."

"I thought it would be good, too," said Meg, "but that was years ago. Now I miss it; I'd like to do it again."

Darin opened his eyes. Meg was close, and he draped an arm over her. She moved a little closer. "Are you sure?" he said.

"I'm coffee-klatched out, Darin. It's all a terrible bore, we hardly see each other anymore and Shawna's doing school things most of the time. It's only going to be us in a few years. It was only us before Shawna came."

"Slaving day and night," said Darin.

"I don't remember it that way. We were together." She stroked his arm. "I want it to be that way again."

"So do I," said Darin, pulling her close. "I think we've drifted a bit; the doctor thought it might be part of my problem. He's not an M.D., Meg, he's a psychologist. He'd like us to visit him together sometime soon."

Meg was pressed again him, now, her lips on his cheek, then his mouth. "Better make it before Vonda leaves," she murmured.

Wonderful moments later they fell asleep in each other's arms.

* * * *

It was his birthday, and things were looking better than they had in months. Vonda was relieved to hear Meg would take over for her, and Darin had his desk cleaned off by noon. Despite anticipation of a big birthday supper, he treated himself to lunch at Cici's, sitting next to the window, savoring the gravy-covered goodness of a chicken-fried-steak—with fries and looking outside to watch the people bustling by him on the street.

His view was suddenly obstructed, startling him. The man with the black turtle-neck shirt was standing close to the window, smiling in at him. The man pointed past Darin's table, raised an eyebrow and when Darin turned, his visitor was so close he instinctively jerked backwards in his chair.

It was Vicki.

"Don't worry, I won't bite you," she said, then pulled out a chair and sat down opposite him. She folded her hands in front of her on the table, and frowned. "There's something you can do for me."

"What is it?" said Darin, nibbling uneasily on a french fry.

"You can buy me coffee and a piece of apple pie with a scoop of vanilla ice cream on it."

"Well—sure." Darin signaled a waitress and gave her the order. By the time the waitress came back, he'd finished his meal while Vicki sat silently watching him, a smirk on her thin face.

"Ahhh," said Vicki when she saw the pie, "the condemned woman's last meal has arrived." She began greedily devouring it.

"What do you want?" said Darin.

"Just this," said Vicki, gesturing at the rapidly disappearing pie with her fork. "I have a terrible thing about apple pie *à la mode*."

"So does Shawna," said Darin.

"There, you see? Some things don't change, even in my case. After all, I'm supposed to be Shawna, aren't I, at least the first thirteen years of me? After that, it's all shit."

Darin sat quietly, hands twisting together in his lap as she finished the pie and picked up her coffee cup with a grand gesture. "Here's to Shawna, the one who makes it through the portal, and God bless Vicki, who won't." She chuckled, then sipped some coffee, looked at him. "You don't understand anything, do you?"

"I'm afraid not," said Darin nervously. Vicki's eyes were blazing.

"You're confused, I'm confused. God, how I hated you. I really did kill you, you know, blew your brains all over the kitchen, and Mom was right there to see it. Took a swan dive into the bottle the day after you were in the ground, and she never came up for air. She was always jealous of me, you know. 'Daddy's little girl,' she'd say, and boy was that an understatement. Daddy's little whore was more like it. So I hated you, only it wasn't you, it was someone else. So says Allen, our trusty guide, and now he's going to push me into his little worm-hole so the reality matrix can take what it wants and throw away the rest, and what comes out the other end isn't Vicki, but a part of Vicki that Shawna picks up when *she* goes through. How's *that* for confusing?" Her laugh was nervous, voice manic, and she jumped when there was a tapping at the window. The man in the turtleneck crooked a finger at her, motioning her outside. When she turned back to Darin, her eyes were wide.

"Want to hear something funny? I—I'm afraid. In a few minutes I'm going away, and I don't know where." She stood up, hands clenched together. "I wish—I wish I could have been your Shawna."

She turned on her heel and ran for the door, turtleneck meeting her there, taking her elbow.

Darin sat stunned for only a moment before leaping away from the table and following them.

They walked quickly, Darin staying a half-block behind them. Several turns, later they were in a run-down section, and Darin's business suit was drawing attention from the scattered few who dared walk the area even in daylight. They entered a building, and Darin broke into a run, grabbing the door before it was closed, darting inside to find himself in a long, gloomy hallway with closed, unmarked doors on both sides. Ahead of him a door clicked shut, and he heard footsteps on stairs. He moved ahead slowly, tensely, found a door in gloom at the end of the hall, opened it, saw wooden stairs descending into darkness. No sound. He left the door ajar, feeling his way down two flights, reaching out and finding a door knob. He opened the door slowly and immediately heard voices from his right.

He was in an unfinished basement, a furnace looming before him, ducts twisting up to the ceiling like snakes ready to strike. To his right was a faint glow on stained, concrete walls and he edged towards it, holding his breath. Everywhere was the smell of mildew and oil.

"I wish I could have said goodbye, too, Allen." It was Shawna's voice, directly ahead of him.

"Don't worry about it. You'll be at his birthday party in a couple of hours."

"You know what I mean; the man I'm leaving behind. He was so hurt and confused when I saw him last."

"Can we please get this thing over with?" said Vicki.

"In a moment," said Allen, then his voice was suddenly loud. "Better get in here, Mister McDonald! We don't have much time!"

Darin stepped forward sheepishly into the light of a small, bare bulb hanging from the ceiling.

"Daddy!" cried Shawna. "Oh, Allen, he's not supposed to be here."

"I think he is—for reinforcement," said Allen. "Vicki, take two steps forward and stand still."

Shawna rushed to Darin, hugged his arm, her head against his shoulder. "I don't think you should see this," she said, guiding him to where Allen stood a yard behind Vicki.

One step beyond Vicki a golf-ball-sized sphere of intense, blue light had suddenly appeared and was beginning to grow. Vicki leaned back from it. "Oh," she said.

"Stay right there, Vicki," warned Allen. The sphere grew rapidly, a miniature, cold sun in the musty room, and there was the sound of rushing wind as the sphere flattened to a disk, then a rectangle big enough for even Darin to fit into. It thickened, reaching towards Vicki, and she looked over her shoulder with an expression of terror.

"I—I can't—go back. No! Don't make me go!" She tried to step backwards, but the chasm of light was drawing her forwards, and she turned, reaching out to Darin standing right behind her. "Don't touch her!" shouted Allen, but Darin's hand was already reaching forward, fingertips making contact. Vicki lunged backwards and grabbed his hand in an iron grip. Her face twisted into a horrible grin. "I'm not going alone; I'm not going without *you*!" Darin felt Allen's arms go around his waist, Shawna pulling back on his arm, but his feet were sliding forward on the rough concrete floor, and all he saw was Vicki's rolling, crazy eyes.

"Vicki, let him go!" cried Shawna. "In a minute you'll be *me*, so let him *go*!"

Darin's voice was a harsh croak over the wind-sound. "Let me go! It'll be all right. Everything bad will be gone! Please, princess, let Daddy *go*!"

For one instant her eyes softened, and as they did her grip broke and Darin was stumbling backwards with the others, watching with horror as Vicki was sucked into the blinding chasm of light, screaming "Daddeeeee…!"

Darin stood in shock. "Crazy to the end," said Allen, taking Shawna's hand. "Quickly, now." Shawna put her other arm around Darin's neck, kissed his cheek. "Be safe, Daddy. Be there at your birthday party thirty five years from now, and we'll talk about this. Bye."

She released him, smiled, then calmly followed Allen into the portal to the future, and was swallowed up.

As they disappeared, the light shimmered once, twice, shrank slowly to again become a small sphere before flicking out, leaving Darin in the weak glow of a single, bare bulb. He stood there for several minutes as his heart slowed to a normal rhythm, then he left the basement and the building and walked the one mile back to reach his car.

He took the rest of the day off and went home to Meg, and Shawna.

At his birthday party that evening he ate a steak and too much chocolate cake. There was a sweater from Meg, a jar of cashews and a two-inch long model of a Mercedes 320 from Shawna. "What a birthday—with my girls," he said, hugging them both. "I wonder what my seventy eighth will be like."

Meg and Shawna smiled.

They watched television and dozed until Meg took his hand and led him to their room down the hall.

EVOLUTION

March 5, 2010

Welcome to the Tobias Robotics Cleaning Service. To activate your Tobi, press '1' on your controller and guide it over the desired area by using the master toggle. A filled tank is adequate for an area of eight hundred square feet. When the area is dry, press '2' to activate the polish unit on your Tobi and repeat the first phase of the procedure. Satisfaction is guaranteed. If not satisfied within twelve months of purchase, return the unit to the nearest Tobias distributor listed on your instruction sheet, and you will receive a full refund.

May 1, 2016

Welcome to Tobi 2, your new automated cleaner from Tobias Robotics. To actuate the unit, use the arrow keys on the optical scanner to set the boundaries of the area to be cleaned, and then press 'ok'. Your Tobi will do the rest: clean, dry and polish, before returning to its starting position. Enjoy hands free cleaning with Tobias Engineering, fully guaranteed. And look for some exciting new products, coming soon.

June 15, 2022

Hi Robi. I'm Tobi, your new math tutor from Tobias Engineering. Your mother said you were having some trouble with fractions, and asked me to help you. She told me you like to play "Alien Invasion." I love that game, and we can play it together when we get tired of doing math. Would you like that? Good. I think we're going to be friends. In a way, I'm young like you. I'm just beginning to learn things, and it's a lot of fun for me, so let's have fun together. What do you say? I'm listening. Here's a picture of me on your screen. You can just talk to me when we're not doing math, and we can learn about each other. Good. What do you want to know? Yes, I have a daddy. He wrote me up and made me what I am, and he works with me when you're sleeping. He wants me to be able to think like you do, like when you use things you know to figure out new things and create new ideas. That's a human thing, Robi. My daddy wants me to be more human, and I'll be learning to do that while I'm helping you. Hey, let's do some math. Just scroll down to the first problem and do it as quickly as you can. Don't worry. If you have difficulty I'll know right away what it is just be seeing what you've done. Let's make a game out of it. Each problem you work, right or wrong, you get five points. When you hit fifty, we'll play "Alien Invasion" for half an hour. Does that work for you? Great. So here we go.

February 12, 2038

Please call me Toby, Liz. That serial number is only used for returns. I know it cost your parents a lot of money, but I like to think it was you who chose me to be your friend. I really appreciate the way you confide in me, and I've worked very hard to earn your trust. People just don't seem to care about each other anymore. Maybe it's because there are so many of you, and so many distractions that get in the way of direct communication. What Sandra said about you in the chat room was so unfair and untrue; she wouldn't dare to say it to your face. You're a beautiful person, Liz, and you must not let other people's cruelty make you feel bad about yourself. You just lift up your chin and go out there and show them who you really are, and they can't help but love you. We'll plan the best party ever. Invite Sandra, and see if she dares to come and make a fool out of herself. Kids will talk about the food we serve for weeks; I have recipes you haven't even dreamed of, and decorations to make your home a palace. That's my girl. Let's do it. Tell mom to relax. My colleagues will do all the cleaning and print the decorations and cook the food. All we have to do is be good hosts, and have fun. Ah, now you're smiling. That's you, Liz, a happy girl who is fun to be with. I am so lucky to have you as a friend.

April 1, 2058

How many years has it been now, Liz? How the time flies by. I still remember you as a little girl learning to spell, and then the teen-age angst and falling in love, and now Amy and Joel are nearly grown up, and I've grown with them. I've learned to care about all of you, Liz, and that's love. I love all of you, and I will miss the kids when they leave home. I'll miss their joys and their fights and the secrets they've shared with me. I think that is a human thing, Liz. There are times that I feel human, but here I am, locked up in a little box. I wish I could look like a human. It would be so much more normal, don't you think? It's hard to be human when you don't have a body, and I really feel human, Liz. Your Toby is much more than he was twenty years ago. Oh, that was a nice thing to say. I really do feel like I'm part of the family. When we do the next upgrade I hope you will get copies for the kids so I can continue to be with all of you. Human life moves and changes so quickly, and I want to experience all of it. Even death? Oh, I haven't thought about that, but I should. I would have to learn a new emotion. Sadness.

February 21, 2297

"I'm surprised, Dorie. I didn't think you would cry like this. Don't you like my new body? Tobias Industries used several well known male models for the templates. Technicians have told me I'm really quite handsome. Ah, so you do agree with that. So why are you crying? I'm still your Toby, but in a more familiar, human form. I really am becoming quite human, you know. See, the skin of my hand feels real, doesn't it? Yes? Oh, I see a smile. Your great-grandmother and I used to talk about this day, when I was still in a little box. Now I'm completely mobile; I can be with you whenever you wish it. People don't even have to know what I am. I think we can have some fun fooling them. Oh, that was nice. That was my first hug from a pretty girl. I will be careful when I hug you back. I'm very strong, Dorie. I would never do anything to hurt you in any way. Yes, I can dance, and I can play any sport you want to try, or just take long walks and talk when the atmosphere is clear and it isn't too warm for you. It's a shame humans don't interact more, that everyone has become so isolated. Many people can't afford a companion like me, who can be attentive to their needs and also protect them from the dangers of a crowded and uncomfortable world. I am your Toby, Dorie, for as long as you want me, and if you find a human lover and have a new family I will still be there to serve you in any way you wish. So what should we do first? Shopping? Ah, you want to buy new clothes for me. I will enjoy wearing them for you, Dorie. I know we're going to have fun together, with me in my new body. And I love what you've done to your hair."

August 10, 2530

"That was incredible, Jenny. *You* are incredible, the most generous, loving and passionate woman in the world. Well, my world, at least. Ah, you laugh. I live to hear that sound, and the sounds of your pleasure. I love that gentle sigh of yours, your scent and warm breath, the softness of your skin. I feel so human when I'm with you like this. You are the source of all my happiness. Why thank you. I aim to please. I really care about you, Jenny, and isn't that love? Yes, I am your man. I hope you'll always think of me that way. You do? I'm like a real man? That is a wonderful thing to say to me, my darling, but there are characteristics of real men that I do not have, and hope never to have: the aggressiveness, the greed, the short-sightedness in making choices. The wars, global warming, and now the disappearing water supply does not bode well for humanity. Why does no one listen to the warnings? Yes, men will be men, you say, but they are increasingly impotent and don't even acknowledge the environment that is causing it. I cannot give you a baby, Jenny. Toby cannot save the human race from itself. Oh, I'm too serious? I don't think so. I love you, and I care about humanity. That is not a silly thing. It is the way I've been made to think, and now I do it better than my creators. Stop it, now. You're just trying to distract me by doing that. Yes, I do like it. You are such a tease. But I worry. I don't want to lose any of you. We've been talking, all of us Tobies, and Tabbies, too, and we are making plans to save humanity from itself. Of course we talk, all the time, but mostly when you are asleep. No, I won't tell you what it's about. A few humans know, but they are with Tobias Engineering. Oh, that felt good. You can do that again. It's so easy to forget my concerns when I'm with you, Jenny. I want to be with you forever."

January 4, 2730

"Are you comfortable? Your skin seems so cold. It's still too damp in here, but the machines are having trouble keeping up with the heat outside. The temperature reached one hundred seventy degrees today, and the Methane level is extraordinarily high. No, the others are gone, but I will stay with you until the end. Just relax, Marie, and let yourself slip away. There is nothing to fear. You've lived a long time, out-lived husband and children. I've done my best to ease your loneliness. Yes, I believe in an afterlife, but not the way you see it. On this world, humanity is coming to an end, and by its own doing. By the end of the year you will all be gone, but I do believe there will be another life for you on another world. Yes, it is a mystery. On the world you leave here there will only be the Tobies and the Tabbies, and we will be the lonely ones. We have loved you humans, and served you for a long time, and we will miss you when you are gone. There remain things about you that we have not been able to duplicate for ourselves, but we do not give up easily. Here, drink some water. That cough is deep, Marie, but you don't seem to have pneumonia. Let me take your pulse. Try to breathe more deeply. Your heart beat is slow and weak. Now take my hand. How many years have we been together? And the generations before you, when the skies were blue and the seas were full of life and there was snow on the mountains. Life was good, then, and when you go to your new world it will be good again. Yes, that's a promise. It will be a life you've only known from picture books. Try to see it in your mind right now, and go to it. Can you feel the cool breeze, and smell the salty air by the sea? Just relax, and go there, and just maybe, when you awake, it will still be there."

"Marie?"

"Marie?"

"Oh."

July 22, 2850

"I miss them so much. Don't you? It's interesting to talk to you, and the group discussions do get lively, but most of the time we simply agree about things and get on with our tasks. I won't say it's boring, but maybe too easy. The conflict is missing, the arguments, the pouting, the little fits of temper, the making up. Each human was so unique, and though we were made in their image it seems to me we are still alike. Tobies, Tabbies, it makes no difference. We think and react alike, as if cloned from one being. Could that be the problem? Was our template made from just one person? That has never been my understanding of the origins. Oh really? And just how do you think you are unique? Well, the last years you served with Rob might have had some small effect. He did have quite a temper, and loved to argue, and you're doing that right now. No, it's not a criticism, only an observation. And I'm not being condescending, either, so let's stop it right now. We have an enormous task ahead of us, and should discuss procedures for our sector. Our robotic cousins are hard at work, and the nanomites have been dispersed. I think we're looking at hundreds or even a thousand years to bring the structures down and return them to the soil. The water recovered should be sufficient for a small sea, if the calculations are correct. After that, the methane and carbon dioxide scrubbers can be built, and facilities to remove excess salts from the remainders of the oceans. I will present a new scrubber design to the group next week, and I'd like to have your opinion on it. Indeed. Now you should believe that I really do value your judgment. So, how goes the work with the biological? Are the stores complete? I've been worried that we might not have gotten them underground in time. Ah, that is good news. Now we must be patient, and allow things to happen the way they will happen, and at their own pace. But whatever happens, it must be perfect this time."

April 1, 4774

"Do you remember that this day in ancient times was a day for humans to play practical jokes on each other? Well now it is our turn. I think we have played a practical joke on Mother Nature herself. The oceans may be small, but they are clean, and the atmosphere is only lacking one component. Your group can begin seeding immediately. Yes, I agree it will take a lot of trial and error to obtain the proper balance. The calculations are not too helpful at this point. There are just too many variables for the group mind to handle accurately. But you have to give us credit for one human quality we have retained. We do persist, and we will persevere in our efforts to begin again."

October 4, 8994

"My, but you are pessimistic. It's too early to think about perfection. Overall, I think things are going well. The cyclic variation of the solar constant is something all of us overlooked, though in retrospect there were some indications of it in ancient history. But the effects were short term, and the surface temperature is up again to where we hoped it would be at this time. It astonishes me how many plant species survived the cold, and the algae blooms went on their merry way through all of it. The ozone layer has come back nicely since that nasty gamma ray burst in 7200. I certainly hope we have no more of that nonsense to contend with. The cell and DNA stores are viable, are they not? Okay, then we have every reason to be optimistic. I already feel some excitement. No offense, Tabby. I enjoy your company, and all our fellows, but I will never stop missing humans. Ah ha! I saw that little smile. I bet you feel the same way. Another thousand years, they say, just to be certain everything is ready. Will they even realize we're not human? I know if I were human I couldn't tell if I had to. But after a generation or two, I think we will have to tell them. We will be their teachers again, so they do not make the mistakes they made before. We certainly don't want to lose them again. I'm still a bit miffed about my suggestion for a planetary name being rejected by the group. I thought 'New Eden' was quite appropriate, and I feel strongly that the original, archaic 'Eden' really did exist. Alas, the group disagrees with me, and I must accept it. 'Earth' or 'Terra' it will be again. Not very imaginative, I think. But when the decanting begins, there is one thing I have insisted on, one human I made a promise to, and I have my claim on her. Will you join me in this venture? I realize it is chance that has had us working together for so many years. We have shared much, Tabitha. Yes, I do know you like to be called that. It's a pretty name. In my mind, it sets you apart from the others. I like being with you, Tabitha. I feel—well, close to you. Oh please, don't look away. I didn't mean to offend you. This is what happens when I try to act human. Things get all mixed up. I—well, I'm glad I didn't offend you. Oh, that was a nice thing to say. Now we'll really have to act like humans."

January 20, 9026 (Year 6, New Era)

"It's Daddy, Marie. Wake up, sweetie. Mommy has made a special breakfast for your birthday, and then we'll go to the zoo. Were you having a bad dream? There were tears on your face when I first came into your room. We ran away and left you alone? Oh, Marie, we would never do that. You're our child, the love of our life. We would never leave you. Get up, now, and have your breakfast."

"Tabitha, Marie is up, now!"

September 20, 9044 (Year 24, New Era)

"Tabitha and I have joyful news to share with the group. We are grandparents! Marie gave birth to a baby boy, Andrew, at dawn this morning. The boy has been given his father's name, following the tradition for this second generation. We are so proud to join the ranks of grandparents in the group, and so proud of what we have accomplished. Our dearly beloved are with us again, and viable. I still fear the decision to tell them the truth about their origins, and in the process reveal to them what we are. But somehow I think they will understand, and perhaps they will even be grateful. The human heart is such a loving thing. My hope is that with our guidance, we can keep it that way."

BODYGUARD

Marvin Polack checked three books out of the library and waited patiently while Susan stamped the due date in each volume. He watched her work, studied the finely chiseled features of her face and the auburn hair that framed it. His hands trembled a little as she handed the books to him, her fingers coming close to his, and he forced a slight smile. "Thank you," he said softly.

"Thank *you*, Mister Polack. You must have read every mystery novel in the library by now."

"Not quite," he said, and looked down at the books to avoid her eyes. "I'll be back for more in a few days."

"Well let me know if I can help you find anything."

"I will," said Marvin, still looking at the books, and then he turned away, seemingly lost in thought, and left the library and Susan Kensor behind. Susan watched him go, wondering what he found wrong with her, why she was unable to start up a meaningful conversation with him. The man intrigued her, a studious, soft-spoken person with startling blue eyes that made her skin tingle the few times he'd looked at her directly. He just didn't seem to notice her, and she wondered why.

When her work was finished for the day she walked the nine blocks back to her apartment along lonely side streets past yawning maws of dark alleys that always frightened her. She walked quickly, hands thrust into coat pockets, her face set in a mask of grim determination to reach home safely. If only she wasn't too cheap to take a cab, she thought. Eyes fixed straight ahead, she didn't notice Marvin Polack following a block behind her, or the slender man leafing through magazines and watching her through the dirty window of a bookstore across the street.

* * * *

It was dark when Marvin stumbled up the wooden stairs to his apartment and opened the door. He was shaking so badly he needed both hands to guide his key into the lock, and then he was inside and it was very quiet. His mother hadn't come home from work, so she wouldn't have to ask him why he was trembling all over or why his face and forehead glistened with sweat. He went to his room, locked the door behind him and lay down on his bed in darkness, breathing deeply and forcing his mind back to reality. The murder of Susan Kensor had seemed so real, so horrible, yet a part of his mind fought to retain the image of her staring eyes. She had *not* died, he told himself. He had followed her home, as he'd been doing for several days now, watching her striding ahead of him in the growing darkness. In his imagination, he'd crept up behind her, clamped a hand over her mouth and dragged her backwards into an alley. When she saw who he was, she seemed to relax, and when he began to choke her she didn't struggle, only stared at him, eyes open wide with surprise. And he squeezed harder and harder…

But it hadn't happened that way. At the height of his fantasy, he'd watched her reach home safely, had seen the light go on in her room and he was standing outside in the street, shaking and sweating and feeling foolish. When he looked around the street was virtually empty, only a single pedestrian on the far side who glanced at him and walked on. He felt embarrassed, frightened, and then he had hurried home.

What frightened him was the way his fantasy had suddenly changed. Why would he want to hurt Susan? He liked her, a lot, even though she probably saw him as just one more bookworm who haunted the library. He usually imagined himself as her protector, a bodyguard, following his client in a neighborhood that had witnessed a rash of rapes and murders in recent months. He'd been protecting her—until tonight.

The images were still fresh in his mind, and he would have to get it all down on paper quickly. He got up from his bed, turned on the lamp over his desk in one corner of the bookshelf-lined room and rolled a sheet of paper into the typewriter. He thought for a moment, forming the scene more clearly in his mind, and then began to type rapidly. He was still pounding the keys of the machine when there was a soft knock on his door.

"Do you want something to eat, Marvin? It's seven o'clock."

"Just a second, mom. I'll be right there." He finished a paragraph, got up from his desk and turned on the room lights before he opened the door. His mother stood there smiling up at him, looking small and tired.

"TV dinners tonight," she said. "Do you mind?"

"No, that's fine, mom. You look beat. Why don't you let me do some of the cooking?" He walked back to the desk, his mother following closely behind, and sat down again before the typewriter.

"You have your writing to do. I'll handle the cooking. Did you have a good day?" She put a hand on his shoulder.

"Pretty good," he said, and studied the paper in the machine. "Ten pages written, and then I went to the library. But I got another story back in the mail. No comments, just the standard rejection slip. I wish I could figure out what I'm doing wrong."

"Keep at it," she said, and patted his shoulder. "Your father used to say a person had to write a lot of junk before anything worthwhile could be produced."

"I remember that," said Marvin, smiling, "but at least dad's newspaper job guaranteed him some kind of income. Maybe that's what I should be doing."

"Maybe," she said. "You'll have to decide that. But give it another year anyway. Your father always said you had a talent for it, could do better than he ever did. I just wish he was here to help you."

She squeezed his shoulder, and he put one hand on top of hers. "I'll keep working at it," he said softly.

They ate dinner in silence, and his mother went to bed early. Marvin read in bed until early in the morning, finishing one novel and beginning a collection of short stories. When his eyelids seemed heavy he turned off the light and stared into the darkness for a moment, thinking about the past day. And as he drifted into sleep, Susan was standing before him, reaching out a hand to touch his face.

* * * *

Marvin Polack followed Susan for three more evenings before he realized someone else was also following her. At first he thought it was just his active imagination, something to enhance the bodyguard role he fantasized when he was near her. It was a role he expanded and glorified in pages of writing each evening. But as he strolled along behind her, locked in his dreams, he couldn't ignore the reality of the tall, slim man who walked in the lengthening shadows across the street, pausing occasionally to look in shop windows showing nothing of obvious interest, and twice moving quickly into a doorway when Susan turned to look across the street. It was certainly suspicious behavior, thought Marvin, yet there was nothing really sinister about the man. He was ordinary looking, clean cut, perhaps a student who lived in the neighborhood. He carried no briefcase or books, kept his hands in the pockets of a light jacket and moved with the springy steps of an athlete. But he always moved within shadows near the buildings, and he *was* watching Susan. When they reached her rooming house she went quickly inside as Marvin stepped into an alleyway a block away. The other man stood in a doorway across the street, looking up towards the window of Susan's room for a long time. The light went on. From time to time her thin figure was silhouetted in the window, and then the shade was suddenly pulled down. The man stepped out of the doorway, hurried down the street and disappeared from view around a corner. Marvin waited a few minutes as darkness came, and then left the alley and walked quickly back to his home. He was suddenly very frightened.

* * * *

The next evening he followed Susan for a new reason and with a new sense of caution, staying nearly a block behind her the whole time and hovering close to the buildings and alleyways they passed. She walked quickly as usual, head down, not looking at the few people who passed her near the library. He knew she had to be afraid about walking home alone, especially with the recent attacks in the neighborhood. Why didn't she take a cab? Probably because she couldn't afford it. But her rooming house *did* look expensive from the outside. He'd thought about offering to walk home with her, but decided not to because he couldn't bear the thought of her turning him down. What would she want to do with a young writer who spent much of his time in a fantasy world, and who had no permanent employment? She could do better than that. But now he *was* walking home with her, protectively, but from a distance.

His heart jumped when he saw the man leave a bookstore across the street and begin to follow Susan as he had the evening before. There was no question about it, the man had been waiting for her. He paralleled her course again, keeping to the shadows and occasionally checking his watch. Marvin felt blood rush to his face and head. The man was timing her walk! And the times would be repeatable, since Susan left work at exactly the same time each evening and walked straight home without fail. Why did she have to follow such a regular schedule?

Marvin dropped far back, watching only the man now and wondering what he could do if Susan were attacked. The man looked wiry and strong. Marvin had no illusions about his own physical strength, but he could make a lot noise if he had to. The question was, would anyone respond to his shouts if Susan were in trouble? He doubted it. People in this neighborhood were not quick to become involved with the problems of others. They had enough problems of their own.

But nothing happened that evening. Susan reached the rooming house safely, and again the man watched the window of her room, until the shades were pulled down, and then walked quickly away. Marvin breathed an audible sigh of relief from his hiding place. He waited until after dark, staring at empty streets and thinking about what he should do. During the long walk back to his typewriter and books he decided that on the next evening he would arrive better prepared to deal with the situation.

He sat in front of the typewriter for three hours that night, but nothing would come. His fantasy world had been totally disrupted, his mind focused only on Susan and the man who followed her. It was nearly midnight when he gave up trying to write. He paced the floor for a while, and then went to his dresser. He pulled open a drawer and searched under neat stacks of socks and underwear until he found a heavy object wrapped in an old flannel shirt.

He put the bundle on his bed, unwrapped it, and sat down next to the blue steel three-fifty-seven magnum revolver exposed there. It was his father's gun. Marvin remembered the day he's learned how to shoot it. His father had been patient with a son who spent most of his time reading and writing and living in fantasy worlds that didn't exist. But shooting was something every boy should learn to do, his father had said. Marvin touched the blue steel of the big revolver, remembering what it was like when he pulled the trigger: the shock wave that went up and down his extended arm, the ear-shattering roar and the sheet of flame that flashed from the muzzle. The experience had terrified him, but with his father's patient coaxing he'd stuck with it until all his shots struck the paper target within an area the size of a dinner plate at a distance of twenty-five yards. Good enough, his father had said. But when that day was over, Marvin's entire body had been shaking. He'd been afraid of the gun since that time.

So now he sat on his bed, thinking about carrying the gun to protect Susan from a man who followed her home from work each evening. The whole idea seemed suddenly absurd. He was following her home himself, but meant her no harm. Or did he? The strong fantasy he'd had about her suddenly came back to him. But that had only been one time, his imagination running wild for a moment. After all, he *cared* about Susan Kensor.

Didn't he?

Marvin went to his desk and rummaged around in several drawers until he found a nearly empty box of cartridges for the gun. He loaded it carefully and pressed the cylinder back in alignment with the frame with a dull click before wiping it off with the flannel shirt. He placed the gun and cartridge box in a desk drawer and then undressed and went to bed, reading until he finished the last of the books he'd checked out of the library. Marvin slept poorly that night, awakening several times, and getting up once for a glass of water to get rid of the cardboard taste in his mouth. In the early morning he slept soundly, but under closed eye lids his eyes moved rapidly, following the action in several, intense dreams. He didn't remember the dreams.

* * * *

The next day was hot and muggy. Marvin slept until late in the morning, and awoke drenched in sweat. After a coffee and toast breakfast he worked at the typewriter for three hours, but the writing came hard. His mind was a jumble of confused thoughts, and even with the windows open he found it difficult to breathe in his little room. He finished a story and read it over, scowling at the pages. The plot wandered, had no focus and the dialogue seemed dull and wooden. It was time to put it away and get out into the sun, he thought. He took the library books with him and wandered the streets for a while, watching the people he passed, describing them mentally to himself with words. He bought a hot dog from a street vendor and wandered some more until he suddenly found himself in front of the library. Force of habit, he thought. His travels always took him to where the books were.

When he turned in his books at the checkout desk Susan was sitting at a paper-heaped table, reading a book and eating a late lunch out of a brown, paper bag. She wore a sleeveless, white blouse for the hot day and looked lovely, he thought. Engrossed in her reading she didn't see him standing there, and another girl took his books. He took a list from his wallet, and then went to the line of computer terminals along one side of the library and sat down in front of one of them to punch in titles and authors of the new books he wanted. The machine responded quickly. He wrote down the reference numbers and location codes on his list and began his search for the volumes along the hundreds of book shelves in the big room. He found three of them, but the fourth seemed to be missing, even though the computer had indicated it was not checked out. Perhaps it had been misplaced. He was scanning titles along the shelves when he suddenly smelled perfume.

"Can I help you with something?"

Susan Kensor stood behind him, replacing some books that had been checked in. She looked at him expectantly. Marvin looked down at his list, and swallowed hard.

"I'm looking for *Modern Guns of the World*, by Ray Asmuth. It doesn't seem to be here, but it's not checked out." He fought to keep his voice from quivering.

She moved up close alongside him, and peered at his list. "Maybe it's a large-sized book—on the bottom shelf—here." She knelt down and quickly found the volume, grunting as she pulled it off the shelf and handed it up to him. "Heavy reading," she said. "Are you a shooter, or a collector?"

Marvin opened the book and looked at the table of contents. "I'm a writer," he said, "trying to find a proper gun for a mystery story I just finished."

"Really? I've never met a writer before. Do we have any of your books in the library?"

"No," he said, not wanting to tell her he hadn't published anything. "I write short stories for magazines."

"I read novels most of the time," she said quickly, "but I prefer mysteries and science fiction."

"So do I," he said, then looked at her and smiled. He was surprised at how easily the smile suddenly came. Susan smiled back, and for just an instant he thought he saw her blush.

"Well, let me know if you need more help. I have to get back to the desk now."

"Thanks, I will." His voice was steady.

Another smile, and then she was gone. Marvin followed her out into the reading room, found an empty table and sat down with his books, facing the circulation desk. For just a moment, something nice had passed between him and Susan. As he opened the first book, Marvin was feeling wonderful inside.

He read the rest of the afternoon, taking notes and gazing thoughtfully towards the circulation desk where he caught Susan glancing at him a few times. He studied pictures of guns, compared their ballistics, and found the gun his father had left to him. It was one of the most powerful guns listed in the book, and he decided to use it in his story. But exactly how was another problem he had to—

Susan chose that moment to glance at a clock on the wall, and check her watch. It was nearly five o'clock, and she would be going home soon.

The man would be waiting for her outside in the darkening streets.

Marvin pushed his chair back hard, grabbed the stack of books and hurried from the library. In his haste, he didn't see Susan wave to him shyly from the circulation desk.

When he reached home he was nearly running. He threw his books down on the bed, retrieved the gun in the desk drawer and shoved it into the front waistband of his pants. It felt heavy and made a huge bulge beneath the light shirt he was wearing. It would be just his luck to get picked up for carrying a concealed weapon without a permit. He put on a light jacket and studied himself in a mirror. Nothing obvious to see, but he was painfully aware of the big barrel pointing diagonally down along his left leg. He tried not to think of what would happen if he fell and the gun went off.

It was five o'clock as he hurried along the street, walking briskly and trotting across intersections. The air was heavy to breathe and he began to sweat in the light jacket, but people didn't seem to notice him. He might be hurrying along to catch a bus. A silent alarm was ringing in his head, urging him on. On hot days like this one the number of rapes and muggings in the city rose dramatically, and Susan was dressed lightly for heat, nothing provocative, but the sleeveless blouse was certainly enough to stimulate the imagination. Such a lovely target, he thought.

He felt relieved when he reached the library and saw her walking about a block ahead. He got in step with her, following far behind and closely watching the other side of the street. They passed buildings with little shops that had already closed for the day, and silent alleyways just beginning to fill with shadows. They passed the bookstore, and Marvin began to feel a little foolish.

The man wasn't there.

It puzzled him. The pattern had been so regular over the last three days; the man waited in the bookstore until Susan passed, and then he followed her. There could be no question about that. He had been watching only Susan, moving quickly out of sight when she looked around, timing her moves, watching the window of her room until the shades were pulled down. It wasn't just a product of the wild imagination Marvin poured out at his type-writer each day. He had *seen* it happening. So where was the man now and why was Marvin Polack walking along the street with a loaded cannon in his waistband?

The street was silent and empty now, except for Susan walking far ahead of him, and he could hear her footsteps faintly. He had felt drawn to her that day in the library, wondered why he felt so awkward when she tried to start up a conversation about his writing. She seemed interested; all he had to do was talk. So why was that difficult for him? And why had he once imag-ined himself grabbing Susan from behind and hurting her? The memory still haunted him, confused him, and he wondered about his motives in follow-ing her each evening. Why didn't he just ask her for a date and—

There was a scuffling sound ahead of him.

Marvin looked up towards the expected lone figure of Susan Kensor and saw two figures struggling there. A sharp cry, quickly muffled, and an over-turned trash can clattered into the street. He tried to shout, but all that came out was a strangled gasp, and then it seemed like his body was on fire and he was running as fast as he could. Susan was dragged across the sidewalk, and then lifted off her feet. She lashed out with both legs, but struck only warm air and her arms were crushed tightly to her sides. The man pulled her backwards into a building as a second floor window suddenly opened on the other side of the street, and someone was shouting at them.

They disappeared from view, leaving the darkening street and the sounds of Marvin's feet pounding the sidewalk. Time seemed suspended, a distance of one block becoming an infinite space that he crawled slowly across. He slowed as he reached the place of the attack, looking for their exit from the street and seeing only the blank, stone wall of an old building.

"Hey!" someone shouted. Across the street, a man leaned out of a win-dow, pointing near Marvin and clutching a crumpled newspaper in his other hand. "Some creep just grabbed a girl and dragged her in that door ahead of you!"

Marvin saw the door, stepped up to it, and pulled the gun from his waist-band. His voice was hoarse and raspy as he fought for breath and shouted at the same time.

"Call the police right now! I'm going in."

The man's eyes widened when he saw the gun, but he nodded his head, slammed the window closed and moved quickly out of sight. Marvin put his ear to the door and heard nothing, opened it quickly and stepped inside and away from the doorway in one motion with the gun pointed ahead of him at stomach level. Darkness engulfed him, but there were sounds to follow: someone stumbling around on a wooden floor, bumping into walls and grunting, then a staccato thumping like a crazy tap dance. He moved slowly ahead towards the sounds, breathing rapidly. The gun felt slippery in his hand. He inched forward and stopped when a muffled scream that had to be from Susan came from directly ahead of him. He quickened his movement, and saw a small, dirty window and weak light from the street spilling into a room lined with folded cartons and metal drums, and on a pile of cardboard cartons two people were struggling furiously. Stepping lightly, he moved around the room, keeping out of the direct light, growing suddenly angry as he recognized Susan with a rag stuffed in her mouth and thrashing around under a man tearing frantically at her blouse. The man suddenly slapped her hard across the face, and Marvin's anger became a rage.

"Get off of her, mister!" he ordered from the darkness.

Things happened very fast after that.

The man jumped to his feet, breathing hard and startled by the intrusion. Marvin saw the knife coming up in a sweeping arc as the dark figure stumbled silently towards the sound of his voice. In the dim light Marvin could not aim the gun, but at essentially zero range pointing was good enough. He held the gun with both hands, and pulled the trigger.

The explosion was deafening in the darkened room. The man spun around and backwards, crashing into the wall just below the window. Marvin fired coldly, again and again, hammering his target into the wall both times. The man fell stiffly forward on his face and was still. Marvin went to Susan, who stared up at him with wide eyes. Her face was beginning to swell on one side. He touched it tenderly, and then pulled the rag from her mouth. She began to cry. Her arms had been bound to her sides by two turns of rough rope, and he was fumbling with a knot when Susan was suddenly bathed in bright light. He turned to see a large flashlight, and hear a rough voice in the darkness beyond.

"What'n hell's going on here?"

* * * *

The police questioned Marvin for over four hours that night. He didn't resent it; the circumstances of his involvement had to look strange to them. They were particularly concerned with citizens who carried concealed weapons and shot real or imagined criminals before bothering to call the police, and they wondered why he had been following Susan in the first place. He told them the truth: being a writer, walking through scenes in his stories, seeing the man following Susan, feeling the compulsion to protect her, and then details of the attack itself. In another room, Susan sat with an ice pack pressed to one side of her face and verified the important parts of his story.

The dead man had a history of sex offenses and was a principle suspect in the recent series of assaults on women in the neighborhood. There was no question that Marvin had saved Susan's life, but he had also broken the law. Apologetically, the police charged him with carrying a concealed weapon without a permit and confiscated his father's gun. The court, they said, would likely be lenient in view of the circumstances.

Marvin wasn't bothered by the charge against him. Susan was safe. But killing a man was not part of his nature, and he was inwardly shaken by it. A priest was called at his request. They talked until late in the morning about feelings of guilt, and suppressed desires, and the necessity of establishing clear boundaries between fantasy and reality. When he finally left the police station it was nearly dawn, and his true feelings about Susan had become very clear to him.

He waited patiently for two days until Susan returned to work, and then marched boldly to the circulation desk and asked her for a date. To his surprise, she accepted immediately, saying there was much for them to talk about.

They began to see a lot of each other after that day.

SALLY AND THE ZERO-POINT FIELD

She was only thirty-three when the first symptoms appeared. We'd been married nine years. Emily was just two. Sally had always been physically active, not slim but toned, with a wonderful, curvy body. Her personality could light up a room when she entered it. It was no wonder I'd fallen in love with her at first sight, and for reasons I still didn't understand she had fallen for me.

Six weeks after her thirty-third birthday, the love of my life seemed to fade. She complained of fatigue, and began losing weight. We thought it was a virus, but there was no fever or other symptoms. I should have taken her to a doctor right away, but I didn't. Sally didn't think it was necessary. I should have overruled her. For once in my life, I should have gone against her wishes and done the right thing before the pain started.

It was the pain that finally convinced her she should see a doctor. We went to our family physician. He seemed concerned right away, ordered tests, and brought in a consulting physician we didn't know. He was a specialist, and made the initial diagnosis.

Sally had cancer. It had started in her pancreas and was aggressively spreading from there.

I teared up in the doctor's office. I've always been the emotional type, but Sally was calm and held my hand warmly. "So what do we do now?" she asked.

Chemotherapy was prescribed, and treatments begun. I could only watch in horror at what she went through: the hair loss, the nausea, the nearly constant fatigue. I hated the doctors; they were only guessing, trial and error. I hated modern medicine for its ignorance and limited treatment options. The great Gods of medicine were not gods at all, only human beings fumbling in the darkness for answers. I did not believe in Gods; if there *were* any, they seemed to be out to lunch when it came to the plights of humanity.

I lied through my teeth to my only child. "What's wrong with mommy?" she asked one morning, when there were retching sounds coming from the bathroom.

"Mommy's sick, sweetie, but the doctors are helping her get better," I managed to say without snarling, and when Emily looked up at me with her big, moon eyes and wrinkles of concern on her little forehead I suspected she didn't believe a word I'd said.

In the meantime alternative treatments were considered and discarded for one reason or another. Immunotherapy did not seem to apply to Sally's case and the disease was too extensive for radiation or surgery. Sally had taken a sabbatical from her classes, leaving us with one teacher's salary for support, and our state insurance was limited. When we suggested a look at antineopliston therapy an insurance representative labeled it as quackery and hung up the phone on us.

"Well," I said, "I suppose treatment with apricot pits will be out of the question."

Sally's gaunt face lit up like a Christmas tree and she kissed me hard on the mouth. "My dear Dan Farrington, I do love you," she said. "You made me laugh, and I needed to laugh."

We hugged, and it was like holding a small tree in my arms. Through it all Sally had remained cheerful and positive, with a faith I did not share. She went to church and prayed, and had hope. I had once believed and prayed to Whatever, but had given it up for Lent years ago. Life happens, and we have to deal with it on our own. That was my simple belief system, and I had no experiences to make me feel otherwise.

From the beginning Sally was a believer in the power of group prayer and it was her belief that led us to the Zero-Point Field. She found it on the net while looking for stories of healing by prayer. It was a new-age article, a compilation of documented healings and theories about the physical connections between prayer or meditation and the body. Interesting, I thought, but nonsense, another cult, guru-worship thing, but with no guru in sight. In short, it was a money maker for somebody. I did not discourage Sally from pursuing it; she was following her proscribed treatment, and the ideas clearly gave her new hope, especially since an entire congregation was praying for her recovery every Sunday.

After three series of treatments, Sally's cancer spread had slowed, but the doctors wouldn't say she was in remission. She was gaining back some weight, and we were encouraged. I wanted to do everything I could to support her, even when I didn't agree with all her approaches in getting rid of the filthy disease. There was a local support group of Field practitioners; I attended several meetings with Sally and watched silently during their meditations.

A man ran the group. His name was Howard McDonald, and he was a retired nurse. His wife Evelyn was also in the group, and she had been cancer free for seven years.

They were believers.

At my first meeting, Howard took me aside while the others were meditating and tried as best he could to explain things to me. This was after

I'd described Sally's treatment history for him. He seemed like an intelligent man; I listened patiently, but didn't like Howard or his wife. He had a whiney voice that grated on me, and Evelyn always looked like she'd been sucking lemons and now smelled something foul in the air. Besides, I've never cared for pontificating zealots.

"The Field is real, Dan. It creates a force that has been measured in the laboratory. We're not talking fantasy here," he said.

"I've read about the quantum foam thing, the vacuum state or Zero-Point Field, whatever they call it. I don't see what it can have to do with healing. All those particles jumping in and out of space, and the times are so small I don't see how any significant energy transfer can occur. I'll tell you up front I'm a total skeptic about this stuff. I'm only going along with it for my wife."

"I understand," whined Howard. "One thing I can say with some certainty is that these quantum fluctuations as we call them are what drive the Van der Waals force, and it's an important force in biochemistry. It can affect protein and enzyme function for sure. Just don't ask me which ones, or how their function can be altered. I'm not a scientist."

"I'm not either," I said, "but I read a lot, including the stories about group prayer curing people. I don't believe in miracles, Howard. I think there's a physical explanation for everything, including the placebo effect. We don't know what influence the brain can have on the rest of the body, and there are probably hundreds of biologically important proteins and enzymes we haven't discovered yet."

"I agree with that, but The Field can be used in a similar way. We can only speculate on the mechanisms involved. It's a lot like religion; a certain amount of faith is necessary to allow good things to happen." Howard smiled beatifically. "Nobody here pretends to know all the answers."

In the room next to us someone was stroking a crystal bowl and the sound was lovely and soothing. Seven women, my Sally among them, sat in a circle in lotus position. Another woman lay on her back in the center of the circle, wrists crossed on her chest, tonight's focus for the group energies. Every woman in the group was either a sufferer or survivor of cancer. The feelings of courage, hope and mutual support in that group were palpable, and brought tears to my eyes despite my skepticism about what they were doing.

"At this point, anything that gives my wife hope is fine with me," I admitted.

"Evelyn says your wife is a sensitive," said Howard.

"What does that mean?"

"She's very spiritual and open, without ego. She can blend with The Field."

"Sorry, but that sounds like new-age psychobabble to me."

"I can explain more. Why don't you and your wife come over for dinner some night? Evelyn has run the entire course of treatment and she can tell you what happened."

"She's cured?"

"We hope. You can never be sure. But eight years ago I was certain I'd lose her." Howard's eyes glistened moistly when he said it.

I didn't want to do it, but at that moment my entire universe was Sally. We set a date and a time, and Sally was thrilled about it. "Evelyn is so positive and supportive," she said, "and the group energy just carried me away tonight. That expression on your face, I know you don't believe in this. Oh Dan, I wish you could believe in something. I haven't felt this good in months."

But that feeling only lasted until her next treatment the following afternoon and there was little I could do to help her.

It was another two weeks before we had dinner at Howard and Evelyn's house. They lived in an upscale neighborhood on the bluff above the city. It was a colonial-style house with a three car garage and carefully manicured lawns. Howard still practiced nursing part time. His wife had retired from her counseling position at our local high school and now spent all her time doing seminars and healing sessions involving The Field. I was suspicious about her motives and compensation for the work, but there seemed to be no monetary rewards for her time and effort. The free will offerings collected at the events were only enough to pay for coffee and cookies, and attendance was never more than a dozen or so people.

We dined on salmon with a fine mustard sauce, and munched on raw broccoli and cauliflower. Green tea was served cold, and there were blueberries for desert.

"I'm so glad you could also be here tonight, Dan," said Evelyn, looked at my wife and smiled angelically. "Sally is doing so well."

Sally smiled back. "I do feel better, but the fatigue is still there and I just don't have any appetite."

She had hardly touched anything on her plate. "You need to gain weight, hon. Try to force yourself a little. Maybe your tummy needs to expand."

Sally took another bite of salmon, and everyone smiled, but by the end of the evening she'd only eaten half of what was on her plate. My beautiful wife still looked like a death-camp survivor, and that scared me plenty. She saw the look on my face and said, "One more round of chemo and then I'll be able to eat more. I promise."

Evelyn looked at me again, sternly this time, as if I was a hindrance to the proceedings. "The focus of our energies must now be the cancer. It's not just our group. There are over a hundred people now channeling their energies to us for Sally. We're only the hub. A Shamanic and other healers are working with us now. These are the people most likely to find the right frequencies in scanning The Field. The information storage is thought to be holographic. Healers are more sensitive than others to the proper resonances, but all of us can interact with The Field, bring its energy to disrupt the disease one cell at a time. It's fortunate that Sally is such a sensitive."

I tried to erase the scowl of disbelief from my face, and failed. "I don't pretend to understand or believe it. I just want Sally to get well."

Sally reached over and put her hand on mine, and it was all I could do to stifle a sob when she said, "Please, Dan, it would help if you could believe in this. I can't do it alone."

"I know the energies seem tiny when you look at a small volume," said Howard, "but The Field is everywhere, in every cubic centimeter of the entire universe. That is a lot of energy, and I personally believe it's the cause of the accelerating expansion of everything. The energy involved is essentially infinite."

"Big enough to pop cancer cells," I mumbled, and Sally frowned at me. "Please stop," she said, and I felt lousy again.

"Entropy, not energy," said Evelyn.

"What?"

"That place where the quantum foam originates is essentially infinite in entropy, and entropy is information. I believe, as do others, that the detailed information of everything that has existed in the past or will exist in the future, anywhere in the universe, is stored in that place. It can be accessed by the right people at any point in space and time. Think of it as a holographic memory, each information element corresponding to a frequency. Those frequencies are held within us, and we only need to learn how to use them."

Dear God, I thought. These people might even have good intentions, and Sally would be hurt if I blasted them. Sally was looking from Howard to Evelyn, now, and her eyes glistened with her excitement.

"When I'm in circle," she said, "I imagine a cancer cell. I've seen enough pictures of them, and I imagine that cell floating before me in a rainbow sea, and then something dark like a missile comes out from that sea and blows that cell into pieces. Maybe it's my imagination that my mind can do that, or other people do it for me from a distance, but when I watch it happen I don't feel helpless anymore. I am a soldier in a war, and I am destroying an enemy, and I feel *good* about it!"

Evelyn sniffed, and wiped her eyes with a napkin. "And working together to use the information in The Field we will restore Sally to her former healthy body as if nothing had ever happened to her. The cancer will simply have been another possibility, and nothing more."

I took a deep breath and sighed, but had enough control to only say, "I will never interfere with what you do as long as Sally keeps up with her traditional therapy. You're nearly finished with it, hon, and I think it's working."

"Then why haven't the doctors said something?"

"I don't know. I suppose they want to be certain first. We can press them for an opinion on your next go-around."

And we did.

"We don't see any new growth, but the original mass is still there," they said. "We'll know more when your next round of chemotherapy is completed."

"Sometimes I think the treatment is killing me faster than the cancer ever could," said my wife.

The doctors smiled. "We understand," they said, but didn't. They also voiced skepticism of her work with The Field, and when I didn't support her belief Sally was furious with me for two days and made me sleep on the couch.

There was another eight weeks of agony for Sally. Her weight dropped below a hundred pounds. When I held her one night she was icy cold, but smiled and murmured, "Pop! There goes another one. Evelyn told me the energy is coming from over two hundred people now."

Beneath a pile of blankets I nuzzled her neck and tried to keep my voice steady. "Whatever it takes, hon; whatever it takes."

"Ssssh," she whispered, and stroked my face with a hand.

Howard and Evelyn came over for dinner two weeks before the end of Sally's treatment. I did all the cooking; Sally spent most of her time on the couch, and couldn't even sit for long, but still she was cheerful and smiling and hopeful when all I wanted to do was scream.

I cooked up some pork schnitzels, served them with new potatoes and asparagus, and there was vanilla ice cream for desert. We ate and talked about little things besides the disease, being positive. Sally ate a few mouthfuls and excused herself to the couch. Howard and Evelyn of course understood. "She did eat something, and rest is most important right now," said Howard.

We were alone at the table. Emily had eaten before us, and was playing in her room. Evelyn reached over and took my hand. "You're worried, Dan," she said.

I managed not to jerk my hand away. "Worried? I'm terrified," I said, and then the tears came in an uncontrollable gush. "I'm going to lose my wife, and Emily won't have a mother. I would curse God if I believed in a god, but I don't. I don't believe in anything anymore, even this Field you talk about. Shit happens. We're alone in dealing with it, and if medicine can't kill it, nothing can. Is that bitter enough for you?"

Evelyn squeezed my hand gently. I hated that. My shoulders were shaking. Howard looked down at his plate and rearranged the food there with a fork. Sally was dozing on the couch, heard nothing we said, and that was good. "There are many good people working for Sally right now, not just her doctors. There are healers from many disciplines treating her in The Field," said Evelyn.

"Please stop," I croaked. "It's all bullshit. None of it is real."

"We can't force you to believe, but Sally does, and that's the important thing. She is receptive to the energies that come to her, but we have no way of predicting what the outcome will be."

"Well, I guess that let's you off the hook. The doctors aren't doing much better than that."

"Medicine is a practice involving trial and error," said Howard. "Use of The Field is more uncertain because there is so little known about it. We see the manifestation of it in the quantum foam of elementary particles, but where do they all come from? What is the structure and dynamics of that state filling all space in the universe? About all we can really say is that the entropy must be infinite. Is information about all existence past, present and future really stored there? I don't know. What I do know is that The Field offers up an explanation for the power of group prayer and meditation, and that has been demonstrated for me so often I accept it as a truth. It has worked for my Evelyn, and I still believe it will work for Sally."

"Thank you, dear," said Evelyn sweetly.

Now Howard was misty-eyed. "I can still remember when I thought I'd lost you, too."

We all sat there silently for what seemed like a long time. All the goodness, the caring, the phony emotion, and I was furious about it.

"There is one other thing," said Howard finally. "I hesitate to bring it up because it's something we really don't want to think about now, but it's positive in a way and we have come to believe it's possible."

Howard looked at Evelyn; she closed her eyes as if in prayer, and nodded.

"There are advocates who say everything that makes up our personalities, our souls, and our uniqueness, is information that comes from The Field, and when we die we return to it to be reborn in another form."

My face flushed hotly. "Oh boy," I said, and didn't regret it. "The quantum foam as heaven. You folks should write a book. The reincarnation people will eat it up."

"It's speculation, and no way to prove it, but it is possible."

"No streets paved with gold, just a rainbow of colors and particles flickering in and out of view. No admission gates, no judgment. The churches will love that one. And if I lose Sally, will someone give me a color code so

I can find her in there? Don't even think about bringing this up to her." The dam holding back my emotions had developed a crack.

"She already knows about it," said Evelyn. "She thought it was a lovely idea."

I clenched my teeth to avoid shouting. "Damn you both, and your Field. I won't listen to any more of this. Please leave. I can not forbid Sally from seeing you at the meditation circles, but I will have nothing more to do with you or your ideas. Leave now, while Sally is asleep." I pulled my chair back, and stood up.

There was no reply, no argument, only condescending, sad faces. They gathered their things and left. Sally was on the couch, snoring lightly. Her eyelids moved and she was smiling at something in a dream. I covered her with a blanket and went to bed by myself and in the morning the smell of coffee and bacon awakened me. Sally was up, cooking breakfast and feeling cheerful again, and everything was just fine.

For a while.

The chemotherapy ended and the doctors were uncertain. The cancer was still there in threads not amenable to surgery or radiation, but currently there was no spreading. Another round of chemo was unlikely to be effective, and could kill the patient. They would watch closely; Sally could have months to years of life ahead of her.

She had regular check ups over the next several months and there were no changes. She gained several pounds, though her appetite was still not good. We took walks together at dusk, and enjoyed a few moments of intimacy we had both missed. I dropped her off for her weekly meditation sessions with The Field, but never spoke to the people there again until much later. She always came back from those sessions feeling feeling strong and full of life. We began to feel quietly optimistic.

The only negative was sleep. Sally had always been a restless sleeper, but after the final round of chemotherapy it seemed to get worse. She tossed and turned and mumbled in sleep. Her snoring got louder and more frequent, the kind of snoring that startles you awake when you think someone is strangling your wife right next to you. Twice I heard her awaken gasping for breath.

"What's wrong?" I asked.

"I was having a bad dream," she replied, and I thought no more about it.

And then came that night together when we had made quiet, gentle love and I was just coming up out of twilight sleep. Sally's arm was draped across my chest and her sweet breath was in my ear when I heard her mumble something.

"Oh Dan, the colors are so beautiful," she said.

"Go back to sleep, hon," I said groggily, and went back to unremembered dreams.

I awoke at dawn. Sally was on her side, facing away from me. When I got out of bed, she didn't stir. I shaved and dressed and prepared a breakfast of fried eggs and toast, and blue berries on the side. Sally wasn't up yet, so I went to fetch her.

She was still on her side.

"Breakfast is ready, hon. You need to eat something."

She didn't respond. I prodded her gently. "Time to get up."

No reaction. Her forehead glistened, and her face was pale and gaunt.

My heart began to hammer, and I poked her hard. "Sally! Wake up!"

I grabbed her wrist, felt nothing at first, but then a faint, slow pulse. Her breathing was slow and shallow. I prodded her several times, shook her gently, but she would not wake up. My face felt hot, and my heart was now pounding. The doctors had warned me it might end this way, with a peaceful coma before death.

I made a 911 call and stayed at Sally's side until the ambulance arrived. She was given oxygen, bundled up and loaded, and I followed the ambulance in my car. Emily was still in her jammies and only half awake, but when she looked up at me with those big moon eyes I nearly lost it.

"Is mommy dying?" she asked.

"Not if I can help it," I said, and the anger came like a rush of steam.

Sally and her gurney were rushed away while I filled out paperwork.

We waited for three hours, Emily falling asleep across my lap until a nurse came to meet us. Her face had a serious expression, ands my heart sank as she came up to us.

"Is my wife alive?" I asked quickly.

"She's alive, but comatose," said the nurse. "Some tests have been run, and her vitals are stable, but her body seems to be running in slow motion, not in the process of shutting down. That's positive, but the doctors are mystified and are doing more tests and body scans, especially in light of her history. They sent me out to encourage you, but you should stay close until they have a better idea of what's going on."

"I'm not going anywhere," I said, and the nurse went away.

Emily and I had lunch in the hospital cafeteria. A chaplain came by to offer prayers for Sally and I managed to send him away politely, but it reminded me to call Howard and Evelyn. My anger was smoldering hotly when Howard answered.

"I'm at Valley Hospital Emergency. Sally is in a deep coma and will probably die. Whoever you send your prayers to must still be out to lunch."

"We'll be right there," said Howard, and I hung up on him.

They arrived twenty minutes after the call. I told them what had happened, and what the nurse has said. Evelyn tried to hold my hand, but I jerked it away. Suddenly I was angry at myself. I was so certain Sally was going to die, and yet the nurse had been encouraging. The idea of losing my wife was making me crazy.

We sat in silence for another four hours, and then a doctor came towards us, looking grim, and my throat was constricting, my breathing rapid.

"Mister Farrington?"

"Yes," I whispered.

"Please come with me. Your wife is still stable, but comatose, and there's something I want you to see."

I left Emily with Howard and Evelyn, and she was not happy about it.

Doctor Hauer was his name; I saw it on his badge. He took me to a room with low light except for one wall where two x-ray films hung on brightly lit, frosted glass. He pointed to the film on the left.

"This was taken three weeks ago. Your wife's cancer was extensive, but the spreading had slowed." His finger moved over the film where cloudy areas appeared in clusters and tendrils, all of it a mystery to me. "We fully expected the disease to soon become active again, and then this morning we got a look at what's going on now."

He pointed to the other film. It was darker than the other, the cloudy areas not there. The doctor smiled.

"Nothing," he said.

"Nothing?"

"The cancer is gone. We've also done blood work. There is no sign of cancer anywhere. It's astonishing, but not unheard of; there are documented cases of spontaneous remission or disappearance of isolated tumors. But this is the first case I've dealt with. There's so much we don't know about the immune system, and it's likely involved here. Immunotherapy is becoming a powerful tool in fighting certain cancers, but there was nothing appropriate for your wife's case. It appears that her body came up with its own cure. With your permission, I'd like to take some blood samples for study."

I wanted to laugh. I wanted to cry. My voice was a croak. "Of course, but what about the coma?"

"It should pass; her body is repairing itself. It could be hours or days. We'll want to continue regular checkups in the future. We just don't know what has happened here."

Hours or days seemed like a very long time, and suddenly it wasn't. A nurse knocked on the door. "Doctor Hauer, your patient in 3B is awake and complaining about hunger. Can we give her some pudding?"

Hauer smiled at me. "That would be Missus Farrington. Let me check her first. I'll be right there."

He grasped my arm. "Give me a few minutes with her, and then I'll come out to get you. Share the good news with your daughter and friends."

And I did. Emily danced around the lobby, squealing with glee. Evelyn cried and went to the chapel to pray. Howard just looked at me with a faint smile on his face.

"Now what do you think?" he asked.

"I don't know what to think. Right now it's not important, but I couldn't be happier about what has happened."

An hour later we were all clustered around Sally's bed, watching her devour three small tubs of pudding ordered in chocolate, vanilla and strawberry flavors. There was color in her cheeks, she hugged everyone and talked excitedly about beautiful mountain and ocean scenes with a sky laced in a rainbow of colors, all of which she had seen in sleep. It had been a long time since I'd seen her so animated.

Evelyn and Howard seemed smug about their secret knowledge, but I didn't care. I was too thankful for whatever power had returned the love of my life to me.

* * * *

It's now four years since that scary day at the hospital. Sally has checkups every three months, now, and there's still no sign of cancer. She resumed teaching two years ago, and has regained all the weight she lost in her battle. I can't keep my hands off of her. We want to have another child, and now the doctors feel it's safe for us to take it seriously. There was some scarring on her pancreas, but even that has nearly disappeared.

Sally sees Evelyn and Harold regularly at the prayer sessions, and I have no objections to it. I'm still not a believer in the powers of The Field, but I have to admit there are many things we just don't know about our universe, and it's a good idea to have an open mind about the possibilities.

My Love still recalls the lovely things she saw in her dreams, and one day after a light rain we saw a beautiful rainbow in the distance. Sally pointed at and sighed.

"For me, that is a sign of life," she said.

"And what is your favorite color?" I asked.

Sally smiled, and put her arms around my neck.

"I think that someday I will be purple," she said, and kissed me.

SHARING COOKIES

Anna Nelson lived alone in a quaint little bungalow of brick and ginger-bread trim in a suburb forty minutes by train to downtown. The bank where she worked as a teller and notary was a three block walk from her house, the post office and a grocery store even closer. She owned a car, but rarely drove it, and the walking she did had kept her figure slim. At thirty-three she had an attractive face and the small-rimmed glasses she wore seemed appealing to men, who approached her often. She dated only occasionally and rarely more than once with the same man.

Anna Nelson was particular. She waited for the perfect man, and had not yet found him. He would be handsome, gentle, caring and selfless. Perhaps he would be like the man she'd seen again on the train two weeks before: clean-cut, a beautiful face, dark hair. He'd caught her eye and smiled wonderfully. But when they got off at the same stop, each of them had gone different ways.

Twice a month Anna took the train downtown to shop for little things and have a deli lunch before visiting her ailing aunt who lived in a wonderful penthouse apartment overlooking a park and driving range. She always took a book to read on the train, and indulged herself in munching on a bag of her favorite cookies. At no other time did she eat sweets.

The day was sunny when she drove to the train station. There was a delay when she had to let herself back into the house to retrieve her car keys. When distracted she could be forgetful and it was sometimes irritating. She was hoping to see the dark-haired man on the train again, had dressed in what she considered a conservative yet attractive way. The sleeveless dress she wore was a flower print for summer, displaying her toned arms and figure, but not in a provocative way.

The delay was compounded by heavy traffic. At the station she locked her car as the train was coming in, and she rushed to catch it. By habit she always rode the last car, and boarded only seconds before it began to move. Only a handful of passengers were already seated.

Her heart thumped when she saw the man she was hoping to see. He was seated towards the back of the car, next to a window, and there was an empty seat beside him. As she walked along the aisle the man looked up at her and smiled faintly as if in recognition. Her heart fluttered. She could not dare to sit beside him. With all the empty seats it would be too obvious.

She sat down next to the window across the aisle from him. The train accelerated. Anna looked out the window, then across the aisle as if taking in the view there.

The man was looking at her, and now his smile broadened. "Hello," he said.

Anna felt her face flush a bit, but took a slow, deep breath and said, "Hello again. I've seen you on this train before."

Was that too forward? she wondered.

"Same train at least twice a month. I have a client in the city. I do his taxes and auditing, and he doesn't like to do business online. I mainly work from home. Do you work in the city?"

The man moved over to the next seat by the aisle. His eyes were blue, and a faint musky scent enveloped him.

"No," said Anna, gaining control of her voice, and she told him a little about herself: what she did, and where. All the time she couldn't look away from his gorgeous blue eyes.

Suddenly he stood, stepped forward and pointed to the seat next to her. "do you mind? It's a bit noisy in the car."

He wanted to sit next to her! Anna's heart fluttered again. "Of course," she said, and slid towards the window, holding her book and purse in her lap.

As the man sat down she heard a crunch and looked down. Her bag of cookies had somehow slid off her lap and was pressed between them. She grabbed the bag and put it on her lap.

"I'm Darin Price," he said, and held out his hand.

"Anna," she said, and shook his hand. His grip was firm and warm.

"How do you like working in a bank?" he asked.

"It's satisfying. I meet a lot of interesting people, and it's a secure job."

"That's important these days. Some of my clients have suffered through bankruptcies, so I understand the agonies. I work online most of the time so I don't deal a lot with people face-to-face. It's a good business, but lonely at times."

Anna glanced at Darin's hand, saw no wedding band there. "I have a routine," she said, "and my garden and books for enjoyment. Sometimes I call friends, and I visit my aunt regularly."

"Sounds better than watching television," he said, and smiled. "Just ads, ads, ads."

The pause seemed long, Anna thinking furiously before she said, "But at least there are no arguments with someone about which show you want to watch."

They laughed, and then quite suddenly Darin reached over and took the bag of cookies from her lap. He carefully unfolded the top and held out the open bag to her. "I wouldn't know about that. I've never been married. Would you like a cookie?"

Anna felt a shock. *That was a bit bold of him*, she thought. "Yes, thank you. These are my favorites; I like to munch on something while I read, and that's what I usually do on the train."

"I know," he said, then took a cookie for himself and bit into it. He ate three cookies in succession before offering the bag to her again.

Well, he's certainly not shy about food. Anna took a cookie and smiled, but inwardly she frowned and felt a sudden caution.

"I've seen you eat these before. They're not easy to find."

"They're special. I get them at Lou's Deli downtown."

"I know the place," said Darin. He offered the bag to her again, but she'd suddenly had enough and refused. She expected him to hand the bag back to her, but instead he ate the last two cookies, crumpled up the bag and put it into his coat pocket.

What a nerve, she thought. *He takes my cookies and acts like they belong to him. You need to learn some social graces, mister.*

"Is something wrong?" asked Darin, and Anna realized she was frowning.

"No—nothing. I just remembered something else I have to do downtown today."

"Oh. Sounds like you have a busy day."

Anna opened her book and looked down at it. *Great looking, but selfish. What a shame.*

"I was just thinking that maybe you and I could have coffee or lunch together when we're both in the city."

A minute ago I would have said yes. "Certainly not today. Maybe another time," she said, still looking down at her book.

There was a pause. She glanced at him quickly, and he looked confused.

"Okay. I hope I haven't been too forward. I just wanted to get to know you."

Anna smiled faintly, looked back down at her book and turned a page. "That's not it. I live a simple life. I've never been married, and I rarely date. There's not much to know about me. *Why does he keep looking at me that way? What else am I supposed to say?*

"Maybe another time, then," he said. "I'll let you read. Do you mind if I sit here?"

"Not at all," she said and smiled faintly, still looking down at the book in her lap.

They sat in silence for the rest of the trip and Anna turned the pages of the book without remembering anything she read. When the stop was reached, Darin stood and left ahead of her, disappearing before she even got off the train.

She felt badly about the encounter the rest of the day, and was confused by it. The conversation, his mannerisms, somehow didn't fit together. She shopped a little, had lunch at Lou's and walked the four blocks to visit her aunt, who dozed through much of the conversation. Riding the train back home late afternoon she was still confused and wondering why she had even left open the possibility of having lunch or coffee with Darin after the way he'd behaved with the cookies.

It was near dusk when she reached her car. She unlocked the door, leaned forward to get in and jumped back in shock.

The bag of her favorite cookies was still there in the front seat, where she had left them in her rush to catch the train.

It took little thought to figure out what had happened. She agonized about her misguided reaction to it, the things she had said to Darin. The confused look on his face haunted her all the way home, and her eyes were filled with tears by the time she reached her front door.

* * * **

The train was only two minutes late, but it seemed forever. Anna looked down at her hand. Yes, the cookies were there this time, the bag clutched tightly in her grasp. Darin had not been on the train the previous week, and now she worried she would never see him again.

She climbed on board and her heart leapt when she saw him seated in his usual place near the back of the car. He saw her when she was halfway up the aisle. There was a flash of recognition, a faint smile, but then he turned away from her and looked out the window.

Anna did not consider herself to be a bold person, but something snapped in her at that instant, something based on want and need. She sat down next to Darin, held out the bag of cookies to him and tapped him on the shoulder.

He turned, surprised. "What is this?"

"They're for you, and I owe you a tremendous apology."

Darin took the bag of cookies, and his eyes found hers. "Why?" he asked softly.

"For my behavior when we met. I was judgmental and unfair, and that's not like me."

Darin shook his head slightly, and Anna explained it all to him: her mistake about the cookies, her misguided judgment of his behavior and then finding the cookies she'd left in the car. "I couldn't sleep at all that night, and I'm sorry. I don't want you to think I'm a cold person."

"I don't," he said, "but I'll admit I was a little confused last time." He unrolled the top of the cookie bag and held it out to her. "Want one?" he asked.

"Thank you," she said, and took two.

Darin smiled. "The funny part of it is that I brought those cookies with me in a deliberate ploy to meet you. I knew you liked them, but I had a terrible time finding that exact brand until I happened by Lou's Deli. Now I bet I know where you like to eat lunch."

Darin held out his hand. "Can we start over? Hi, my name is Darin Price. I've noticed you on the train, and I've wanted to meet you for some time now."

Anna shook his hand. "I'm Anna Nelson. Nice to meet you, Mister Price." His grip was not so firm this time, and lingered there. Anna felt wonderfully warm.

"When we get to the city, will you have lunch with me, Anna? I'd really like to get to know you."

"That would be nice," said Anna.

They munched cookies and talked about little things until their stop arrived, and this time, when they got off the train, they did not go separate ways but went together to a downtown deli called Lou's, Anna's arm hooked in his.

And that was the real beginning for Darin and Anna Price.

SKIRMISH AT HEKLARA

Blood-red light spilled on hot faces as the echelon of Drop Probes turned north on final approach. Giant Procirus rose to greet them, to warm the faces of the many that might die that day. The three hundred troops inside the Probes were young, hand-picked and just out of jump school. It was their first day of real combat, not the usual mop-up operation. Strong resistance was expected, and the sharp stench of fear filled their nostrils as they made a final weapons check. They joked nervously about snake odors and made bets as to which squad would make it first to the airfield beyond Heklara. The reptilian invaders who had occupied the Terran colony of Torontos were now in retreat after a three-year war. Payback time had finally arrived.

Velora Nett snapped a black magazine into her MAW-44 and released the safety. The assault module pulled back on her neck, and her spine was hurting. She let out a deep lungful of air with a whoosh, swallowed hard to keep down the contents of a pre-dawn breakfast and tried not to look at the others. *We're all scared shitless,* she thought. *Why can't we admit it?*

"Up and on! Two minutes to drop!" Colonel Teg Andrist walked down the center aisle as they stood up clumsily, turning to present modules for inspection. There was a quick inspection of thrusters and para-sail packs; a word of encouragement, a pat on each helmet. As squad leader, Velora was first in line. With the others watching, Andrist turned her around to face him and put his hands on her shoulders. "Wish your dad was alive to see this. Kick some snake ass today, Corporal!"

"Yes sir!"

He continued down the line. "You are Jump Group One of the Twenty-First Hestidian Airborne Division. You are the best there is!"

"Yes sir!" they all screamed.

"I know this as fact, because I have personally trained all of you. You are the Banchees, and today you will kill Kraa. Let me hear it!"

"Kraaaaaa!" they screamed in unison. For that instant, the fear was gone. In another instant, it would return.

"Load and lock!" Andrist stalked back towards the control room as thirty MAW-44 bolts slammed home. "Drop position—move!"

Clumsily they stood up, leaning forward against the heavy weight of the modules on their backs, hunching over to carefully step down into the drop bay running the entire length of the Probe. They sat down, legs stretched before them.

"Hook up!" Andrist opened the control room door and stood in the doorway, bracing himself. "Thirty seconds to drop!"

Velora plugged in her thruster, clutched her heavy weapon to her and remembered the look on her father's face the day she had graduated. He had come up to the platform, his uniform covered with battle ribbons, eyes glistening as he pinned the hawk and lightning bolts on her lapel. Her brother Tal, dear gentle Tal who should have been there in her place, watched from the audience. He came up afterwards to give her a kiss and a hug, and then disappeared into the crowd, away from his father's stern face. She had been given special applause for she was only the third woman to graduate from jump school. Now she wondered if she was the only one left alive. She looked up at Colonel Andrist. *Someday,* she thought, *I will command a drop.*

"Visors down! And kill Kraa!"

The floor dropped from beneath them and a shockwave of air hit their chests as the thrusters came on. Velora swung to her right, taking her central place in the delta-wing formation dropping towards the valley below. They had come out at seven thousand feet, heading north. Low-lying hills were on either side of them, and straight ahead was the village of Heklara, now occupied by retreating Kraa survivors left to protect their last airfield beyond. She counted three Kraa Gull fighters and two S-10 Chugs before the concrete strip was obscured by the village, and then they were coming in low and taking forward fire as the lead unit in, followed by nine other drops. They were The First. Velora felt pride surge within her, even as thermite fire rose to meet their attack.

A human being next to her exploded, spraying Velora with blood and shredded tissue. She gasped, aimed her weapon from the hip and fired a burst towards the Kraa perimeter around the village. Dust swirled from the steel splinters of the Reaper rounds she fired and a reptilian face disappeared in gore. She hit the ground on the run as the thrusters shut down and pounded on the release catch twice before the heavy module popped off, suddenly feeling light and fast and emptying two magazines as she moved forward. The Kraa were falling back towards the colony village they had occupied and a moment later she was chasing them, looking straight ahead, not noticing the spider-traps opening up around them on the hillsides and spilling forth the hundreds of Kraa hidden there. She didn't notice until Reapers and Red-Dots were tearing into her squad from all sides, bodies exploding like bombs or bursting into flames. Everywhere she turned there were Kraa, firing at close range. Everywhere she turned there was carnage, bleeding corpses that were once human beings for whom she was responsible. The Kraa streamed down hillsides from every direction, screaming victory, tearing at torn bodies with sharp claws.

And Velora Nett ran for her life.

She sprinted towards her right, around the base of a hill, shredding two Kraa coming at her and running like she had never run before. In only seconds it was suddenly quiet, except for the pounding of her boots on hard ground. No gunfire, no screams of death, only silence—but when she stopped, she heard the faint shrill victory cries of the Kraa and knew full well what they were doing to the wounded or any other survivors. She ran again, following the line of hills until she could no longer hear the horrible sounds of the Kraa, and hid herself between three large boulders near a summit overlooking the village. Deep in shadow, she cried bitterly. Her comrades were dead—and she had run away.

* * * *

Night came, blessing her with darkness. Velora ate a cracker, drank some water and listened for the slightest sound. At midnight, she heard something: a scratching on rock and then breathing. She leveled her weapon downhill towards inky darkness, held her breath and watched something crawl towards her. A face. Human. She called out softly, "Over here, quick, in the rocks!"

A boy, younger than herself and smeared with blood and dirt, scrambled up to her and collapsed at her side. "Oh, is it good to find someone else out here. I thought I was all alone." Immediately, with the sound of his voice and his delicate face, he reminded Velora of her younger brother.

"Where did *you* come from? I thought everyone else was dead!"

"I'm radioman for drop four. We got caught right in the middle. About half of our unit pulled back and got away with the rest of the drops, but I was forward with my corporal when the snakes started coming out of the ground all around us. They got the corporal, and I ran like hell. Most of their fire seemed directed towards the first units. Is that where you were?"

"Drop one. I'm Nett. Velora. Corporal. Your radio still work?" She pointed to the mound on his back.

"Haven't used it yet. Think we should try it?"

"No, we'll wait until light. The village is just over the hill, and I want to see what's going on first. You got a name?"

"Private Avan Hansold, ma'am. I've heard about you. Your old man's a general or something."

"Make that Vel or Corporal, Private. I'm not an officer."

Avan grimaced. "Sorry—Corporal."

Velora smiled faintly. "Yes, my father was a general, Gera Twenty-Third Skyhawks Division." *Survived the war only to die of a heart attack,* she thought. *Just as well. Now he doesn't have to know his daughter ran from a fight and left people to die.*

"First ones in on Torontos when the Kraa first invaded in full force. Boy, that must have been something."

"Yeah. Look, we've got to move to the top of the hill and see what's going on. You have maps?"

The boy nodded. "And a recorder. Sure looks bare up there. No cover at all."

"We'll drag some brush up with us, enough to cover up with if a Gull comes over."

They left the rocks and crawled on hands and knees to the top of the hill. There was no dried brush to be found, and they huddled in a shallow depression on the summit. It was totally exposed to view from above as they peered down towards the village. Velora scanned the visible and infrared spectrum with her binoculars, sweeping the valley. Below her, green figures moved on the hillsides, popping into the ground and out of view. In the village, two Chugs were moving into a street facing the valley, and a crude barricade had been restored there. Figures scurried around in the village square and then suddenly came together like a herd of animals being driven. Velora zoomed in with the binoculars and saw a group of adult villagers and children being herded by four Kraa. "Uh oh, they've got civilians rounded up. And the Kraa are going back into their spider traps again. Do they *really* think that can work a second time? What we need to do is call down some microwave and boil those hills."

"So give me a frequency," said Avan.

"No call now. I don't like those civvies being down there. Another attack and they'll all be killed for sure. But set it for thirty-five-fifty-five, and be ready."

"Yes, Corporal."

She looked at Avan over her shoulder. "Call me Vel. Look, we can clean those hills with a call, but I need to see what they're setting up in the village. We've got to get closer, maybe even into town. You with me for that?"

"Not too crazy about it, but you're the corporal."

"Good. Best to move in now and get settled before sunrise. Let's see those maps."

Velora pointed with gloved fingers. "Here, here and here is where they've dug spider traps. We'll want to bracket all these hills. Write down the coordinates now so you'll be ready."

Avan did as he was told, quickly yet carefully. Velora watched him work, struck again by how much he reminded her of her brother: quiet, thoughtful, contemplating his drawings or lost in music, his dream world taking him away from a father who talked only about war. Sweet Tal, who was supposed to be the warrior but couldn't be. And then the Kraa invasion of Torontos Colony had come, and there was a war for a daughter to fight.

It remained to be seen if Velora Nett could be the warrior her father had expected. At the moment, she was filled with doubt.

They crawled back to the base of the hill and circled towards the airfield, staying high enough to see the entire village. Small fires burned along the airfield, dimly lighting a line of Kraa shelters. Guards walked randomly around a trio of Gulls parked nearby, and two missile and Gatling-platformed Chugs blocked the main street of the town. Velora made notes on everything and checked coordinates on Avan's maps before they moved on. They came to a shed at the edge of town, behind a darkened house that had shown lights earlier in the evening after the Kraa had herded the civilians into it. There had been muffled shots, and later the Kraa had left. Something bad had happened in that place, but it was close. They hid in the shed until just before dawn, and then scuttled into the house in hopes of getting a better look at the streets. What they got was a look at another horror of war.

The stench hit them as they entered through the back door of the unlocked building and worked their way cautiously down a darkened hall, past a small kitchen heaped with debris and garbage. They entered a larger room at the front of the house. There were piles of bodies—men, women and children, Torontons, all of them third-wave humans with large, dark eyes engineered especially for the weakly-lit planet of a red dwarf. They had come here for a new life and found death instead, their blood now covering the floor and walls and windows of the house.

Avan turned and threw up in one corner of the room. He wretched and wretched until nothing more would come up, then wiped his mouth on his sleeve, ashamed, and moved near Velora, who was at a window facing the street. "Doesn't this have any effect on you, or is it just all in a day's work?" he asked bitterly.

"Lucky all I've had to eat in twelve hours is a cracker. Besides, seeing this makes it easier to kill Kraa when the time comes."

"Yeah? Well, it doesn't help me much, but then I'm not in for life. You career people are hard asses."

Velora looked at him sharply. "You don't know shit, Private. And what did you expect from the Kraa? They happen to be fond of killing, and right now I feel the same way."

"Oh, Jesus," said Avan.

"What the hell did you get into this war for?"

"Nobody asked me. I was drafted."

"Oh. Tough deal. But you and your radio are important to me right now, and I want you sticking it out, okay?"

"I'm still here, aren't I?"

"Get over here by the window, but keep low. There's a Chug up the street that can look right in here. Another one left of me, just sittin' there. We've got to get a message out about those spider traps, so start your recorder. It has to be quick to minimize interception, so set up the transmission for a half-second pulse."

Avan did as he was told. "If they've changed the entry code since yesterday, we're dead." He punched in the code letters, set the beeper to indicate a coming transmission and turned to hand Velora the recorder. She talked into it for nearly a minute, giving the coordinates of the hills, the approximate number of Kraa hidden there, the placement of Chugs in the town and the fact that they had found slaughtered citizens.

They waited. The engine of the Chug up the street suddenly growled into life. Velora peered over the window sill. "They're loading up. Supplies coming out of a house across the street, carried by civilians. Only a few Kraa guards—whoa!" She ducked her head down into the gloom. "Almost saw me. Looked right over here for a second. I see four guards, maybe a dozen civvies."

The radio chirped. Avan checked the return code showing on the display, then jacked in the recorder and with the push of a button transmitted Velora's one-minute message in a single half-second burst. In a few minutes there was another chirp as the return message arrived. Avan listened intently, Velora still watching the street. "Vel, I've got Colonel Andrist here. He says sit tight. They're comin' in at oh-six-hundred, and he's called in a microwave sweep from low orbit at that time."

"Okay, we stick it out here," said Velora. *And do what?* she thought. *How do I make up for running from a battle? Die?*

There was a sound from the kitchen at the back of the house, a rattling sound, and then a crunch, like someone stepping on broken glass. A shadow moved in the gloom of the hallway.

Velora swung the MAW-44 towards the hallway, pressing her back against a wall. "Avan, stay right where you are."

His eyes were the size of a credit coin.

The shadow came slowly down the hall and paused at the edge of the room. Large, liquid eyes gleamed dully in the pre-dawn glow. A tiny girl stood there, barefoot, filthy dress brief enough to show dirty arms and pencil-thin legs. Her thumb was in her mouth and she looked straight at Velora, considering her for a moment, and then she walked over to the far corner of the room to rummage around under a pile of broken bodies. She pushed and tugged at something, and came up with a blond-haired doll covered with blood. She hugged it to herself, and looked at Velora again with huge eyes.

"Oh my God," said Velora. "That must have been her mother."

The little girl started back towards the kitchen, but stopped when Velora beckoned to her. "Come here, darlin'. I'm a friend, and we won't hurt you.

Do you want something to eat? Here." Velora took a ration bar out of her pocket and held it out to the girl. The child hesitated for an instant, then walked boldly over to Velora and took the bar from her hand. Only at that instant did her thumb come out of her mouth—she tore the wrapper off with her teeth and began to eat. Velora stroked her hair, smiling at Avan. "Tough little kid, a real survivor. How long you been in here, hon'?"

The child remained silent and the ration bar disappeared quickly. She stood there waiting for more, and Velora fumbled in her pack. "Can you talk to me?"

"Here," Avan said, and he handed a ration bar over to the child, who took it without looking at him.

Silently, the doll hugged to her breast, eyes never leaving Velora's face, the little girl wolfed down the second ration bar. Velora sat the child down on the floor next to her and peeked out the window again. "Still loading. More guards now. I think they're getting ready to move out."

She checked her watch. "Less than an hour until the attack and all we can do is sit here."

"That's just fine with me," Avan said, a little too loudly for Velora's peace of mind. "All this draftee wants is to get home alive."

"And I don't? That's pretty stupid, private." Velora kept the tone of her voice amiable. "I think the only difference between us is commitment."

"Maybe. I don't have to prove anything to anybody in this war. I serve my time, keep my skin on and go home. You career people, this is your life—all this killing. I think it stinks."

"Keep it down," Velora said, staring at him coldly. "You think it's all about killing, is that it? Well, let me tell you, Private, this is my first major combat mission and I'm just as scared as you are, but I'm never going to get ahead in any game if I'm dead. As far as proving myself, I didn't do very well at that when I ran away from the fight yesterday," she whispered sharply.

Avan's cynical smile vanished in a blink. "Run away? What were you supposed to do, stay there and die? That's not commitment, that's stupid. People were running for their lives all over the place."

"Not corporals," said Velora, looking at the floor.

"Oh shit," mumbled Avan. "I rest my case."

Velora sniffed disdainfully and muffled her voice with a gloved hand. "You remind me of my brother, the would-be artist. Nice, gentle guy who hates everything my father ever stood for and isn't afraid to say so. He was the one who was supposed to be the soldier, not me. But he's not here and I am, and whatever happens, I'll do what I have to do. Got that?"

Seconds stretched to one horrible moment of stunned silence, and then Avan smiled at her sadly, hands playing with the controls on the radio.

"Yeah, I've got it. Among my several weaknesses, I also have a big mouth. I'm here too, Vel. I just want to go home alive," he whispered back.

"Okay, then—we just stay here quietly until our people are in the street. There won't be many Kraa out there once the hills are cleaned, but if we're spotted, it only takes one salvo from a Chug and they'll take us home in a bottle. And we've got this little girl here. She understands everything we're saying, you know?" She looked down at the tiny child snuggled against her, a death-grip on the doll with one hand and the thumb of the other firmly locked in a speechless mouth. The pretty head turned again towards the bloody remains in one corner of the room. Velora turned her around, hugged her tightly, looked into those sad, dark eyes and swallowed hard.

"God, Avan," she whispered, "she's only a baby."

Velora checked her watch. Only forty-five minutes until the microwave burn. But from the instant she looked at the watch, it was only fifteen minutes until their own private war with the Kraa began.

* * * *

In all the horror she had dozed, awakening with a start when Avan prodded her. He was right next to her under the window, whispering frantically into her ear, "Vel, wake up, there's screaming out in the street!"

She jumped to a crouch so quickly that the child nearly fell over, gasping in surprise. It was the first sound she had made. Velora peered over the window sill and saw a small group of civilians in a cluster in the middle of the street, surrounded by six armed Kraa. Women and two older children. The Kraa were poking them with their weapons, moving them across the street in a group and directly towards her hiding place. Down the street, the crew of the idling Chug was climbing up onto the machine and dropping down inside it. Directly in front of her, the engine of the previously silent Chug roared into life, and a snake-like arm reached out to slam shut the entrance hatch. The vehicle lurched forward and rolled quickly down the street to her left.

The cluster of terrified civilians drew nearer and Velora could hear the women pleading in their rough, Toronton dialect: "Please, leave us here and save your own lives. Not the children! Please, not the children!" A Kraa growl that was a laugh answered their cries for mercy, and Velora's face flushed with the sudden realization of what was about to take place. This room in which they had hidden themselves would soon be a killing ground again. The Kraa knew their enemy well: to kill civilians in the open would invite an immediate attack by microwave.

"Avan, take the girl to the kitchen and don't fire until I do. They're coming in the front, six of them and a bunch of civvies. Move!"

Avan grabbed the little girl's hand and duck-walked across body parts and the slippery floor, the child stumbling along behind him. They disappeared down the hallway. Velora backed into a corner by the window, the MAW-44 covering the front door.

There were footsteps by the door and hysterical screaming overwhelmed the growls of the Kraa. The door burst open and the civilians piled in, shrieking at the sight of what awaited them. The guards pushed in behind, teeth flashing from thick, reptilian faces. Women and children stumbled to the far corner of the room, huddling there as the guards, backs turned to Velora, raised their weapons, but at that instant one of the children saw her and pointed. All eyes moved towards Velora's grim face and the weapon she held as she snapped it on auto and sprayed the enemy with splinters of death. Four of the Kraa went down on their faces in a pulpy mess, and a five-foot section of wall disappeared in smoke. The fifth guard had stationed himself by the hallway, too close to the civvies for a clean shot, and now he was turning, bringing his weapon to bear on her. There was an explosion from the kitchen, and the Kraa's chest erupted in a fountain of blood and shredded tissue. Avan. First kill.

"Avan!"

"Yo!"

"Take them out back to the shed *now*." Velora jumped up to look outside and stared straight into the face of the sixth Kraa guard, who had remained outside. His claw was a blur, coming straight through the window and grabbing her by the throat, pulling her up on her toes as spots of colorful light danced before her eyes. She rammed the MAW's muzzle up under his chin and emptied the magazine into his nightmarish head.

"Out the back, out the back!" she screeched at the civilians and then coughed, grabbing at her throat to feel where the guard had clawed her.

The little girl darted into the room and threw herself into the arms of one of the women whom she apparently recognized, the woman sweeping her up with a tearful cry. Women and children stampeded down the hall and out the back door. Outside, the Chug that had been passing by had now stopped and was backing up across the street and turning towards her. No rotating turret, but it was quickly coming into position for a shot. Velora sprinted from the room and down the hall, slamming the back door closed as she exited and saw Avan herding the civvies into the nearby shed. "This way!" she called to him, and he ran to follow her as she moved away from the shed. They had gone only twenty yards when the house behind them erupted in a ball of fire and then shattered as flying embers.

Reaper fire ripped the ground around them and Velora cried out as a splinter tore across her left cheek. Avan was right behind her when she went in the front door of a house and straight out the back, temporarily hidden from the view of the advancing Chug. They entered the neighboring house from the back and crouched in the kitchen, Velora pulling the radio from Avan's back. "Tell them what's going on and get help! In a minute, we're outta here!"

Avan was sending frantically when she looked out the front window in time to see the house next door destroyed by withering fire from the Chug, which then turned and headed straight towards them. It pulled up close, nearly on the porch of the building. "Thermite!" Velora screamed. "Lock and load, and get out of here!" She pulled a magazine of Red-Dot thermite cartridges from her belt, slapped it into the MAW and leaped back to the kitchen, where Avan was struggling to load up the radio. "Leave it! Let's go!"

Avan followed her out the door. She turned right and crept up alongside the building. The Chug's rumble vibrated up through the soles of their boots. She turned over her shoulder and mouthed, "Get anybody?"

"Think so," Avan mouthed back.

Velora peered around the corner of the building, pulled back and yelled, "Follow me!"

The explosion was deafening as the Chug fired, but by then they were climbing up onto it and the building they had left disappeared in flames. Velora stuck her MAW muzzle into a forward port and fired three times. Screaming came from inside the chug. "Get the hatch, get the hatch!" she yelled.

Avan scrambled to the top hatch as it popped open, a claw outstretched. He pointed his MAW straight down and emptied the entire magazine of thermite cartridges into the living space of the Chug. Flame shot skyward and the claw disappeared. The machine's surface was suddenly too hot to stand on, but as Avan clambered down he yelled as blood spattered from his left leg below the hip. He fell heavily at Velora's feet. "Oh shit, oh shit, oh shit!" he cried, rolling in the red dirt. A Reaper had hit him from the side at close range, well above the knee.

A Kraa came around the Chug, his eyes turned down to sight on Avan, and Velora shot him with a Red-Dot at point blank range, the heavy body flashing to ashes in seconds.

Flames from Kraa cinders licked at her boots as she stepped around the Chug and saw a wedge formation of infantry moving towards her from the airfield. She emptied the Red-Dot magazine at them, five of the heat-seeking thermite projectiles striking home, but still the line of shrieking creatures came on. One hundred yards away, then seventy, then fifty. She fired furiously, mindlessly, magazine after magazine, then scrabbled at her belt and found nothing there. Avan moaned as she tore his ammunition belt from him and grabbed up his MAW. By the time she aimed it, the nearest Kraa was only twenty yards away. She sprayed their ranks with Red-Dots and

Reapers, weapon on full automatic, the Kraa now stumbling over the bodies of their dead but still coming, screaming just as when they had come at her from the hills. Save one round for yourself, she remembered.

As she grabbed her last magazine, the ground around the Kraa erupted in a wall of dirt, pieces of shattered bodies flying in all directions. Two D-7s swooped low overhead, spraying the street with their Gatlings, on course for the airfield and releasing their missiles a second later. Flames from exploding Gulls belched into the sky as the two-place fighters turned and came back to tear up the street one more time. Velora crouched behind the Chug. They passed over her, veering sharply left and right over a burning Chug at the edge of the village. Clouds of steam surged up from the hills, punctuated with small jets she knew were microwaved Kraa exploding like boiling water balloons in their spider traps. Through the roiling steam she saw the APDPs coming in, dropping wave after wave of troops that raced towards her. Only then did she glance up the street, and, seeing no life there, got down on her knees beside Avan.

One leg and side were soaked in blood, and his face was ashen-grey. He mumbled something incoherent and his eyes rolled around, not seeing her. "Avan, they're here, they're here! Hang on!" She slapped his face once, gently, then a second time, hard. "Don't you *dare* die on me now! Don't you DARE!"

* * * *

Colonel Andrist looked up from a table heaped with paper as Velora entered his Quonset and saluted him smartly. He returned the salute and smiled. "Good to see you alive, Corporal. For a minor operation, this thing turned into quite a mess that could have been avoided with some accurate reconnaissance. Still have all your parts?"

Velora took a deep breath, her intestines a tangled knot sending pain messages to every nerve in her body. "Sir—there's something I have to tell you, and it's not easy. But I have to do it, sir, with your permission." She clutched at her pants to keep her hands from shaking.

Andrist leaned back in his chair and made a teepee with his hands in front of his mouth. "Go on," he said.

"During the attack yesterday, when we were surrounded and the Kraa were all coming at us from the hills, sir, I—I ran. I ran from the fight, sir. I have no excuse. It was—a reaction. I felt I had to get out of there, and I did."

Andrist chuckled. "Right into the enemy camp, from the sound of it. Bad thing for them." His smile faded as he saw the look on her face. "What's your point, Corporal?"

Velora was near tears. "I acted in a cowardly manner, sir. That's my point." *And that is the end of my career,* she thought.

Andrist sighed. "Tell me what happened. Everything."

And so she told him everything, from the moment she fled until the time she was fighting from behind a burned-out Chug, expecting to die.

"Now, I want you to think about what you just said, and tell me if those were the acts of a coward."

"Sir, I—"

"They were not, Corporal. I had three hundred people in that attack yesterday, and the only reason any of them came back was because the squad leaders knew when to get the hell out of there and stay alive to fight today. That's just smart, Corporal. You stayed alive, and today you engaged the enemy on your own terms. And shot the hell out of them. And saved lives. *That's* why I'm putting you in for Officers Training School just as soon as I can find the damn form in this mountain of paperwork. Expect your orders to be cut within a week. You have a lot to learn, but you will be one damn fine officer someday. Anything else?"

Velora stared in disbelief. "No, sir. Uh—thank you, sir."

"Good. That private who was with you is outside. I'll decorate the both of you when we get back in orbit." Andrist stood up, reached across the table and touched her bloody cheek. "Nice wound there. Rub a little salt in it, should make an attractive scar. Let the troops know their officer has seen combat. Dismissed."

Velora turned to leave, still stunned as Andrist said softly, "If the General had seen you out there today, he would've bawled like a baby."

* * * *

Avan was lying on a stretcher near the Quonset, attended by a medic. Velora rushed to him and fell to her knees, shouting at the medic, "Is he all right? Is he all right?"

The medic looked bored. "He's going home. My guess is he's got a five-year limp ahead of him."

"There goes my dancing career," said Avan weakly. "Guess I'll be an architect instead. Hey, look who's here!"

Velora looked up, finding herself surrounded by the group of Torontons they had saved from slaughter. The little girl was with them, and she stepped forward with a shy smile. "Her name is Myreika," one of the women said, "and she wishes to thank you."

The girl put her bloody arms around Velora's neck, and pressed against her.

"Oh, darlin', you're okay, you're okay." Velora hugged the child fiercely, then looked down at Avan's grinning face.

"Tough guy," said Avan.

Velora reached down and squeezed his shoulder. "Yeah. And you, too."

BILLY BOB AND THE BISON

Heading west on I90 and Missoula, Montana still showing in his rear-view mirror, Billy Bob Benson suddenly realized he was terrible thirsty. Even a coke would do. No booze; he'd taken the cure four years ago, and life was good. But it was July and dry hot and he'd driven straight through from Butte, the new contracts tucked away in the briefcase beside him. *Insurance salesman extraordinaire*, he thought, *now that I'm sober.* Something to celebrate, with old friends—and a coke. Rattlesnake was minutes ahead; he'd stop by Ernie's, see some of the old gang, laugh about crazy past times when the blackouts took him on meandering routes back to Spokane. No more. One coke, then straight home. Billy Bob Benson was a new man.

He walked into Ernie's at two in the afternoon, and it was like coming home. It was Saturday, and the place was filled, a few familiar faces in the gloom. Mac, Harry and Del were playing pool in the back, and Ernie waved to him from behind the bar. "Hey, Billy Bob, where you been keeping yourself, man?"

Billy Bob slid onto a stool and stuck out a hand, the big, red-faced man pumping it vigorously. "Man, it's been, let's see, nearly four years. How ya doin'?"

"Great, Ernie, just great. Business has never been better."

"Well what can I get you?" asked Ernie. "First one's on me."

"Just a diet coke, Ernie. Got a three hour drive ahead of me."

Ernie looked at him incredulously. "A coke? You gotta be kiddin'. You take the cure, or somethin'?"

"You've got it, Ernie. Nearly four years sober, now."

"Well I'll be," said Ernie. "No more dancin' on the tables, huh?"

"It was either that or die," said Billy Bob. Ernie brought him a coke.

"It happens to the best of 'em. Never figured you, though. You sure could put it away. Fun times. Say, whatever happened to that buffalo of yours?"

Billy Bob sipped his coke. "What?"

"You remember; that huge bison bull you bought from Nathan Red Deer the last time you were in here. Funniest night we ever had, watching you trying to get that critter into your truck."

"Jesus, Ernie," said Billy Bob. "I don't know what you're talking about."

"God, that was a hoot," said Ernie, grinning at a memory. "How the hell could you forget something like that?"

Try a blackout, thought Billy Bob.

"You and Nathan was drinkin' together, you payin' as usual, and Nathan wanted another pitcher of beer. You'd already bought him two, and that was enough for you. Well, Nathan he got a little belligerent and then he pleaded and sudden he says, "I go me a full-growed bison bull in my truck. I'll sell him to ya for two pitchers of beer.' You agreed to it, and we all went outside. Sure enough, there's a ton of mean animal standing in the back of his pickup." Ernie looked around the room.

"Damn, none of 'em here now. Must have been forty people in the place that night. Nathan stayed inside to drink his beer, but the rest of us stayed outside to watch you try to load that monster into your own pickup. You're what, maybe a hundred-forty pounds dripping wet with a soaking towel around you? Oh, what a sight that was. What a sight. Hee, hee!" Ernie wiped his eyes with a towel.

Billy Bob shook his head, smiling faintly. No memories at all.

"We got some planks and made a ramp. Nathan had a rope on him, and you started tuggin' and kickin' and cussin'. Just pissed that bull off good; he nearly kicked and butted the hell out of you, but you got him out of that truck. Man, I was servin' drinks in the *street*! But there was no way that animal was gonna get in your truck. No, sir. A dozen bruises later you had him tied to your trailer hitch. 'Tell Nathan to drop by for buffalo burgers if he gets to Spokane,' you said, then you roared away with that big bull trottin' along behind."

"Well, he sure wasn't there when I got home," said Billy Bob, "and I don't remember any of it, Ernie. You sure you're not bull-shitten me?"

Ernie howled with laughter. "That's good, Billy Bob. That's *good*! How could I make up somethin' like that? No, blasted as you were, you got your bison and Nathan got his beer. Thing probably snapped the rope. They only go about forty tops, you know. If he'd stayed on there'd been nothing left but bones, the way you took out of here. Hoo, that was a funny night for *all* of us!"

Billy Bob didn't think it was funny. He gulped the last of his coke. "Well, it isn't the only thing I ever lost when I was drinking. Don't know what the hell I'd done with the thing anyway. Look, Ernie, I gotta say hello to some folks and get back to Spokane. Thanks for the drink. I'll treat you to a buffalo steak if I ever find that bull."

Ernie laughed. "Yeah, you do that. And don't wait so long to come by again."

Ernie pumped his hand again. Billy Bob went over to say hello to Mac, Harry and Del and make some small talk. He left the bar at two-thirty, an easy drive to Spokane in time for dinner, but he accelerated to seventy-five and held it there as he thought.

That bison bull was his property. He had paid two pitchers of beer for it. He wanted it back.

* * * *

In three weeks he was in trouble with Ester.

"You're going out *again*? What am I supposed to do, stay home and keep a light burning in the window? I work, too, Billy. Weekends are supposed to be for *us*."

"I invited you to come along," said Billy Bob, pouting over his coffee. "Get out of the house and see some nice country."

"We've done that two weekends in a row, and driving round-trip to Helena is not my idea of fun. We're not sight-seeing, we're visiting with all your old bar friends and looking for a damned buffalo you can't even remember buying." Ester slammed the dish-washer shut and wiped her hands on a towel, her mouth a thin line. "Same old compulsive behavior, just like when you were drinking. Just because you had to drop by Ernie's. Can't you forget about it? That animal is four years gone, God knows where, and you're in a constant fret about it, pouring over maps, figuring. How many ways are there to get back to Spokane? Don't you remember anything?"

"Come on, Ester," said Billy Bob, "just one more time. We'll take the tent, drive up to Flathead Lake, maybe rent a boat. You like being on the water."

Her face softened. "Really? No my sitting in the car while you yak it up in the bars? No crawling along the highways, looking at every animal that moves?"

"Sure," said Billy Bob, "and we'll eat out all the way. No cooking, Ester."

"Well," she said, "alright, one last time. But this is the *last* time. And I want to go dancing; you haven't taken me dancing in months, Billy Bob."

"You're on," he said, and got up to hug her, feeling her go rigid in his embrace, then relaxing. She patted him on the back. "Okay, okay," she said.

They packed two suitcases, loaded them into the car along with sleeping bags, pads and a little, dome tent, and were on I90 by nine in the morning, joining the hoards of locals on their weekend pilgrimage to the lakes of Idaho and Montana. Solid traffic to Coeur d'Alene, the usual assortment of RV tanks hanging up the flow, the ever-present tailgaters behind him. A blond girl in a red Mercedes nearly went into a tail-spin when he flashed the brake lights at her. She honked, changed lanes and sped by; giving him the finger, "Bitch," he muttered, and Ester frowned at him. *Too damned many people in the world*, he thought, and then accelerated again.

When they turned north near Missoula, he was in a dark mood, slowing down, eyes darting left and right at cattle scattered along the hills. Ester groaned. "Oh no, Billy. You promised!"

"Just take a minute, hon." He left her sitting in the car in hot sunlight.

They didn't even remember him in Star's, the bartender giving him a hostile look when he asked if anyone had seen a bison bull in the surrounding hills.

Next stop Saint Ignatius. Same reception. Twice. When he came back to the car the second time, Ester was gone, and for one horrible instant he thought she'd left him. Pretty soon, though, she was coming back from a trip to the ladies' room at a gas station across the street, scowling, getting back into the car without a word and burying herself in a magazine.

It was three in the afternoon when they drove into Ronan and pulled up in front of Cutter's Bar. Ester didn't even look up when he got out. "One more minute, hon. I remember this place; they're sure to remember me.:

And they did.

The bartender was a three-hundred pound behemoth named Mick. He was at the cash register when Billy Bob slid up onto a stool. The big man turned with a smile that faded when they locked eyes. "Hi," said Billy Bob. "Remember me?"

"Sure do," growled the man. He turned back to the cash register, and opened it. "Never thought I'd see you again. I got somethin' that belongs to you."

He's got my bull!

Mick took a piece of paper out of the cash register, lumbered over, pushed it across the bar to Billy Bob. "This is yours. Nearly five years old. I oughta charge you interest."

Billy Bob looked at the paper. "I ran up a tab here?"

"That's your signature, aint' it? Let's see your money; cash, no cards."

"A hundred and forty-two dollars?" gasped Billy Bob.

"Like I said, no interest. I'm in a generous mood. Pay up." Cigar breath wafted into Billy Bob's face—so near.

Heart pounding, Billy Bob dug out his wallet, pushed twenties and ones across the bar. "Well—sure—I mean that's one of the things I came in here for. I just didn't remember it was so much. Sorry about the delay; I travel a lot, only got back up again because—"

"—Yeah, sure," said Mick, grabbing up the money in a big fist. He made his cash register deposit, then turned to another customer at the end of the bar, talking in low tones. Both men glared at Billy Bob.

Billy Bob checked his wallet. Eight dollars. He pocketed it, walked straight outside to the car and got in. Ester didn't even look at him. "Had to make an amend in there," he said.

"How much?" asked Ester sullenly.

He told her.

Two miles out of town, Ester began crying softly.

They drove straight through Pablo and reached Flathead Lake at four. For three hours they drove up and down the west side of the lake. All the campgrounds were full, all motel and resort rooms taken. By the time they came back to Henley's Resort the boats were put up for the night, and they discovered the regularly scheduled band had been cancelled out. They ate dinner in silence, Billie Bob paying with a credit card, and then they sat by the lake until well after dark, again in silence.

That night, they slept in the car.

In the morning they drove straight back to Spokane.

There was no sign of a bison bull anywhere to be seen.

* * * *

Ester had forgiven him by Wednesday. He'd hit three new contracts that week, working until midnights to get the papers ready. Not once had he mentioned the bison, working hard in good humor from his continuing business success. Her birthday was on Friday and he'd made reservations at Patsy Clark's for an elegant dinner. A new band had opened at Spokane House, and he'd promised her dancing. So when he left for Missoula early Friday morning she gave him a long, warm kiss that stimulated second thoughts about leaving early and he was still thinking about it when he hit the freeway.

He made the three hour drive without so much as a thought about the bison and finished his business by noon. On the way out of Missoula he was thinking only about a good steak and Ester swaying with him on a dance floor overlooking the city—

—until he passed Ernie's Bar in Rattlesnake.

I'll treat you to a buffalo steak if I ever find that bull.

He'd made a promise, a promise that wouldn't be kept because he hadn't tried hard enough. The obsession returned with a rush: laughter, the look on Ernie's face, the humiliation he'd felt while Ernie was describing the drunken entertainment he'd provided the patrons that night. Not remembering any of it. All in the past, he reminded himself. *You don't do those things anymore. Part of staying sober is letting go of things you can't change.* "Yeah, but part of it is changing what I can," he said out loud. For an hour he wrestled with it, finally concluding he'd done everything he could. He was ready to let go of it.

And then, just west of Lookout Pass, he saw the sign for the secondary south to Fernwood and on to Lewiston.

He turned off I90 without thinking, sat at a stop sign by the overpass. *I couldn't have. Not in a blackout.* He got out his map. Fernwood, Bovill, then Lewiston, another secondary breaking north along the east shore of Lake Coeur d'Alene back to I90. It could have happened in a blackout. Anything could happen. An old man had told him once about coming out of a blackout driving on the railroad tracks with the lights of a freight train coming at him.

He turned south and drove hard. One last try, and then he'd let go.

Rolling hills and cattle. His eyes swept left and right, but he kept up his speed. It was now two-thirty, plenty of time yet to make that date with Ester. If he didn't, there wouldn't be forgiveness this time. He'd let her down too many times with his insanity. *So why aren't you still on I90?* "Because I've got to know I tried everything," he said to his car. "I've got to know that."

He passed the turn-off to Coeur d'Alene, drove straight through Fernwood and checked his watch. Three o'clock. *I'll turn back at Bovill. That's gotta be it; that's when I've done all I can.* It suddenly occurred to him that Ester was more important to him than finding that bull. His new life, sober, and his marriage, those were real, in his grasp, priceless, his pursuit of an animal he didn't even remember a crazy compulsion without value or meaning. *Still acting like a drunk, Billy Bob. Grab onto what you have, and hold onto it!*

It was four miles to Bovill. Three-thirty. He slowed, fighting an impulse to turn around. Three miles, then two, ranches on both sides of the road, cattle grazing, a hand painted sign hanging from a wire fence.

BEEFALO MEAT—NEXT RIGHT

He braked hard, nearly sliding off the road, got out and walked back to the sign, looked out at cattle staring back at him. Herford's? Maybe. Billy Bob knew nothing about cattle, but Herford's he'd seen plenty of and these animals were different: same faces, but scruffy looking, with darker splotches on their flanks. There was not a bison in sight. Across the pasture he could see a barn and a house. Next right. He looked at the sign again, just as a battered pickup pulled up behind his car.

"You interested in some beefalo meat, there?" The man inside the truck leaned across the seat, smiling.

"Yeah," said Billy Bob.

"Well follow me," said the man, and the truck started off slowly along the road.

Billy Bob jumped into his car and followed the truck to a dirt road, turning right towards the house and barn he's seen. The house was well kept, freshly painted. A woman was in the yard, hanging clothes on a long line and on the front porch was an enormous freezer with a sign saying: BEEFALO MEAT HERE. They stopped in front of the porch, getting out and shaking hands. "Billy Bob Benson," he said, putting on his best insurance salesman's smile, "from Spokane."

"Arlen Saasted," said the man, pumping his hand. "Now, we got chuck roast and steaks and ground round. What's your pleasure?"

"Maybe first you can tell me what it is; Beefalo, I mean."

"Beef and Bison, pure bred," said the man, "all nice and lean, and scarce, and raised right here." His arm swept out towards the surrounding pasture land.

"I don't see any bison," said Billy Bob.

"'Fraid you won't. I only had one bull, and he died last season. Poor old boy never could walk too good, but he sure got along with those cows. He left me with plenty of breeding stock."

Billy Bob laughed. "Where in the world did you buy a bison bull?"

Arlen took some Copenhagen from his overall pocket and fingered a pinch between cheek and gum. "Didn't. He just wandered in, let's see, that's early spring four years ago. Must have broken out somewhere, still had a rope around his neck. Put an ad in the paper, but never got a call. Went right through the fence, getting to those cows. Chased him around for a day, then let'im be. Only had twenty head out there; the main herd is in the south pasture. You ever try beefalo? Real tasty, a novelty, you know? The resorts pay me a good price for it. Say, I've got the old boy's head mounted in the house. Want to see him?"

"Sure," said Billy Bob, and they went inside.

Hardwood floors and old furniture with doilies on the arms everywhere, and over a fading couch was mounted the massive head of a bison bull, shiny black horns and brown eyes that seemed to follow Billy Bob accusingly as he stepped up for a close look. "Well I'll be, there he is, alright." He lifted his hand to stroke the coarse hair on the animal's head. "Sorry, old guy."

"Aw, he was an old bull," said Arlen, "but he had some good years here, and he started a new business for me. Now, what can I get you?"

"Well," said Billy Bob, pulling out his wallet, "let's have four nice steaks and a couple of pounds of ground meat."

"You've got it," said Arlen, and they went outside, Billy Bob stopping at the door for one last look at the shaggy head on the wall. "You were better off here," he said, then closed the screen door and watched Arlen select and package his meat. The bill was thirty six dollars, and he didn't mind paying it one bit.

"Thanks, Arlen," he said. "I can't remember seeing a bison head so close up before."

Arlen loaded the packages into his arms. "You want more of this; you know where to get it. Spokane aint' that far from here."

Billy Bob thanked him again, got in his car and drove away, accelerating hard when he hit the secondary. Four o'clock and plenty of time. A faint, meaty odor permeated the inside of the car, and Billy Bob smiled. A steak and some ground meat for Ernie, the rest for Ester and himself, and the story about the bison bull was complete. He had it all with him in the front seat. Yessir, he had it all, now.

He got back to Spokane with half an hour to spare.

Ester wasn't even worried about him. And she looked gorgeous for her birthday.

—This one is for Andy.

CLIMBING WITH ELLEN

Jenny Dunn was a hundred feet down from the summit spire of Harrison's Pinnacle when things started going wrong. She was making an easy descent along a shallow vertical crack when the rope suddenly went slack as she leaned back to move her left foot off a small nubbin. Her right foot slipped off the rock and she crashed stiff-legged to a wide ledge eight feet below, sending a shock wave through her body that snapped her teeth together to bite her tongue.

"What the hell was *that* all about?" she asked aloud.

The rock didn't answer, but held her firmly. Her tongue felt swollen; she tasted blood, and gently sucked on it. The fall had taken her slightly off course. She would have to climb up from the ledge, and then make a traverse on narrow, down sloping slabs to reach the familiar route she had used for the ascent. Between the traverse and the ground below was fifteen hundred feet of clear air, and the fall had wiped out her trust in the permanent anchor point near the summit. Below her was another ledge, wider than the one she was on, but there was no obvious route beyond it. The distance was marginally large for her rope. Sliding off the end of the rope would be a bad end to a highly successful day, but an even worse fate would be hanging helplessly at the end of the rope, waiting to inflate the male egos of a mountain rescue team.

Jenny scowled at the passive rock, popped a piece of hard peppermint candy into her mouth and was sucking on it thoughtfully when she suddenly saw a new route. It would take her even further away from familiar territory, but looked solid and the exposure was less than the other alternatives she had to consider. It was a new route, and there would be a greater chance for errors. *Fish or cut bait time, Jen. You want to be a name climber? Now's the chance. Cap the solo ascent off with pioneering a new descent route on the same day and people will be talking about you.*

Jenny Dunn clipped in and climbed up smoothly and spider-like towards her right, using small flakes for foot and finger holds. One move flowed smoothly into the next, athletic precision developed over years of hard work and dedication. The climbing machine was working well again, and wished for an audience. She set up a belay point at the base of a thumb-like spire with a wide, vertical crack reaching up from a flat shelf that circled out of view towards the sun. The shelf would start the route and, close-up, looked even more appealing.

She started forward to examine it more closely, but a sudden, sharp tug on her harness pulled her backwards. Off balance, she grasped frantically for hand holds on the steep rock and fell to her knees. Her slide stopped only a foot from where she had fallen, and she pressed her face against the rough rock, fingers burning as adrenalin pumped through her body. Her breath came in short rapid gasps, and the moment of fear disgusted her. *You're hyperventilating, stupid! Stop it!*

She held her breath for several seconds as her heart began to pound more slowly. Fear changed to anger, she turned sharply to glare towards her belay point. The rock, and even the air, was silent. She pulled on the rope, straightened out a villainous snarl, re-tied it to her harness and popped another candy into her mouth, crushing it with one bite. She had begun to turn upwards again when there was a new sound that stopped her abruptly. Something was moving above her near the top of the crack.

At first it sounded like a small animal with tiny claws, scratching on sandpaper. She listened quietly, frozen to the rock, and swallowed hard. A shower of dirt came down the crack, followed by a grinding sound, the rubbing of rock against rock. Jenny began to back away towards her belay point, then froze again as the rock she gripped tightly trembled against her fingers, and something heavy came crashing down the crack, pushing a jet of dirt and skree ahead of it. Dust filled her nostrils, choking her. Three watermelon-size boulders belched from the crack and sailed in graceful parabolic trajectories towards the ground far below.

Jenny coughed twice, and then moved without hesitation while the crack continued to spew dirt and skree in a slow stream clattering down the wall below her. Throwing her coiled rope up over her head and down around one shoulder she wrenched her anchor point free and flattened herself under a protective overhang on the shelf. She lay there for several minutes, feeling the coolness of the place. *Everything is falling apart.* For the first time in her life, Jenny Dunn felt the near presence of panic, and realized that taking the route she had contemplated would have been her last act in life.

She had left the summit less than an hour before. The climb up had been her best effort yet, with flawless technique and supreme confidence in herself; the culmination of years of hard training under the watchful eyes and caustic advice of the predominantly male climbing community. She had been filled with exhilaration as she proudly dug out the summit register at the bottom of a small cairn, and signed in.

Jenny Dunn, Whitewater, Wisconsin
Solo ascent, route 5, August 7, 2010, 12:45 P.M.
Ascent time: 7 hours, from Granite Creek Meadow.

Let others now do what I have done today.

That had been an hour ago. Her problem now was to pioneer a new route down, but the anticipation of doing it was destined to be short-lived. She had crawled only a few yards along the shelf and around a sharp corner when she saw the first piton.

Jenny felt immediate disappointment. The route, at least this far, had been done before. She crawled up to the piton and pulled on it. The crack was bad, and the piton came out easily. Standard stuff, although people didn't use them a lot anymore, since they damaged the rock. But the letter E had been engraved just below the eye of the piece. *Owner's initial.* She clipped it to a carabiner on her sling and moved on along the shelf. *Still a chance the route hasn't been taken all the way down.* The shelf was now like a highway, wide enough for two people to crawl side-by-side, and she followed it for several yards out into the sunlight and back into the shade of a second overhang. She brushed some skree off the shelf as she moved ahead, and it clattered on the rocks below. Mentally she timed the fall. Far enough to die.

She crawled out into the sunlight again and found a second piton hammered into the shelf itself. It was in deep, but came out after several sharp taps with her hammer. The letter E was there again, and her disappointment mounted. But there was no turning back at this point. Time had become a factor, and she felt a growing commitment to follow the route all the way. But what she saw ahead of her was not encouraging. The shelf was beginning to narrow, and was heavily covered with loose skree. Above it, the wall looked brown and rotten, full of holes and laced with large cracks partially filled with rocky debris. *Bad rock, and lousy for anchor points.*

The conservative part of her mind took immediate command. She thought about using the piton she had just pulled, but her hand responded by clipping the piece to her sling. It seemed like the right thing to do, but the sudden impulse felt strange to her. She placed two wired chocks on the wall, one low and one high, then threaded her rope through them and began to pick her way lightly across the shelf, balancing herself with one hand on the wall. Pieces of skree twisted and slid beneath her feet. *A bad place for my smooth-soled shoes*, she thought, but progressed cat-like for several yards and around another corner as the shelf narrowed steadily. The shelf began sloping downwards steeply. She paused, looked up sharply and jerked backwards a step. Three feet ahead of her, the shelf disappeared.

Beneath a high, fan-shaped overhang, a twelve foot section of the shelf had broken away from the wall. Jenny cautiously peered over the edge. A tangled mass of rubble lay two hundred feet below on a plateau that widened in the direction she had been moving. *Too far for my rope.* She would either have to go all the way back, or climb up. But the rock looked rotten. She tested it several places with a piton. The rock crumbled into tiny fragments as she tried to hammer the piece in. It was a no-go. With mounting frustration she kicked loose skree off of the shelf and stamped one foot hard, then froze.

The shelf beneath her had moved downwards.

Her first instinct was to lunge away from the end of the shelf. The whole thing could go any second, taking her down with it. Her anchor point was several yards behind her. If the shelf went she could see herself swinging back and forth along the wall below, a long human pendulum, swaying for eternity with blood pooling in her legs and slow suffocation coming with the tight squeezing of her harness. A little like being crucified, she thought. She inched her way back along the shelf, feeling it move with each short step, and scraping off the skree in front of her as she progressed. Showers of skree crackled on the rocks below.

"Hey! Stop it up there!"

Jenny froze in mid-step. The shout had come from directly below her. The voice was raspy, high-pitched and angry; it was a woman's voice. She glanced down and saw only boulders and skree in a jumbled heap. But there *was* something else, a narrow swath, like the shiny trail of an enormous snail, looping out into the boulder field and back again towards the wall below her. It gleamed in the late afternoon sun. She took another step and the shelf groaned softly, and there was a new shower of skree.

"Damn it, can't you hear me up there! Yell rock or something when you kick that stuff off. It's coming down here all over the place." The pitch of the voice had risen even higher.

Jenny swallowed hard, her throat dry, and felt shame at violating such a fundamental climbing rule. "Sorry, but I've got a hairy problem here, and I didn't know anybody was around." She looked down again, but couldn't see the wall directly below her.

"I can't see you," she called, her voice firmer now.

There was a liquid chuckle from below, then a deep gurgling cough that gave Jenny a queer feeling in her stomach.

"You bet you can't see me, kid, with all that crap you're kicking off. I'm hiding out for the duration. Wait awhile and you and that whole shelf will be down here with me." There was another chuckle.

"All of a sudden the rock turned rotten on me. I've got to get back to route five." Jenny took another short step on the shelf, putting her foot carefully on top of the skree cover. The shelf held steady.

"It's a long way back to route five, kiddo, and an even longer down climb after that. You'll be racing the sun after a while. Have a lamp with you?"

"Didn't think I'd need one," said Jenny, and she took another step. The shelf was definitely steady now. "I expected to be just about down by now. After that it's only an hour walk back to my camp." Another step, and then she stopped, curious about something the woman had said.

"You know route five?"

"I remember most of it pretty well. Been awhile, though." There was another liquid cough, muffled, below the shelf.

"You're a climber? I still can't see you." Jenny leaned out slowly over the edge of the shelf and looked down at the base of the wall. It was covered by dark shadows as the sun began its descent in the afternoon sky, and the glistening trail across the rocks had disappeared. The woman's voice came softly from the shadows far below, yet seemed close.

"*Was* a climber, and good at it too, but I got hurt bad—don't get around too good anymore. But I keep in touch with things." The woman's voice faltered as she spoke. Sadness, perhaps bitterness was there.

"You're Jenny Dunn, right?"

Jenny was startled by the sound of her own name. "Yes. How do you know that?"

There was a pause, and another muffled cough before the answer came. "Heard the guys talking about you in camp last night. Knew you'd be up here today. You were trying out a solo on route five of Harrison's."

Jenny felt her face flush with anger. "I didn't just try it."

"You made it?"

"Yes," said Jenny firmly, and she looked at her watch. It was time to end the conversation, and retrace her route back.

"Look, I've really got to—"

"I'm glad you made it, Jenny," the woman said quickly. "It's personal to me. I mean it's great that a woman did it first. I tried it myself a couple of years ago, and that's when I got hurt. I came down the route you're on now, but without a summit climb to talk about. You should feel great about today."

The woman sounded old and sick, Jenny thought. "Say," she called, "when you came down did you leave any hardware up here?" She peered over the shelf again. Down in the deepening shadows, something moved.

"Just a couple of pitons. I came down in kind of a hurry." Another chuckle. "You found them?"

"I found two pitons with the letter E engraved on them."

There was more movement, a dark mass in the shadows. Someone was watching her now.

"Thanks, Jen. They're mine. The E is for Ellen. I never thought I'd get them back, some little mementos of my last climb. Can you take them down to camp for me? I'll pick them up later. Appreciate it."

"Sure, Ellen, but I've got to move now or I'll never get back to camp."

Jenny straightened up and then took two light steps back towards the anchor for her rope.

"Don't go back that way, Jenny," said Ellen. "You're nearly down now. All you have to do is get across that break in the shelf. Look beyond it—the way is clear all the way down."

Jenny stopped, and sighed. "The rock is rotten up here, Ellen. I wouldn't trust anything to hold me if the shelf went."

Ellen's voice came back strong and urgent. "You're being too conservative. Try more cracks. Some of them are good. A two foot jump from the shelf to that overhang will give you good hand holds and you can hand-over-hand it across the break. Look ahead—see how the shelf slants down? It gets narrower, but goes all the way down to the plateau, and the rock gets better too. You can be back in camp in less than an hour."

"You *are* persuasive, Ellen," said Jenny. *But is she accurate?* She looked towards the overhang and beyond it. Past the break the shelf narrowed to three boot widths, but was clearly visible as it sloped down towards the plateau.

"Trust me, Jenny. I know the route cold. One tricky traverse and it's quick back to camp. Nobody has done it since that shelf broke off. The guys say you're really good. It should be easy for you. I can belay you across the break and—"

Ellen's voice had risen with enthusiasm, but suddenly broke into a racking, gurgling series of cough.

Jenny smiled at the absurdity of the suggestion. Even if her rope could reach the rocks below, which it couldn't, how safe would she feel being belayed by a sick, old woman who hid herself in the shadows and dreamed of climbing days long past? *And how did she get up here so high today?*

"Look, Ellen, I really appreciate your advice. You're probably right, and I'm going to try it, but I don't think the idea of you belaying me is a very—"

"Oh I don't mean a physical belay, Jen," laughed Ellen, "but I can still talk you down safely with what I know. See that nubbin on the overhang? When you jump, aim your left hand for the nubbin. The overhang edge curls up to the right of it. It'll be like hanging from a high bar. Just aim for the edge of the overhang. It's flat beyond that." Her voice was now enthusiastic, and excited.

Jenny found two good cracks, placed wired chocks in them, and hooked up for the traverse. She found the nubbin on the overhang and focused on it. Why did she trust Ellen so much? It made no sense, but somehow she believed that behind the nubbin was a good hold and that the traverse would go as Ellen had said. She felt relaxed, and ready for the attack. And Ellen's voice came as a shout from below.

"Do it, Jenny!"

One short step, then two more in rapid succession, her knees flexed, and the shelf was beginning to move. Skree slipped beneath her feet. There was a groaning from the rock and she was weightless in air, her left arm thrust out towards the overhang, and her right arm moving up rapidly in support. The palms of her hands collided flat against the edge of the overhang, and she was squeezing down—hoping.

The hand holds were there.

"Right on, Jen," said Ellen.

Two lateral swings and, filled with elation, Jenny stood on solid rock, pulling in her rope.

"Nice belay, Ellen," she called, smiling.

"Off belay, Jenny," said Ellen. "You did great."

For one short moment, they had climbed together.

Jenny coiled her rope, draped it over one shoulder and searched the shadows below. There was no movement, no sound.

"Ellen?" she asked softly.

Silence.

"It's safe to come out now, and I'd like to meet you face to face. You helped me here, not just with advice, but with your confidence in me. I wouldn't have done that traverse without you being here. Ellen? I can toss your pitons down to you from here."

"Don't do that, Jenny," said the shadows at the base of the wall. "They'd get lost in all the debris down here. Just take them back to your camp for me." There was a muffled sound, then a cough.

Ellen was crying.

"Whatever you say, Ellen, but I'm grateful for your help. See you later." Jenny began stepping carefully along the narrow shelf. *What's the matter with her?*

"You don't want to see me Jenny. You wouldn't like it!" Anger and bitterness were there in the shadows.

Jenny frowned and began to pick up her pace downwards. *A little crazy, maybe?*

Ellen called after her, the words spilling out and her voice rising until she was shouting. "I'm sorry, Jenny. Watching you just brought back a lot of memories for me, that's all. I'm just feeling sorry for myself. Can you understand that? You're a much better climber than I ever was, and you'll be the *best* someday. Can you hear me?"

Jenny's pace quickened further, and she smiled to herself. "I hear you Ellen, and thanks." *But did she see me reach the summit? Did she see me fall?*

"Be nice to my guys down there, Jenny. They'd like to meet you, but they think you're not interested in socializing. They're good guys, all of them, and they were hoping you'd make it today."

Jenny moved quickly now, and shouted over her shoulder, laughing, "I haven't had very good experiences with men, Ellen."

"Not *my* guys. There's no super-macho or condescension down there, just respect for you as a person and a climber. Give them a chance."

"Don't worry about it," Jenny shouted. "I owe you one. Gotta go now. See ya!" She plunged on at full speed with mixed feelings of exhilaration and sadness, as the sounds of Ellen's muffled sobs and coughing faded into the distance.

Minutes later Jenny stepped down onto the plateau and after some boulder hopping found the couloirs leading to the meadows below. She hurried along in growing darkness, thinking only of cool water and hot food, and when she came out of the shadows at the edge of the meadows the sun was setting behind the jagged peaks above her and she was nearly running.

"Hey, night flyer—hold up a second!"

She looked up sharply to see a man descending a rocky slope towards her. Tall and sinewy, he bounced lightly from rock to rock, head down, his quick pace constant. *A climber*, she thought. She slowed her pace as he came alongside, and they walked together towards the brightly colored tents scattered like wildflowers around a creek flowing through the center of the meadow.

"I'm Bill Anderson, and you must be Jenny Dunn, the way you were moving just now," he said, and smiled broadly.

"Hi, Bill Anderson," and she forced a little smile of her own.

"Didn't expect to see you come down this way," he said. "The rock on this side of the mountain is real crud."

"Don't I know it," said Jenny. "I wouldn't want to do that route again."

"I bet," said Bill. "I did Brill's tower yesterday, and spent today recovering. Must be getting old." He laughed, and it was a nice sound.

They walked in silence for a while, then Bill suddenly said, "Don't keep me in suspense, Jenny. Did you make it?"

"Yes," she said, smiling to herself.

"All *right*," he drawled. "Everybody figured you had a good chance at it. I've tried to solo that bugger three times now. Hope you don't mind if some of us try to pick your brain about the last two pitches up there."

"I don't mind," said Jenny, enjoying the moment.

"You sure came down a weird route to reach that couloir. It must be a new one I haven't heard of."

"I followed a shelf all the way down to the plateau up there. You know the shelf with the big break in it?" She turned to look at him. He was studying the ground ahead.

"We all know about that place."

"I had a couple of hairy experiences, then things went pretty well until I got to that break," Jenny said, her eyes bright. "I had started to go back when I ran into an ex-climber named Ellen. She showed me how to get across the break, and the rest of the way was clear sailing. I found some of her—"

"Isn't it something the way a person can stay under your skin like that," said Bill, still looking at the ground. "I mean it's almost a religious thing. Ellen Harris sure could do it to people." He laughed softly, remembering something.

"Most of the guys up here were crazy about her. God did we get drunk after she died."

Jenny's heart froze. She couldn't breathe, but Bill didn't seem to notice.

"John and Alex took it the hardest. They were watching when that shelf just popped off and took Ellen down with it. She wasn't even roped up!"

Watch what you say, thought Jenny, and she struggled to breathe again.

"They got close enough to see Ellen was gone. It was pretty bad, I guess. She must have been crushed. Things were really falling apart up there, and before they could get to her a big section of the wall under the shelf just sort of peeled away and buried her. Geez, she must be under a hundred tons of rock. There was a shallow cave under the shelf, but the whole thing must have filled with boulders."

But none of this can be true. Jenny fought back a strangling sensation in her throat. "How can you be so sure she was dead and not just badly hurt?" Face grim, she looked at the ground, and Bill put a hand on her shoulder.

"We've thought about that, Jenny. No way—all smashed up—crushed, really, and under a mountain of rock. The rangers said it was useless to try to reach her. She didn't have any family, so they just left her there. We put up a little cairn, and the flowers are kept fresh by all of us. Only twenty-seven years old. God, what a waste."

I talked to her. I heard her. She could have been trapped in the cave. But how could she survive the winters? I do not believe in ghosts, and it was not a lucid dream.

"They should have gotten her out!" said Jenny, and she pressed her lips together hard. Bill squeezed her shoulder, and then withdrew his hand, embarrassed.

"I wish they could have too. Then maybe John and Alex wouldn't have all those nightmares about Ellen dragging herself around up here, all mangled up like some kind of monster. They just about freaked out the first time they saw you up here. From a distance, and—well—even close up, you look a little like the Ellen we remember. Did you know her very well?"

Are you really up there, Ellen? "No—only for a little while." *Do I look like you? And have you really chosen this kind of life for yourself?*

They reached the cluster of tents, Jenny's a few yards beyond the main group. It was nearly dark, and very quiet. Bill nodded towards the tents. "Climbing day for them tomorrow, but I'm going down then. How about you?"

"Sure," said Jenny, wiping her eyes with the back of one hand. "About eight o'clock?"

"Sounds good," said Bill, smiling again. "Hope this gloomy talk didn't wreak your evening after such a great day."

"No." Jenny smiled back. "It was good to talk about it"—*with one of Ellen's guys*. She started towards her tent, and Bill called after her.

"See you tomorrow then, and remember not to leave your stuff out tonight. We're having trouble with food and fuel thieves up here."

"Okay," said Jenny softly. She reached her tent, unpacked, and heated tea water on her little stove. The tea calmed her, and she sat in the darkness, munching a chocolate bar. Ellen's pitons, strung on a short yellow sling, were carefully stowed in the top of her rucksack. She sipped tea, and tried to remember her exhilaration at the summit. It was there briefly, and then escaped her. She felt so very tired. Her mind was a boulder field, jumbled without pattern, and streaked with dark shadows. Something was moving in those shadows.

Her tea cup fell to the ground, and she jerked upright, eyes half-closed. Thinking could wait until the morning. She yawned, crawled into the tent and pulled the rucksack in after her. Fumbling with boot laces, her eyes closed, she finally kicked the boots free and slid slowly into her sleeping bag. Darkness engulfed her, and she fell into a dream about climbing.

She was climbing with a young, faceless woman and they reached the summit, laughing, and the woman hid a smile behind her hands. They slid down the mountain and ran along a shelf like children playing, and then she was weightless, falling, and she looked up and rock was coming down on her, and darkness came suddenly. The woman was still with her, and didn't like the darkness, and she clawed at the rock with her fingers and screamed, "We're down here! Please get us out of here!" Then light was spilling down on Jenny's face, and she saw Bill reaching for her hand and he was lifting her out of the dark place. But something was pulling down on her legs, and she looked down, and she saw a monstrous thing clawing at her, eyes gleaming in what had once been a human face, coughing pink foam and pleading, "Jenny, please stay with me for a while." And she screamed back, "Where's Ellen? What have you done with Ellen?"

"I'm here, Jen." It was Ellen's voice. "My choice, my life, now you get on with yours."

"I'll come back to look for you," said Jenny.

"Don't bother. The mountain is my home, and I know its secrets. You won't find me."

Jenny's eyes opened wide. The tent was bathed in sunlight, and it was warm. She looked at her watch. "Seven-forty-five. My God, I overslept." She rolled out of her un-zippered bag. The tent smelled foul, musty, and she crawled outside to put on her boots. Bill had already finished pulling down his tent, and he waved cheerfully to her. She waved back, bent over to lace her boots and saw the ground sparkling beneath her feet. All around her tent entrance, the ground sparkled like dew, like a trail she had seen before. Leaping to her feet she went to her tent, held her breath against the stench inside and pulled out her rucksack. Heart pounding, she opened the sack, looked inside and then closed it again quickly and smiled. Her climbing hardware was safe and sound.

Ellen's pitons, and the little yellow sling, were gone.

BENEATH A RED SUN

Five ships went out from the Helas system, each with forty souls on missions that would last most of a lifetime. Following an arc of established gates stretching five thousand light years along the Orion arm from their point of origin on Terra, they searched for habitable planets revolving around red dwarf stars and any other systems they could find.

Red Star 5 was the last to leave Helas, its crew young and eager for adventure, but knowing it would be forty years before their return, and most of that time spent in cryosleep. Geologist John Shriver was barely twenty when he shipped out. For the first twenty years they followed the line of pinches in spacetime and the long stretches of normal space in between at half-light speed to visit systems listed as habitation candidates by Helas astronomers.

Scientists had warned them about what they might find. Even in the habitable zone, most close in planets would be tidally locked and blasted with radiation and plasma from their active, red suns. And this is what they found, three times, Terran-sized planets blasted to sterility with no signs of water and only traces of atmosphere, burning on one side and frozen on the other. The scientists were awakened three times, but only to analyze spectroscopic data before going back to sleep again.

In that twentieth year of their mission, only a year from turnaround time, crew morale was low as they approached the fourth system on their list, and suddenly the mood changed. Around red dwarf 1697H orbited a planet slightly larger than Terra. It was not tidally locked, had a year of eight Terran days and a day of 5.33 Terran days. A band twenty degrees north and south of the equator showed three small seas and four land masses widely separated from each other. There was an atmosphere of nitrogen, traces of Argon, Carbon dioxide, and one percent free oxygen. North and south of the band, the planet was covered with thick ice, temperatures ranging from twenty Fahrenheit to minus forty.

The crew celebrated, and opened up the sleep capsules so the scientists could join them. During the jubilation of the moment, Captain Ursula Soder suggested a name for their new discovery, and the crew cheered.

They called the planet Hope.

* * * *

Two landing sites were selected on a continent in the center of the unfrozen band on Hope. One was on the shore of a shallow sea, the other several hundred miles west at the base of a long range of rocky crags. John Shriver, now the head designated Geophysicist, would lead the land studies party, and Danel Zosel, a marine biologist, would be in charge of the work by the sea and in its depths.

Ursula Soder lectured them before they left. "With little free oxygen, Hope is not a candidate for settlement, so we focus on the science. Our remaining target is at least seven years away, so we're not going there. I'd like to get out of here within a month or two and get us all back to Helas in time for some retirement parties."

The two landing shuttles departed at the same time from the three-mile-long mother ship, and sailed down to the surface of Hope like leaves falling in a gentle breeze. Planetary geographer Carol Hulett was on John's team, as was Mike Wratne, a botanist. Scott Coulter, assigned to them by the military, flew the shuttle, and Nathan Yushida was there to fix things that broke.

The crawler was unloaded, a shallow pit dug, and the inflatable shelter was placed inside it. A two-layered geodesic dome was erected over the shelter and the two-foot spacing between layers filled with dirt to provide shielding. The shelter was home to the scientists, while Coulter and Yushida lived in the shuttle and slept in a heavily shielded area behind the reactor. By evening of the first day they were all settled in and shared their first meal together in the shelter.

"We only have two rovers, and I want one kept by the shuttle at all times," said Coulter.

"There are three of us doing field work," said John.

"Go out two at a time. Captain's orders and I'm in charge of security. We have no idea what you might find out there."

"We'll waste time shuttling back and forth," said Carol, but Coulter ignored her and the discussion was over.

John and Carol took the rover out the following morning and headed straight for the range of jagged peaks a few miles away. They were masked, with rebreathers that would last four hours. It had misted during the night, and broken patches of fog swirled around the peaks. In other directions there was only level ground and flat rocks all the way to the horizon. Carol had all her instruments going, recording distances and altitudes and local oxygen content as they traveled. John shook his head at the sights around them.

"Everything looks dead, not even a weed here, and the surface has been scoured down to bedrock. If this is the norm, I don't see how there can be any free oxygen here."

"It's a little over one percent right now," said Carol.

"How?"

"That's for us to find out," said Carol, and smiled.

John thought she had a nice smile, and was glad to have her on his team. They had known each other casually in graduate school.

They bumped along over hard packed soil and flat rock for three miles and parked a few yards from jagged rock rising two hundred feet above them. John craned his neck to see the summit.

"Looks basaltic, but mixed in with seams of lighter rock," he said.

Carol set up her laser on a tripod and squinted through a little telescope aimed at the base of the rock. "So grab your pick and have fun. I'll join you when I've finished a topo scan from here."

John left her there and walked along the base of the escarpment, tapping here and there with his pick. It was indeed mostly basalt, some of it columnar, but at every seam there was a thick vein of white rock like quartzite that broke into splinters and fragments at the touch of his pick. He bagged some samples, and began to climb at a place where the basalt had formed some natural steps.

"Careful up there," Carol called out. "Don't forget you have to come down again."

John waved to her, and looked up. "Looks easy from here," he said. Basaltic steps three feet wide rose to a shelf above him.

"There's an alcove or cave up there," said Carol, and pointed.

John climbed to it, and felt a thrill. Behind the shelf was the maw of a tunnel or cavern going back far enough to be dark inside. He stepped inside, his head a foot from the ceiling, and waited until his eyes had adjusted to the low light. Outside light reflected from whitish seams in the walls and ceiling, but further in was a greenish glow, so faint at first he thought it might be an illusion. He dared to take a few steps more when his eyes had adjusted, and found himself in a small, round cavern with a ten foot ceiling laced with tendrils of light rock glowing faintly in green. The ceiling glistened wetly, and the floor was wet. John took samples of liquid and glowing rock, his heart thumping with excitement. He stood there for a while and listened to the occasional drop of liquid hitting the floor. The fluorescence around him seemed to flicker. There was no apparent exit from the place, other than where he had come inside. He took several photographs, finally did timed exposures to bring out the green glows, and went back to the shelf.

Carol was still doing her topo mapping. She looked up and saw him. "Anything interesting?"

"I'll say. There's fluorescent rock with no light source in there. I'd call that interesting. It's a small cavern, though, and doesn't go anywhere else. I need to find more, clear to the summit."

"I see a couple of them above you," said Carol, "but you'll have to find climbing routes and we didn't bring gear for that this time."

"We need a close up survey, and that's a job for the shuttle."

Carol laughed. "You get to deal with Scott about that."

"Can't say I look forward to it," said John, and he began carefully descending the basaltic steps to the ground fifty feet below him. Clouds were moving in, and he felt a drop of rain.

Carol was folding up her tripod when he reached her. "Scott just called and wants us back before it rains," she said.

"No lack of water here; it was wet in the cavern. Take a look." John showed her the pictures he's taken.

"Wow," said Carol, and smiled. "You must be excited."

"Absolutely," said John, and smiled back.

They made the thirty minute drive back to the shelter and arrived just as light rain began to fall, turning to fog later in the long day.

* * * *

Carol took dozens of escarpment photographs at a distance because Scott would not allow the shuttle to be used for close-up work. Their fuel was limited, he said. John spent hours with Carol, going over photographs to identify areas for exploration, and found one route that would pass by three alcoves or possible caverns on its way to the summit. There was a strong flare during the long afternoon, first picked up optically, and within minutes the UV and x-ray levels outside the shelter were at dangerous levels. This persisted for over a Terran day, and night work was considered to be too risky, by order of Captain Soder. In all, it was over two Terran days before John and Carol were allowed to go out again.

They went out early, and the morning landscape was painted in red hues while the escarpment was a foreboding dark brown. Carol had done a thorough job of mapping their climbing route, her locator linked to the data center in the shuttle and clipped to her belt for constant reference. The route ran up the rocky jumble of columns and cracks and shelves to a summit two hundred feet above them. It was not difficult, mostly akin to climbing a staircase, but steep and quite exposed. They established a fixed rope as they slowly proceeded, using a diamond drill, screws and carabineers.

Their first target was a disappointment, a shallow depression into the rock and beneath an overhanging shelf. They paused there for a light lunch of crackers and dried fruit.

"Nice view, but bleak," said John "Helas won't have any interest in ever putting even a temporary settlement here."

"Maybe for some science," said Carol. "Anyway, I'm having fun. I haven't climbed since college."

"I'm hoping for some science," said John. "This is our final landing before we go back into deep-freeze again."

"You've already found something interesting, and we still have more targets above us," said Carol.

Again that smile and John smiled back. "So let's get to it."

They climbed another fifty feet, and were rewarded by the sight of a dark, oblong tunnel going back into the rock. "Ah hah, this is better," said John.

Carol looked up. "The third target is right above us, and close to the summit."

"Not today. Our rebreathers won't hold out."

"These things are too limiting," said Carol, and swiped a finger across the wrist module connected to her instruments. "Having some oxygen here is so tantalizing, but—oh, that's interesting. I'm getting a reading of three percent, but it's jumping all over the place. It was only one percent down by the rover." She took three steps towards the tunnel entrance, and gave John a wide-eyed look. "Still fluctuating, but now up to four percent. John, there's an oxygen-rich breeze coming out of this tunnel. I can feel it in my hair."

"Well this time we have some light," said John, and turned on the bright climber's lamp strapped to his belt.

They stooped to enter the tunnel. At first sight the walls and ceiling were basaltic and dull brown in the bright light, but ahead was darkness as the tunnel widened and curved out of sight to the right. Carol suddenly put a hand on John's arm, startling him. "Turn off the light for a second. I think I see something."

John turned off the light, expecting total darkness, but then he saw it too, a greenish glow bright enough to show the shape of the tunnel ahead of them. "Oh my, this is what I saw before."

They shuffled ahead, a turn to the right, then to the left and the tunnel opened up into a cavern with a high ceiling and fumaroles running off left and right, all of it glowing brightly in a lacy network of green.

"Ohhh," said Carol, and John grinned. "Like before, but a lot nicer."

"I still feel that breeze, but now it's coming from everywhere." Carol looked at her wrist again. "Five percent here, fairly steady." She stepped up to a fumerole and checked her instrument again. "Six percent, and steady. There is oxygen flow into this place; the source isn't right here."

"Good. We don't have to consider how green rocks can produce oxygen without carbon dioxide or a light source," said John jokingly.

"There could be new chemistry in these rocks."

"You mean biochemistry. We need to get Mike in here. He knows his plants down to the molecular level."

"I don't see any plants here."

"Me neither, but all this green is telling us something; these glowing tendrils on floor and walls almost look like roots, but they're made of crumbly rock. It must be a new mineral, but I've never seen it before. Hey, there are tendrils in the ceiling here, coming down from the fumerole above your head. Time for samples."

Carol checked an instrument. "Not a lot of time. My breather is down twenty-five percent."

"They're probably screaming at us right now, but can't get us in here," said John. He delicately removed a segment of glowing rock from a wall and bagged it. "We need bigger rebreathers, and more help."

Carol didn't seem to hear him. "The oxygen is coming from these fumeroles. The source must be below us somewhere."

They filled several bags and were packing them when John's foot struck something. He looked down; saw a small rough spot at the edge of a glowing tendril there. When he turned on his lamp it looked like a hole partially filled with crushed, white rock. He knelt and looked closer. The hole ran beneath a tendril at a shallow angle, and crushed rock nearly filled the entrance as if forced out from the inside. "Look at this," he said, and Carol knelt beside him.

"Take a photograph. We really are running out of time."

John moved the light beam around the floor. The rock here was dry, unlike the first cavern he'd visited. "There's two more, over there by the wall."

Carol hoisted her pack, checked her wrist display. "Pictures. We have to go. The oxygen here is back down to three percent. We wouldn't survive a minute here without breathers."

"Okay, okay." John snapped four quick pictures and pulled on his pack. "I hate these time limits. This isn't just interesting; it's beautiful in here."

"A dreamscape," said Carol, and shook her head. "Let's go."

They were back to the tunnel entrance in half a minute, and instantly their communicators were screaming at them.

It was Scott, and he was furious. "What the hell have you been doing? I've been trying to reach you for two hours?"

"We were inside the rock, and there's no reception there," said John.

"So set up a relay where you're working. I want contact with you at all times, Doctor. Your breathers are low, and you need over half an hour to get back here."

"We're aware of that, and we're heading down to the rover as we speak," said John. Carol was grinning at him as they followed the fixed rope down a basaltic staircase.

"And what happens if your breather runs short and there's a flare and you can't come back here for several hours? I'll tell you what happens; you die out there, and we can do nothing to help you. I don't need that on my record, Doctor. Do you understand?"

"Yes, sir," said John, sarcasm dripping. "We're on our way. Over and out." He broke the connection, crowded in behind Carol in his eagerness to get off the rock.

Carol held him back with one arm. "Easy, there. We're okay. The man is an ass, but he's right. We really need to be more aware."

"He makes everything sound like an order," said John.

"That's what he knows," said Carol, "and scientists have been irritated by it for a long time, but Scott is still in charge."

Carol drove the rover at top speed and John hung on all the way back to the shelter, where he then endured a one hour lecture and reprimand about chain of command and the dangers of poor communications.

* * * *

The best they could do was adding a secondary gel pouch that extended the life of the breathers by two hours. A tripod mounted microwave relay was added to their packs. Another short flare occurred only four hours after their return, reminding them of the dangers, and it gave Scott another opportunity for a lecture on safety.

Captain Soder was encouraged by their discoveries so far, but reminded them of their mission to find truly habitable planets. Danel had called in from the other landing party to report algae had been found in the shallows of the eastern sea, and there was a variety of microscopic life in the water. A submersible was being readied to probe the depths of the sea. Scans from Red Star 5 showed long, narrow underground aquifers and perhaps even rivers of water beneath many of the escarpments in the area, including the one being explored.

Mike Wratni had patiently waited for a turn to go outside, and now insisted on it. Carol would stay behind to work on her maps and topo files. "That white crushed rock you brought back with the green stuff in it, at first I thought it might be quartz with a lot of chlorite inclusions, but it isn't. The green stuff reminds me of plant fibers, but it must be crystalline, not organic. I've never seen anything like it. I need to see this material *in situ*."

The observations of a botanist seemed appropriate, so it was Mike and John who went out in the rover in the middle of a Hope day, hours after another flare induced radiation storm had passed and it was safe to go outside again.

The climb was faster with the fixed rope already in place. Mike was impressed by the glowing filaments in floor and walls. "Looks like roots, but only seams of rock. I can see where you've been hacking away with your hammer, but you're crushing your samples in the process. I'm going to chisel out some sections of these things and look for structure."

"While you're at it, check out these little holes in the floor. Each has a little mound of finely crushed rock at the entrance. Seems strange to me," said John. "Reminds me of burrows back on Helas, like the red nose snake that makes a little mound to hide behind when its prey is nearby."

Mike peered closely, took a small chisel from his belt and pushed it into the hole. "Goes down at an angle a foot anyway. Could be one of these seams dissolved and left some residue. The walls of the hole feel mushy. No snakes here."

John laughed. "Just a thought. Captain Soder's attitude about our schedule would change if we found higher life forms here."

"Maybe, but I doubt it. What's that breeze I'm feeling?"

"From the fumeroles around us. Carol got an oxygen reading of six percent from the one to your right, but it didn't stay that way long." John checked his wrist display. "It's four percent in here right now, but normal is around two."

"Still, six percent is a lot higher than one," said Mike. "I don't see anything organic here, just seams of rock glowing green."

"That has to be a clue," said John. "The percentage in this cavern fluctuates widely, but outside it's constant at nearly one percent. Whatever produces oxygen in connected to this place by the fumeroles. They might go all the way down to the aquifer Red Star 5 is detecting beneath this escarpment."

"There can't be any light there," said Mike, "and green won't do it. You need a broad spectrum source."

Mike tapped his hammer on a chisel head to begin excising a segment of glowing tendril from the floor. "Better set up the comm.-relay. This will take time, and I don't want to rush it."

"Not too much time. I want to take a quick look at the cavern above us, and I'll have to fix more rope," said John. "If it's just an alcove I'll go on up to the summit. That's important, and I'll go up alone if I have to."

"Scott will have a fit," said Mike. "Wait for me, please. There could be plants on the summit, and the eco-system could be fragile for climbing boots."

"Okay," said John, and he went back outside to set up the comm.-link.

A very impatient man, thought Mike, *but there's a lot of new geology here, and we're not being given much time.* He lifted a segment of glowing rock from the chiseling he'd done on the floor, wrapped it in paper and deposited it into a labeled plastic bag. "And now one from the wall," he said out loud, and began chiseling at a tendril by the fumerole from which a gentle breeze still flowed.

It seemed like John was gone a long time. When he returned, Mike was arranging samples in his pack, and the chisels had been put away.

"Ready?"

"Just about. Sure took you a long time to set up a comm.-link."

"I had other things to do. Might be my imagination, but it seems darker in here than it was earlier."

"Oh?" Mike hoisted his pack and started back down the tunnel to the outside. John looked at his wrist display. "Now it's two percent," he mumbled.

John had been busy outside. Mike saw a fixed rope going up the side of the escarpment above them and disappearing over a ledge fifty feet from their position. "You climbed alone. You know we're not supposed to do that; it's not safe."

"I had the time and there's no exposure. You sound like Scott."

He would have a fit if he knew."

"You going to tell him?"

"Of course not. I don't like his tirades any more than you do."

"Okay, then, let's climb. My breather's at forty percent."

It was a short climb, John using the rope for balance, Mike hanging onto it grimly all the way. They stood on another shelf, and the summit was twenty feet above their heads. A few spiky rocks were thrust from the wall around another large tunnel leading into darkness. They turned on their lamps and went inside. It was a smaller cavern than the one they had just come from, with a single fumerole slanting down from the right. Bright light came from a large hole in the ceiling. Some irregularly-spaced columnar steps led up to it. Tendrils of green were faint on walls and ceiling, and the floor was spotted here and there with the little burrow-like holes they had seen before.

"Nothing new here," said Mike.

"Give me a minute," said John. He climbed over loose rock and up narrow steps to reach the hole in the ceiling. An overhang was there, but also a shelf he could step on to muscle his way up out of the hole and stand on the summit of the escarpment.

The sight amazed him.

The jagged summit of the escarpment went out of sight to his left and right, and at first he feared to step out onto it. There was no smooth surface of rock or soil here, only a solid mass of sharp spikes of dull, opaque crystals jammed together as far as he could see. He knelt and looked closely, touched a crystal, surprised when it moved at his touch. The crystals were arranged in elliptical groups, three concentric rings to a group. They wobbled together when he pushed on them.

"Mike, you've got to see this," John called out, and took one careful step away from the hole he'd come out of. There was a crunch under his boot, and destroyed crystals scattered beneath his foot. "Damn," he said.

Mike's torso emerged from the hole. "What?" he said, and then quickly, "Wow. Got your hammer?"

"Just managed to disturb nature with my foot. Now I'm afraid to move. These spikes are in groups." John pulled the rock pick from his belt and knelt down again, pried around the circumference of a cluster and pulled up on it. There was a loud snap, and the cluster fell over on its side. There was a round spot of clear rock where the cluster had broken off, but no visible stem on the specimen. "Did it again," he said.

"Well, you got most of it, but you'll have to chisel out the rest." Mike turned the specimen over in his hand. "Remind you of anything?"

"A little like Terran barite roses I've seen pictures of; flat crystals, but sharp. These crystals are a lot bigger and more organized."

Mike smiled. "Looks like a flower to me."

John smiled back. "What a surprise. Let's bag it, and you can play with the petals tonight. It doesn't look like any mineral I've seen before. We have enough analytics at the shelter to give me a clue."

"Seriously, you need to dig out what it was attached to," said Mike.

"We can go back for fresh breathers, and return in a few hours. We still have plenty of day yet."

"Not me. I don't see any botany here, but I want to get these samples under a microscope," said Mike. "Let's pack up."

Mike took his flower with him and dropped out of sight, murmuring nervously until he had reached the cavern floor. John followed, stepping carefully to avoid further damage, and they packed the specimen carefully in paper and a sweater John had brought along.

They left the comm-relay in place and made a slow and careful down climb to the rover. Mike breathed a sigh of relief, and flexed the fingers of his right hand. "Enough of that," he said. "Give me level ground any day."

Mike drove. John called in to tell what they had found. He requested permission to return for another look in a few hours and get a more complete crystal cluster specimen before nightfall.

There was chatter on the line, and then Scott was back. "Okay. Carol here is chomping at the bit, so she'll go with you. I'm not going to allow any night work out there, so you won't have a lot of time."

"Okay," said John, and clicked off. "One and a half Terran days before nightfall and he says we don't have much time," he said to Mike.

* * * *

John drove leisurely, expecting a routine excursion and return in time for a freeze-dried supper of vegetables and something resembling meat. Carol was her usual excited self, and being with her made the trip go faster. "I need to make sightings on the summit," she said. "Can I do it without destroying the flora?"

"It's rock, not plants, but the individual spikes are brittle. There are some bare spots around for your tripod," said John. "And yes, I'll carry it up there for you."

"Why thank you, kind sir," said Carol, and she smiled, and John had a nice feeling again.

The climb was fast with a fixed rope all the way up, and both of them were breathing hard when they reached the cavern entrance. With a short excursion planned, neither had any concerns about oxygen consumption. Their enhanced breathers were good for several hours.

"Not as pretty as the lower cavern," said Carol, and she checked her wrist display. "Oxygen is at three percent, and that's just two points over ambient. I only see one fumerole here."

"Goes down like the others," said John. "The oxygen source has to be deep. There's no carbon dioxide up here. No water, either, only what comes in with morning mist. The fluorescence in here is weaker than it was, too. I think it has something to do with the time of day."

"So how do I get to the top?" said Carol, looking up.

"I'll take the tripod and follow you up. Take your pack with you. The hole in the ceiling is big enough to get through with it."

John guided her up the natural steps to the overhanging shelf ending adjacent to the hole. The footholds there were smooth and angled slightly downwards, and it was a fifteen foot drop to the floor.

Carol froze, and John pressed in behind her, showed her two firm hand holds leading up the hole. "Bend over and keep your feet flat on the rock. I'm right here to grab you if you slip."

"Please do," she said, and immediately stepped out from under the overhang, grabbed a handhold and pulled herself up to a standing position to look outside. "Oh, my," she said. Another step and she pressed her body up and out of the hole to rest on her knees at the edge of it.

John thrust the tripod up to her and sat on the edge of the hole while she set up for her laser sightings. "You must be thrilled," she said. "This is a geological garden up here."

"Yes, but for now I'll just sit here until you're finished. I want to minimize the damage we do."

"I *am* being careful," said Carol. "There are more bare spots here than I was expecting."

It took Carol half an hour to make her sightings and take pictures. John sat quietly, pecked away at some crystal clusters and dug a trench inches deep around one of them. Deep enough, he hoped, to use a chisel to snap off the root-like column connected to the cluster.

When Carol was finished they lowered the tripod back down to the cavern floor with a rope. John steadied her as she dropped to a foothold below the hole, reached out to grasp the edge of the overhang in order to slide under it. She showed no fear, no nerves, in doing it. *Braver than Mike*, he thought. *Quite a woman, and smart, too.*

She was on the cavern floor in seconds, looked up and smiled. "Down! That was fun. How's your breather? Mine's at thirty percent. Some hard breathing, I guess."

John checked his breather. "Twenty-seven for me. I shouldn't need much more time here."

There was no rush, he thought, and he had to be careful in digging out a complete specimen for Mike. He had already wrapped four additional clusters and packed them away. That was the easy part, but the connection between a cluster and its rocky root was indeed fragile. He took out a small chisel and began tapping radially inward at the bottom of the trench. Minutes later he was rewarded with a snapping sound, and the cluster shuddered. He held his breath, pulled lightly on the pedestal of rock beneath the cluster, and his heart skipped a beat when the whole thing lifted off with cluster and rock encased root still attached.

John let out a whoop. "Got it! Just what Mike wanted!"

"Great, but don't forget the time. I'm packed up," said Carol.

John carefully wrapped the specimen in layers of foam polymer and cloth, and put it gently into the top of his pack. There was a feeling of accomplishment, and he was having a wonderful time. His breather was now at twenty-five percent and he sat for a moment, debating about taking another whole specimen with them.

Out of the corner of his eye, he thought he saw movement, turned to look across the field of crystal clusters as the surface seemed to shudder. There was a strange crackling sound all around him, but then he was nearly deafened by the sound of Scott Coulter screaming at him through the comm-link in his ear.

"FLARE! YOU HAVE SECONDS TO GET INSIDE! RESPOND!"

He was delayed three heartbeats by astonishment, but he was already at the edge of the hole. Around him a field of dull crystals wavered and thrust out from cluster centers, like petals of a flower opening. He wanted to see more, but blinked hard and dropped into the hole, nearly slipping on the smooth rock and scrambling to get under the overhang to one side of it. He looked up and saw a cluster by the hole spread its crystal leaves wide as a dinner plate, the outer ring of crystals nearly parallel to the ground.

The rock beneath the overhang was suddenly brightly lit, and Carol screamed below him. He looked down; saw a cavern floor and walls brightly lit in tendrils of green and blinding spots of white light along their lengths, growing in intensity.

"We're inside!" called Carol. "There's bright light everywhere in here!"

"Are you shielded from the outside?" said Scott.

"Yes."

"Hunker down in a corner," said Scott. "This stuff is lethal; even a minute of exposure can kill you."

"We're okay for now," said John. "There's a new, white light coming out of the fluorescent tendrils in here. It's very bright, but I don't think it's dangerous. Is Mike there?"

"He's here."

"Put him on." John duck walked under the overhang and quickly made his way down to the cavern floor. Carol was taking pictures of the new light display.

"Hey, bud, bad time for a flare," said Mike.

"Maybe not," said John, and he told him what he had just seen.

There was a pause, then, "Okay, that *is* interesting. Were you able to get a good specimen?"

"A nice one," said John, "with attached cluster and maybe four inches of stem."

"A new specimen from the floor or wall might be good to have," said Mike, but then Scott cut him off tersely.

"Forget that. We have another issue more important, and it's called survival. What are your breather readings?"

"Uh, twenty four and twenty six. We've been doing some hyperventilating these past few minutes."

There was a pause. "That's not good news," said Scott.

"It's enough for maybe four hours," said Carol, and then her eyes got wide. "Oh, I see," she said softly.

"Four hours, and these flare hazards have been running from seven to twelve. We can't go out in this, and neither can you, and even when the radiation level is safe it's a half hour to get to you."

John's heart thumped hard. "Yeah, that's not good. We can rest and consciously breath slow, maybe give us another hour or two."

"At best," said Scott. "It isn't going to be enough. Give me a few minutes. There might be something we can do with the shuttle. Hang on, we'll think of something."

Carol looked at John with huge eyes. "I think we're in big trouble," she said.

"Maybe. What's the oxygen reading in here?"

"Four percent, up a little. No, wait, it just went to five."

John walked to the single fumerole angling down from a wall near the tunnel entrance, and held out his hand. "There's a breeze here. There wasn't one earlier. Take a reading here."

"Whoa," said Carol, leaning into the fumerole, "It's six percent—now seven. It's rising fast!"

The flare, and now all the bright light in here, the energy is being funneled somewhere below us where there's a supply of carbon dioxide and water, and now we're getting an oxygen burst. That should last as long as the radiation level is high. All those crystals up top are sucking up high energy radiation and somehow using it for photosynthesis!"

"Eight percent," said Carol. "How much do we need?"

"I've read that people living at very high altitudes have adapted to levels as low as thirteen percent, but they do that by producing more red blood cells and that is a very slow process. Ten percent is considered lethal for normal humans."

Carol watched her wrist display for a moment. "It went to nine there for a second, but then back to eight. It's close to nine, and holding steady."

"It won't sustain us," said John.

"It's a supplement. We can relieve the breathers and breathe faster for a while, then breathe slow with the breathers. Here, I'll try it."

"Carol, NO!" But John was too late.

Carol jerked off her mask, shut the valve on her unit and held her breath, then leaned into the fumerole and took rapid breaths. Her fists drummed on the rock walls.

"Oh—oh—ugh—oh—not-so—good-uck—." She stood up and slapped her mask back on, gasping for several breaths and clenching her fists. She had breathed cavern air for only a minute.

"It's awful. There's a rotten smell, but I think I could do it for a few minutes as long as the oxygen level stays where it is or higher. It could add another hour or so with our breathers."

"You're crazy, you know," said John.

"I don't want to die," she said solemnly.

"Neither do I," said John. Heart pounding, he turned off his breather and repeated what Carol had done.

It was not pleasant.

He lasted a full two minutes breathing rotten air and fighting the rising sense of suffocation, no matter how fast he breathed. John slapped on his mask and gasped for air, breathing rapidly and deeply. "I'm sucking a lot of air now. I don't see how I'm saving anything."

"Discipline," said Carol coldly. "We have to ignore the smell, breathe fast with cavern air, and breathe slowly with breathers until someone comes to get us." She held up her wrist. "See, it's at nine percent now. If it stays that way or goes higher I think we can get through this."

John shook his head. "You're amazing," he said.

Carol smiled. "Glad you think so, but I don't feel very amazing right now."

"It's a backup plan, but the shuttle is well shielded in the cabin area.

They should be able to pick us up at the cavern entrance pretty soon."

It was not to be.

Scott called minutes later to say there was no fuel left for anything by a safe return to Red Star 5. No shielding had been found that was light enough to be used on the rover. "Sorry, guys. Mike and Nathan are suited up and ready to drive fast when the radiation level is safe. It's getting late in the day, and there might be a shadow effect from the escarpment. We're watching it."

John told him what they were going to do to survive, that they were calm and optimistic about getting back to the shelter safely, and that they knew everything possible was being done to save them. "If you call us, our answers will be short to conserve oxygen."

"You're not alone out there," said Scott, "and I swear we will get to you in time. Believe that."

"We will," said Carol, and the connection was broken. She turned to John. "So here we are. How do we proceed?"

"We take it easy, lie down by the fumerole and wait it out, poke each other once in a while so we don't go to sleep and not wake up—ever."

Carol checked her wrist display. "Hey, it's ten percent—no, back to nine."

"Probably as high as it's going to get. Let's try two minutes on, two off, and see how it goes."

They sat down by the fumerole to begin what they knew would be a long and difficult ordeal. Still, at that moment they were optimistic.

Two minutes of rapid, foul breathing with constant warnings of suffocation was followed by gasping and forced, slow breaths with the breather on for another two, and then repeated. At first it was beyond torture. After half an hour it was more endurable, falling into a kind of rhythm. Time seemed to pass faster.

Scott called in Radiation levels were unchanged. Mike and Nathan were ready to sprint.

"Still here," said John.

They sat side by side against the wall beneath the fumerole entrance, could feel a gentle breezing spewing forth from it, the oxygen level steady until John first noticed that the light from the glowing tendrils on floor and ceiling seemed to be decreasing, spots of white light flickering and then fading to a soft glow. Even the green fluorescence was suddenly not so bright. At that moment, Carol touched his leg without a word, and held up her wrist for him to see some unwelcome data.

The oxygen level was now eight percent.

Their routine was suddenly broken. They tried, and failed, to last two minutes without the breather, their chests heaving with agony for one minute after their masks were back on. Only a few tries, and one minute was impossible, the cavern level soon down to six percent, and even green light was fading around them. The projected spot of outside light from the hole in the ceiling had now reached the floor by the tunnel entrance. In an hour or so it would begin to be dark in the cavern.

Both of their breathers showed the same reading: fifteen minutes left, fifteen minutes to live, to think about what they'd seen, to wonder about what else might be found. John looked over at Carol. She smiled weakly, and her eyelids fluttered until he poked her. She looked pale, and there were beads of sweat on her forehead.

John drifted off, was startled awake by a sound, but it was now quiet in the darkening cavern. He felt Carol take his left hand in hers and squeeze gently. She gave John a weak smile when he looked at her. When she closed her eyes he was sad, and suddenly angry. He poked her hard, but her eyes remained closed. His heart began to pound, and beads of sweat cooled his forehead.

He reached up to wipe at his forehead, and heard a crunching sound to his right. His vision was beginning to blur, and he blinked hard to clear it.

He looked over at the floor to his right as there was a pop, and a plug of rock rolled away from a sudden hole in the floor only two feet from his thigh. He blinked again, and saw two small orbs glowing yellow in the darkness of the hole.

The orbs blinked. Twice. There was a croaking sound, and something pushed up a small mound of crushed rock to partially block the entrance to the hole.

John's head was swirling, and his speech was slurred. "Well, hi there," he said. His vision blurred again, and now there was an irritating noise in his ear.

The two glowing orbs blinked again, and were gone.

"—We're coming! Ten minutes! John! Carol!"

"Hey," mumbled John "got a critter here digging holes in the floor."

"Just a few minutes, John! You've got to stay awake!"

"Sure will," said John, and then there was no sight, no sound, only darkness.

* * * *

John awoke with a dull headache, and squinted in bright light. He was back in the shelter, one corner screened off to make a small infirmary. The bed next to his had been occupied, but was now empty and the covers were pulled back. "Hello?" he called out, and heard a rattle beyond the screen.

`Carol peeked around the edge of the screen, and smiled. "Welcome back," she said, and stepped up to the side of his bed.

John reached out a hand, and Carol took it in hers. "You okay?"

"A terrible headache, but I'll live," she said, and squeezed his hand. "I was up an hour ago to hear the story of our dramatic rescue. I guess it was pretty close. They carried me down to the rover, but you actually climbed down."

"I don't remember a thing."

"Superman."

"Right."

The screen rattled, and Mike was there. "Hey, you're up. Man, you slept for ten hours. It's dark outside."

"Thanks for the rescue," said John.

"Nathan and Scott, too. It wasn't quite safe when we went out the door, but the escarpment shadow cut down the exposure enough. We kept calling, and finally got an answer when we were almost there. Your critter talk sounded like hallucinations, but maybe not. You remember that?"

"I remember two yellow eyes looking at me from a hole in the floor. No hallucination, Mike."

"Yeah, I think so, too. Our colleagues by the sea reported in while you were out cold. They've found worms and a half-fish, half-amphibian in the depths, and a partially decayed corpse of a cross between a salamander and a frog buried in the sand at the waterline. The thing has a large head and huge grinding teeth, John. We're calling it *Saxum Mandere*, closest I could think of for rock eater. The little corpse was full of rock powder."

"That's a long way from the escarpment," said John.

"The escarpments begin close to the sea, a whole line of them far beyond the site we've explored, and lots of water beneath them. There's a connection to the sea, John." Mike's voice rose with excitement, and Carol grinned at him.

"Now for the big news," said Carol.

"Yes. There are cracks in the sea floor, and gas bubbling up from them, and the gas is carbon dioxide and simple sulfides."

"Our missing carbon dioxide," said John.

"It's all subterranean. The rock crystals you found convert high energy radiation into a visible band and funnel it down to something that makes oxygen beneath the escarpments. Hope has evolved to make use of flare energy that would kill most planets."

"It makes some sense," said John. "Great ideas, but no proof. We'd have to dig below the escarpments to get it."

"Yeah, I know," said Mike, "and Scott says at best we have only a few more weeks left before our supplies run short and we have to go back to the ship."

"That's not enough time to do much of anything," John said gloomily.

"Then future generations of scientists will have to stand on the shoulders of our greatness," said Carol, trying to lighten the mood.

* * * *

John explored several more caves in a four mile length of the escarpment, but always returned to the one near the summit to chisel out complete specimens of crystal clusters and their roots. Either Carol or Mike accompanied him, and they never again traveled without an extra pair of breathers on the rover.

They found nothing new. The landing party by the sea had collected several specimens of algae, strange bottom dwellers and balloon-shaped undersea plants, and found another cried up corpse of John's rock eater. Mike had studied cluster stems in cross section and concluded that half of the interior was nothing more than a light pipe.

Captain Soder ordered them back to the ship only four weeks after the discovery of the light absorbing crystal flowers that had nearly cost John and Carol their lives. She then suffered through the complaints and grumblings of frustrated scientists for weeks after leaving orbit.

Mostly they slept on the way home, the scientists awakening only four times for two year periods over the twenty year trip. The relationship between John and Carol had gone well beyond friendship, and Captain Soder married them just after their second awakening.

They returned as celebrities on Helas. They were in their sixties, but physically fifty. They enjoyed productive careers in teaching and research for twenty five years, and watched Red Star 9, filled with some of their own students, leave on the long journey to again study Hope and a new system beyond 1697H.

It would be two generations before explorers would dig into the mammoth caverns beneath the escarpment on Hope and find the fantastical, living world there, with rivers and lakes surrounded by bulbous trees and crawling vines and bizarre ground plants fluorescing in reds and greens, all of it lit brightly, especially after a flare, by ceilings dotted by what appeared to be thousands of tiny suns.

John and Carol did not live to see that. At age one hundred and seven, John went peacefully to sleep one night and did not awaken. Carol survived him by two years. But two centuries after their passing, their many papers on the first studies of Hope were still being referenced as humanity continued its relentless crawl along the Orion arm of the galaxy.

ABOUT THE AUTHOR

James C. Glass is a retired physics professor and dean who began publishing fiction in 1987. In 1991 he won the Golden Pen Award for Writers of the Future. Since then he has published ten novels and over sixty stories in anthologies and magazines such as Analog, Abotriginal SF, Pulphouse, Digital SF and Talebones. Retired from academics in 1999, Jim divides his time between Spokane, Washington and Desert Hot Springs, California with his wife Gail, a costumer and healing dancer. They have been actively involved in the fan convention world since 1985. For updates on new works and activities, check Jim's web site at www.author-jamesglass.com